Also by Ray Hobbs and Publishe

G000115710

Published Elsewhere

Confusion to Zeus!

Ray Hobbs

Wingspan Press

Published in the United States and the United Kingdom by WingSpan Press, Livermore, CA

The WingSpan name, logo and colophon are the trademarks of WingSpan Publishing.

ISBN 978-1-63683-048-3 (pbk.)
ISBN 978-1-63683-962-2 (ebook)

Printed in the United States of America

www.wingspanpress.com

This book is dedicated to those who believe that some partnerships are meant to happen.

RH

Sources and Acknowledgements

Batstone, S., *Wren's Eye View* (Tunbridge Wells, Parapress Ltd, 2001).

Wragg, D., *Fleet Air Arm Handbook* (Stroud, Sutton Publishing Ltd, 2001).

Hanson, N., *Carrier Pilot* (London, Patrick Stephens Ltd, 1979).

Jameson, W., *Ark Royal* (London, Rupert Hart-Davis, 1957).

Thetford, O., *British Naval Aircraft Since 1912* (London, Putnam & Co Ltd, 1958).

Kemp, P. K., *Fleet Air Arm* (London, Herbert Jenkins, 1954).

Winton, J., *Find, Fix & Strike!* (London, B T Batsford Ltd, 1980).

Winton, J., *The Forgotten Fleet* (London, Douglas Boyd Books, 1989).

Lamb, C., *War in a Stringbag* (London, Cassell, 1977).

Brown, E., *Wings on My Sleeve* (London, Arthur Barker, 2006, re-published London, Orion Books Ltd, 2007).

Thomas, D. A., *Malta Convoys* (Barnsley, Pen & Sword Books Ltd, 1999).

Crosley, R., *They Gave me a Seafire* (Barnsley, Pen & Sword Books Ltd, 2014).

The photograph on the rear cover of a Corsair making a deck landing is reproduced by courtesy of the Imperial War Museum.

As ever, I am thankful to my brother Chris, who acted as soundboard and a ready source of ideas throughout the preparation of this book.

Author's Note

I have tried, as far as the text allows, to offer some explanation of the technical terms used in this story, but I feel that a quick reference guide is also useful. I hope my readers find it so.

A 'bottle' was simply wartime naval slang for a reprimand, although I have no idea how the word came to be used in this sense. If anyone can tell me, I'll be most grateful.

HF stands for High Frequency, the range of frequencies used in air-to-surface communications beyond the range of Radio Telephony, or intercom. Despite its name, it represents the medium range, being higher than **LF** and **VLF**, and lower than **VHF** and **UHF**, so it's perhaps as well that hardly anyone bothers with these things nowadays.

A **'tilly'** is a utility vehicle, rather like a no-frills, single-decker bus, used to transport personnel both on and off naval establishments.

Not surprisingly, a **'jenny'** was a Wren, at least until 1990, when female naval personnel simply became officers and ratings of the Royal Navy, and gender difference became a matter to be officially ignored.

WT stood for Wireless Telegraphy, as distinct from **RT**, or Radio Telephony. This was in the days before technology made idiots of us all, and senior officers settled for sending one another emails.

The **cycle** was a measurement of radio frequency until the international term **hertz** was adopted, somewhat belatedly, by the Royal Navy.

A **'run ashore'** was an off-watch excursion from any naval establishment, whether afloat or ashore. Likewise, those who enjoyed the experience had to be back '**on board**', albeit through the main gate, by the appointed time.

The **wardroom** is the naval equivalent of an officers' mess. In

Nelson's time, it was little more than a wardrobe for the storage of clothes and valuables. In time, it became more spacious and luxurious.

Until the 1980s, an **'OD'** was an **ordinary seaman**. Being a new recruit, he was inexperienced and often naïve. The term was also used in a derogatory way to describe someone regarded as ingenuous. Forty years ago, the rates of ordinary seaman and able seaman were combined to form the single rate of 'seaman' so as to avoid undermining junior ratings' self-esteem. After all, no one likes to think of him/herself as 'ordinary', but such are the ways of habit and tradition that the gauche and seemingly clueless continued to be referred to as 'ODs'.

A sailor's **'oppo'**, literally 'opposite number', was his friend. The allusion was to the rating doing the same job on the opposite watch.

A **'buzz'** was a rumour. They were usually played down by those in authority, because, like most rumours, they could get out of hand and have a deleterious effect on morale.

'Bag meal' was naval slang for a packed meal, as prepared in the galley. A saying prevalent on the lower deck when describing a disorganised person was that he 'couldn't organise a bag meal for a banyan,' or, in other words, a packed meal for a beach barbecue/picnic.

The **arrester hook** was fixed to the tail of an aircraft so as to catch one of the arrester wires stretched across the after part of the flight deck of an aircraft carrier, and so arrest the landing aircraft's onward progress. Vertical and short take-off and landing technology has now rendered arrester wires and hooks superfluous.

'A drop of roughers' was a spell of inclement weather, usually regarded with philosophical detachment, but sometimes welcomed, according to circumstances, e.g. U-boats would remain submerged, and enemy aircraft would be grounded, and therefore harmless for the duration of the 'roughers'. Likewise, the ship's officers were less likely to dream up tiresome exercises.

The **'Stringbag'** was the Fairey Swordfish, a multi-purpose biplane, obsolete by 1939, but it went on to become one of the most successful aircraft of the war. It would fly in weather that kept other types grounded, it was completely without vices, and was credited with sinking more enemy shipping than any other aircraft in any theatre of war. It received its nickname from one of its test pilots, who likened it to a housewife's string bag because of the wide range of weapons it could carry. Some say the nickname was also a reference to its multiplicity of wires and struts but, as a long-term devotee of the Swordfish, I prefer the former, more imaginative explanation.

A **'three-badge hand'** was a highly experienced seaman. The badges, a maximum of three, were actually chevrons, worn on the left arm and each awarded for four years' good conduct, or 'undetected crime', as lower-deck lore would have it.

Pompey is navalese for Portsmouth. Various explanations have been offered, the most likely of them being that it is a playful compression of the chart reference and landmark Portsmouth Point.

The **'Owner'** was the captain. '**The Bloke**' was the Commander, or second-in-command of a capital ship, q.v., and **'the Jimmy'** or **'Jimmy-the-One'** was the First Lieutenant, also known by his fellow officers as **'Number One'**. The origins of such nicknames seem to be lost in the mists of time, or possibly the alcoholic haze that attended the rum issue.

A **capital ship** is a major warship. During and before the Second World War, it was usually a battleship, battle-cruiser, cruiser or aircraft carrier. Anything smaller than a cruiser was considered small fry, but the Navy was always good at keeping people and things in their places.

After all that, I leave you now to the important part, the story itself. I hope you enjoy it.

RH

CONFUSION TO ZEUS!

Royal Naval Air Station Hatston, Orkney

September 1943

1

Into the Blue

The door of the WT Office opened, and Leading Wren Stead asked, 'Eileen, will you do me a favour? Will you reach some signal pads for me?' Somewhat unnecessarily, she explained, 'They're on the top shelf and I can't reach them.' At five-foot-eight, Eileen was four inches taller than Jane. Otherwise, they were dissimilar only in hair colouring. Jane's was chestnut against Eileen's dark, loose curls, which were currently pinned up in accordance with King's Regulations. The two had been close friends almost since Eileen's arrival on Orkney.

'Of course I will.' The broadcast wasn't due for another half-hour, so Eileen had ample time. She stood up, straightened her skirt and followed Jane to the stationery store. 'How many do you need?'

'As many as you can manage, if you don't mind. Then I'll put them somewhere sensible.'

The signal pads, both large and small, were on the top shelf, but Eileen was able to reach them by going up on tiptoe, and she lifted them all down, a handful at a time, and handed them to Jane.

'Thanks, Eileen, you're a good hand.'

'It was no trouble.' A memory made her smile.

'What's the joke?'

'One time, when my brother and I had done the washing-up at home, I told him I couldn't reach the top shelf to put the dinner plates away. So, just for fun, he lifted me up so that I could. There were four plates, so he did it four times. My mother didn't think it was at all funny, but she always did have a grudge where other people keep their sense of humour.'

'Have you never been home on leave, Eileen?' Jane knew something of Eileen's problem.

'I did once.' She grimaced. 'Never again.'

'What a shame. What do you usually do?' Remembering herself, she said, 'If you don't mind my asking, that is.'

Eileen was aware that their conversation had attracted the interest of a petty officer armourer, who made no secret that he was eavesdropping. She ignored him for the present, as that kind of intrusion was common among predatory ratings. 'Of course I don't mind. I've stayed with my brother and his wife in London, up to now, but it won't be so easy now I've been drafted here.'

'What's your brother do, then, if he lives in London?' The question came from the petty officer.

Ignoring his rudeness, Eileen said, 'He's a fireman.'

'Oh yeah? Three quid a week for dodgin' the column, eh? A fireman.' He gave a snort of contempt.

Suddenly, Eileen was angry. 'He's a better man than you are,' she said. 'For one thing, he doesn't go around eavesdropping on private conversations and sneering at other men's efforts.'

'He ain't in no position to, is he?'

Jane was sending her urgent signals to back down, but it was too late for Eileen. 'Just bloody-well take that back, you ignorant lout!'

'Who are you callin' names? See these, my girl?' He tapped the crossed anchors on his left arm. 'Let's 'ave a bit o' respect around here.'

She blinked as tears of anger threatened to undermine her dignity. 'Respect? You don't even know what it means!'

What might have happened next was anyone's guess, but Providence intervened when the Duty Officer's door opened and a voice said, 'What on earth is going on out here?' To Eileen's surprise and dismay, it was a man's voice, although the Duty Officer was Third Officer Blane. She froze when a Lieutenant, RN, stepped into the passageway. 'I can't hear myself think with all this noise.'

'I'm sorry, sir,' she mumbled. 'It was an argument that got out of hand.'

'Very much out of hand, I'd say. What's your story, Petty Officer Jackson?'

'This Wren was very disrespectful to me, sir, but if she apologises, I won't take it no furver than givin' her a "bottle".'

'And you know more about bottles than most, Jackson.' Turning to Eileen, he asked, 'What have you got to say for yourself?'

'Well, sir,' she began, now uncomfortably conscious that Third Officer Blane was also observing the proceedings, 'I'll apologise to the petty officer, of course.'

'That's very noble of you, but no one has yet told me what the disagreement was about.'

'I think you should know, sir,' said the third officer, 'that Wren Dewhirst is normally a very respectful and courteous rating.'

'In that case, Wren Dewhirst, would you like to tell me your version of events?' He was rather nice-looking, with well-trimmed, medium-brown hair and gentle eyes, and he didn't seem particularly angry.

'Wren Stead asked me where I usually took my leave, sir, and when I told her that I stayed with my brother and his wife in London, Petty Officer Jackson, who suddenly arrived from nowhere and butted into the conversation, asked me what my brother did. I told him he was a fireman, and that was when he became abusive.'

'I see. The usual cliché, was it, Jackson? "Three quid a week Army dodgers"?'

Scenting trouble, the petty officer said, 'Not in them same, exact words, but that sort o' fing, sir.'

'You should know, Jackson, that during the Blitz, firemen fought fires night after night in appallingly dangerous conditions. I know that because my home and family are in London. Many of those firemen might have had as cushy a time in the armed forces as you've had up to now, because the Blitz was hell on earth for most of them, but they did their duty. It's well worth remembering that before you're tempted to parade your ignorance again.'

'Yes, sir.'

'I'll speak to you again in a minute. Meanwhile, Wren Dewhirst, do try to control your temper. I realise you were provoked, but this could easily have become a disciplinary matter.' With a meaningful look at Third Officer Blane, he said, 'Be thankful it hasn't.'

'Aye, aye, sir. Thank you, sir.'

'You're welcome. Petty Officer Jackson, come this way.'

'Aye, aye, sir.' The humbled P O followed the officer outside, quite clearly, to receive a reprimand.

'Wren Dewhirst,' said Third Officer Blane, 'I can add nothing to what Lieutenant Underwood has said, but do try to remember what he told you.'

'I will, ma'am. I'm sorry I lost my temper.'

'I know you are.' She looked at her wristwatch and said, 'Fifteen minutes to the broadcast. Don't let me keep you.'

'No, ma'am. Thank you, ma'am.'

Back in the WT office, Jane said, 'You were dead lucky with that officer. They're not all as nice as him.'

'He was nice, wasn't he?'

———◆———

The following week, a gastric disorder rendered a large number of officers and ratings unfit for duty, leaving the rest to cope as well as they could. One of those stalwarts was Eileen, who was told at the beginning of one watch to report to the Wireless Repair Workshop. It seemed odd, but she reported to the Chief Wireless Electrical Mechanic, a harassed Devonian, who pointed to a piece of equipment and said, 'You're to take that HF transmitter to Fulmar Sugar Victor Fox and install it, m' dear. It's easy enough. The tilly's waiting to take you to the aircraft.' He showed her the leads and said, 'Plug this into the aerial socket and this into the receiver. They're different sizes, so you can't get it wrong, and when you've done that, secure it with these four snap fasteners.'

'I've never done this before, Chief.'

'So it'll be a new experience for you m' dear. Take a suit of flying overalls from the locker, here, to the heads, and change into them.'

Completely bemused, Eileen selected a suit of overalls that looked as if it might fit her and disappeared into the heads to change. It made no sense that she was having to do work for which she'd received no training, but illness followed its own haphazard agenda, so she finished dressing and returned to the workshop, carrying her tunic and skirt.

'Get a pair of fur-lined boots as well,' the Chief WEM advised her. 'It gets cold up there.'

'Up where, Chief?' She was horribly afraid she already knew.

'In the sky, you silly girl. You have to go up and test the equipment when you've installed it.'

Now, Eileen was filled with dread. First, she had to install something she'd never seen before, and now she had to take to the skies for the first time in her life.

'Now, let's get your parachute harness on.' He passed it over her shoulders. 'Hold these two straps while I bring up the rest.' He reached between her legs, ignoring her look of alarm, to fasten the harness around her thighs, and brought the whole thing together in a buckle at her waist. 'We can't afford to be coy in this job,' he told her. 'Carry the parachute with you, and one of the aircraft handlers will attach it for you and show you what to do. Right, m' dear?'

'Right, Chief.' She was still in shock.

'Chances are, you won't need to bale out. It's just a precaution.'

'I see.' She didn't, really, but she was too dazed to tell him so.

'Now, your Mae West.' He handed her the lifejacket and waited for her to fasten it. 'Okay. Put your cap on in case you meet any officers on your way to the aircraft, but don't try to salute them while you're carrying the transmitter. Some Wrens have been daft enough to. Any questions, m' dear?'

The shock of it all had left her completely mute, so she could only shake her head, pick up the transmitter and hope she wouldn't make too big a fool of herself.

Peering into the distance as she left the building, she saw that there were several aircraft on the tarmac apron leading to the runway. As she gazed in bewilderment, a driver stopped his utility beside her and asked, 'Are you the "jenny" who's going to Sugar Victor Fox?'

'Yes.'

'Hop in.'

She put the parachute and the transmitter on two of the seats and took the next, bemused and on the point of tears.

After a bumpy ride of half a mile or so, the utility came to a stop, and the driver said, 'Here it is, love, and your chauffeur's waiting for you.'

7

'Thank you.' Eileen picked up her parachute and the transmitter, and stepped carefully down on to the ground. A short distance away stood a Fairey Fulmar two-seater fighter that bore the identification letters SV-F. Two aircraft handlers and an officer stood beside it. The officer wore a flying helmet and a fur-lined leather jacket.

'Hello,' he said, smiling. 'You're the Wren with the temper, aren't you?'

With some difficulty, and in spite of his flying helmet, she recognised the officer who'd intervened between her and the horrible petty officer. 'Good afternoon, sir.'

'If I remember rightly, you're a telegraphist, so I don't suppose you've done this job before.'

Still tearful with terror, she mumbled, 'No, sir.'

'Don't worry. I'll show you what to do. Come over here and put the transmitter on the deck.' He led her to the large cockpit. 'Has someone told you about the parachute? The rip cord and the quick-release buckle?'

'No, sir. The Chief WEM said one of the handlers would show me.'

'I'll do that for you when you're on board.' Pointing to the aircraft, he asked, 'Can you see where to put your feet?'

She saw that the places were clearly marked, and nodded, not trusting herself to speak.

'You can't damage anything, so up you go and into the observer's seat. That's the after one. When you're ready, I'll pass the transmitter down to you.'

Feeling clumsier than ever under the eyes of the aircraft handlers, she climbed aboard the aircraft and took the after seat, wriggling until she was as comfortable as she could make herself. Standing on the wing, he took the transmitter from one of the handlers and passed it to her. 'Don't do anything with it yet,' he said.

She'd no intention of doing anything; in fact, she wouldn't have known what to do,

'Right,' he said, 'put it down between the receiver and the radar set, this way up,' he showed her. 'Then, connect these two leads and screw the locking ring clockwise until it's tight.' He watched her make the connection. 'Right, connect the other to the aerial socket. Just shove it in and tighten the locking ring, as before.' He waited until she'd done that, and said, 'Well done. Now press those snap locks shut. Don't be gentle. They're like stokers and Royal Marines. They don't respond to subtlety.' His observation earned a chuckle from the handlers, who seemed to know him well. Again, he waited patiently. 'That's my girl. Now, let's attach this parachute to your harness.' He did it for her. 'This,' he said, showing her a metal 'D' ring, 'is the rip cord. Pull it when you're clear of the aircraft and it'll open the parachute. This,' he told her, pointing to a large buckle, 'is the quick-release buckle. Don't touch it until you hit the ground or the water, because it will separate you from the parachute.' He paused in his delivery to say, 'By this time, I imagine you're terrified out of your wits.'

'Yes, sir.' It was hardly more than a whisper.

'All this,' he explained gently, 'is in case the absolute worst happens, and that's as likely as I am to win a fortune on the football pools. For what it's worth, I wouldn't know how to fill in the coupon, so take comfort in that.' His friendly smile gave her much-needed comfort. 'Now, let's fasten you in.' He handed her the ends of her safety belt and made sure they were secure. 'If things were to go wrong, I'd open the canopy, you'd have to unfasten your safety harness, and then I'd roll the aircraft over to tip us both out. As for the lifejacket, if you ever did need it, one big blow would stabilise you in the water.'

'I had one when I came across from the mainland, sir, but it wasn't quite like this.' She thought she ought to make an effort to sound positive.

'No, you're promoted today, and you can wear a Mae West. I can't imagine how it came by that name, but now, as then, it's only a precaution.' He smiled encouragingly. 'Okay?'

'I think so, sir.' She liked his understated humour. Anyone could see that the lifejacket would resemble a woman's bust when it was inflated.

'Before we take off, this is an HF transmitter, as you probably realise, for communicating with a ship or station when the aircraft is too distant to do it by intercom. Tune it and the receiver to five hundred kilocycles. It's all you need for now. When I tell you to test the equipment, call up George Love How, give our indefinite callsign, Victor Four, and do a simple radio check. There's no need to change frequencies. That's all you need to do.'

'Aye, aye, sir.'

'Good girl. Put your flying helmet on, and then you can communicate with me.' He showed her the intercom switch. 'There, that wasn't too awful, was it?'

'No, sir.'

'You'll be all right.' He waited until she'd tuned the receiver and loaded the transmitter, and then climbed into his own seat. A rating passed him a log of some kind, and then another, both of which he signed. He started the engine, waved the chocks away, and then taxied as far as the runway.

The aircraft stopped, and Eileen heard him call the Control Tower.

'George Love How, this is Victor Four. Request permission to take off. Over.'

The reply came. 'This is George Love How. Wait. Out.'

They waited for approximately one minute, before a green flare burst out of the Control Tower.

The aircraft began to move forward.

Everything was happening too quickly for Eileen's shocked sensitivities. She'd heard the Fulmar described as slow, but it was fairly hurtling along and the wheels were making a deafening, drumming noise against the tarmac. Then, suddenly, the noise stopped, and she was conscious of the aircraft tilting upward. She realised that she was airborne for the first time in her life, and it was a truly exciting, if scary, feeling.

The air station was shrinking now. It had always seemed huge, but now it looked no bigger than one of the small farms she'd known in the West Riding.

The pilot's voice crackled in her earphones. 'I'll take you over the fleet anchorage in Scapa Flow,' he said. 'It'll be something to tell your grandchildren about in years to come.'

'Thank you, sir.' In her nervous state, Eileen was gripping her parachute. The ground was a long way below them, now; in fact, she'd lost the air station completely. She could only hope Lieutenant Underwood could find his way back.

'Carry out your radio check,' he said, 'and then you can relax and enjoy the ride.'

Checking the aerial loading coil again, she put her hand on the Morse key. At last, she was doing a job she understood. She called up

Hatston and sent *INT QRK K*, the operating signal that asked, 'What is my readability?' The single *K* was the WT equivalent of 'Over.'

The response came immediately. *QRK 5 INT QRK K.*'

Hatston were reading her strength five, and their readability was the same, so she informed them of it by sending *QRK 5 AR.*'

With a huge feeling of relief, she reported, 'Transmitting and receiving strength five, sir.'

'Good girl. Well done.'

After a short time, he half-turned and pointed downward to starboard. 'Scapa Flow,' he told her.

It was even more breath-taking than she'd imagined. The fleet anchorage seemed to spread out for miles, and she'd never seen ships like those that met her gaze now. They were so huge and magnificent, they had to be battleships, or cruisers, at the very least.

He flew in a wide arc, giving her the best possible view, it seemed, and then said, 'Time to go home.' Somehow, he knew the course to take, and in what seemed like very little time, they were approaching Hatston.

He called Hatston and requested permission to land, and the green flare appeared with surprising promptness.

Eileen felt a swell of comfort as well as relief as the pilot made his approach. The ground seemed to rush upward at a terrifying speed, until she felt she could almost reach out and touch it. Irrationally she braced herself, and then she heard a short screech as the tyres touched the tarmac, and then the wheels rumbled again. Next, she was thrown forward against her safety harness, and she realised he'd applied the brakes. The aircraft decelerated and taxied to a standstill. The pilot switched off the engine. 'Well,' he asked, removing his helmet, 'how was your first flight?'

'It was wonderful, thank you, sir!' She switched off the transmitter and the receiver to save the battery.

'To say you'd never done the job before today, you acquitted yourself very well indeed.'

'Thank you, sir. I hadn't a clue, really, but you were a great help.'

'I do my best. Isn't it typical of the Navy, though, to drop someone like you in at the deep end?'

She had to be careful. 'It's not for me to say, sir.'

'It's all right. I said it for you.' He waited for the handlers to chock the wheels, before opening the canopy and saying, 'I'll get out first, and then I'll help you out.' He guided her feet into the footholds, thanked the handlers and walked with her to the utility.

'By the way,' he asked, 'what's your name?'

'Nine-seven-two-four-one-six-nine Wren Dewhirst, E M, sir.'

He laughed. 'I can't call you that. What's your Christian name?'

'Eileen, sir.'

'Do you ever go down to the Jolly Fisherman, Eileen?'

'Sometimes, sir.' It seemed a strange question, just as it seemed strange that he should want to know her first name.

'If I see you down there, I'll stand you a drink. I reckon you've earned it this afternoon.'

2

Out of the Blue

The Jolly Fisherman was in Kirkwall, about a mile to the south-east of the air station, and the walk could be bracing in the cold months. Late September was cold enough for the party from Hatston to wrap up warmly, especially against the stiff northerly wind that had caused all flying to be cancelled.

The Jolly Fisherman was a welcome sight, but hardly as welcome as the open fire that greeted them as they entered, and they stood beside it for several minutes before going to the bar.

Eileen's parents would have been horrified, had they known she was frequenting licensed premises, and the practice had felt strange to her at first, but she was always in mixed company and therefore loosely chaperoned, which seemed to make it all right.

In view of their modest income, treating was out of the question, and junior ratings, both male and female bought their own drinks. As a newcomer to alcoholic drinks, Eileen always stuck to what she knew and had light ale. She didn't particularly like it; it was just something that made her one of the group, which was important, as it was the company, rather than the beer, that made a run ashore worth the mile-long walk.

The company was female, however, as the two men had found the dartboard conveniently free, but the two girls chatted easily with each other, enjoying the warmth and the change of scenery. It was very pleasant, and they were denouncing a particularly unpopular PO Wren, when the outer door opened to allow two officers into the pub. The

13

Wrens saw them and continued with their conversation until another officer arrived. They ordered their drinks, and Eileen heard him say to his fellow-officers, 'If I'd known you two were coming, I'd have begged a lift with you instead of driving here.' His observation attracted the usual male banter, but not before Eileen had identified his voice, and when she looked more carefully, she recognised Lieutenant Underwood. In that moment, he saw her and made an excuse to his colleagues.

'Eileen,' he said, approaching her, 'let me get you that drink I promised you.' Noticing Jane's startled look, he said, 'In fact, let me buy you both a drink. What'll you have, girls?'

Eileen broke the shocked silence by asking, 'What's that you're drinking, sir?' It was darker than the beer she was used to.

'It's mild ale. Try it,' he offered. 'Have "sippers" from the other side of my glass.'

Eileen took his glass and sipped some of the dark liquid, tasting it appreciatively. 'It's rather nice,' she told him. 'Could I have a little one of this, please, sir?'

'By all means. What about your friend?'

'This is Jane, sir,' said Eileen.

'It's very kind of you, sir,' said Jane. 'I'd like the same, please.'

'Nothing easier.' He attracted the barmaid's attention. 'Two halves of mild, Katherine, please.'

'It'll be a pleasure, Lieutenant.' She inclined her head towards the door and asked, 'Too windy for you tonight, sir?'

'It's no problem for us, Katherine. It's the Luftwaffe who can't cope with it.' He paid her for the drinks and handed them to Eileen and Jane.

'Thank you, sir.'

'It's very kind of you, sir. Thank you.' Jane was still recovering from the surprise of an officer buying her a drink.

'I said I'd stand Eileen a drink because she did an excellent job the other day.'

'She told me about it, sir. I was quite envious when I heard she'd been up in an aeroplane.'

'You enjoyed it, didn't you, Eileen?'

'Yes, sir, it was wonderful, flying over Scapa Flow and seeing the ships. I'll never forget that.'

'You made yourself very useful as well. Don't forget that.'

'Thank you, sir.'

Glancing over his shoulder, he said, 'I'd better get back to the crowd. Enjoy yourselves.'

'Thank you, sir.'

'Yes, thank you for the drinks, sir.'

'Well, I never,' said Jane when he'd left them.

Before she could say more, the two ratings who'd been playing darts returned to the bar.

One of them asked, 'Did I see you two talking to an officer?'

'Yes,' said Jane. 'He bought us a drink.'

'I go flying with him,' said Eileen airily. Then, taking pity on them, she admitted, 'Well, I did once.'

'How jammy can you get? I'd give anything to go up in one of them things.'

They chatted until closing time, when one of the officers approached them to say, 'It's very cold out there in this northerly. If you'd like a lift back to the station, we can take you all between us.'

His offer was eagerly accepted, and Eileen found herself in his car with Jane and another officer she didn't know, while the two men went in Lieutenant Underwood's car. When they reached *HMS Sparrowhawk*, as Hatston was officially called, they agreed that they would have been frozen silly if they'd walked back. They also agreed that pilots and observers were excellent people to know.

Eileen often heard aircraft taking off at around dusk, presumably to intercept enemy bombers that might attack the ships in the anchorage, but air raids had become so rare, it hardly seemed worthwhile. Having flown, however briefly, in a Fulmar, she tried to imagine what it must be like to fly on night operations. It had been exciting enough in daylight, but flying at night must be incredibly difficult. She would have liked to ask Lieutenant Underwood about it, but she hadn't seen him since that evening at the pub. It was a shame, because he was very approachable, but she had to resign herself to the fact that there were some things about which she could only wonder.

Having made that decision, she was very surprised, a few mornings later, when she met him as she was going on watch. He was in flying kit and presumably returning from a night patrol.

'Eileen,' he said, 'how are you?'

She saluted him and said, 'I'm well, thank you, sir. And you?'

'Jaded,' he said, returning her salute and then pointing skywards. 'I've been hard at work.'

'You must be very tired, sir.'

'I am, but listen. When do you next get an evening off?'

'I'll tell you in a minute, sir.' She consulted the watch bill pinned to the green baize notice board outside the WT Office, and said, 'Tuesday, sir.' She imagined he had in mind another visit to the pub. It would be a very cold walk, but it might be entertaining.

'Good. I'm free all next week. We're being rested.'

'A much-needed rest, I imagine, sir.'

'I can't disagree with that, but do you think you could see your way to joining me for a drink on Tuesday evening? Just you and me, that is. We can go to a place that's more discreet than The Jolly Fisherman.'

She thought quickly. She liked him, and he seemed trustworthy, but it was still dicey. 'It's a bit naughty, isn't it, sir?'

'Only a little bit, and it's not carved in stone. In any case, no one else needs to know.'

'All right, sir. I can be ready by nineteen hundred.'

'Okay, come to the place where the private cars are parked. You know my car, don't you? Anyway, I'll be there early and I'll look out for you.'

'Tuesday, then. Sleep well, sir.'

He closed his eyes wearily. 'I can guarantee it,' he said.

Eileen went on watch happy, but a little on edge. If an officer found out, she would get no more than a bottle for it, but it wouldn't enhance her service record.

She pondered that during the morning, until Jane found her alone and said, 'Who's got a fella, then?'

'What?'

'I saw you talking to Lieutenant Underwood this morning.' Her face was alight with good-natured mischief.

'All right, but keep your voice down.' Eileen told her about the assignation and about her misgivings. In the end, she was glad she had.

'It wouldn't go on your service record. One of the girls in Charlie Watch did the same thing, and they just reminded her that relations between Wrens and officers weren't encouraged.'

'That's a relief.'

'Anyway,' said Jane, 'you're Hostilities Only, so why are you worrying about your service record?'

'I don't know.' She really didn't. 'Maybe I'm just a worrier.'

A sharp look from the PO of the watch discouraged further confidences.

Eileen intended writing to her brother Ted when she came off watch, but she wouldn't mention her date. All letters were censored, so it would be like owning up for no good reason. Instead, she was happy to enjoy the secret.

3

October

The Sharing Kind

Still with a nagging sense of residual guilt, Eileen made her way to the compound where officers' cars were parked, not that there were many. Fuel rationing had caused most private cars to be laid up for the duration, although some car owners still managed to trade coupons.

She was grateful for the fact that Wrens weren't subject to the Naval Discipline Act. It meant that she was free to go ashore in civilian clothing. She was also grateful to the American sailor who'd given her two pairs of nylon stockings before collapsing in a drunken stupor. She'd never have completed the transaction, anyway. One girl had, and she'd regretted it.

She spotted a car that looked very much like the one she was looking for, and then the driver's door opened and he got out, walked round to the other side of the car and opened the passenger door for her.

'Thank you, sir.'

'Not "sir",' he told her. 'Away from authority, my name's Reg.'

'Not Reginald?'

'Only my mother calls me that, and then only when I've incurred the maternal displeasure.' He waited for her to gather her skirts and closed the door.

'It's a nice car. How long have you had it?'

'Only since I came to Orkney. I bought it from a chap who'd been given a sea-going appointment. That's how it works, you see. When I go, I'll sell it to someone else.' He started the engine and drove to the Main Gate. 'Have you got your identity handy, Eileen?'

She handed him her paybook, and he showed it, together with his identity card, to the sentry, who lifted the barrier to let them through.

'Where are we going, Reg?' As she spoke, it felt very strange, addressing an officer by his Christian name.

'We're going to the other side of Kirkwall, where we can relax and escape the notice of people we know.' He cocked his head momentarily and asked, 'What's that perfume you're wearing?'

'It's nothing special. It's impossible to get anything at all special nowadays. Even basic things are thin on the ground.'

'Ah, but it *is* special, because it's special when you wear it.'

'What do you mean?' She suspected he was talking nonsense. Men often did, especially when they were after something.

'Perfume is an individual thing. Chanel Number Five smells wonderful on some women, but not as good on others. Similarly, whatever you're wearing might be very ordinary on some girls, but it has a most attractive fragrance when you wear it.'

'Do you mean that?'

'Absolutely. My sister told me about that, and she works at Bourne and Hollingsworth, the department store in London. At least, she did until she was called up. She's in the Wrens now.'

'Is it a family tradition?'

'Very much so.' They passed The Jolly Fisherman and continued through Kirkwall. 'My father was in the Navy. He was killed when his ship was sunk in the South China Sea.'

'Oh, Reg, I'm so sorry.'

'Don't be, Eileen. It's the Japanese who should be sorry and, hopefully, they will be before very long.'

'I was only sympathising.'

'I know, and I appreciate it.' He took one hand off the wheel to pat hers.

'Reg,' she said, changing the subject, 'you made a big thing of what I did with the transmitter and everything, but all I did was follow your instructions.'

'I know, but it wasn't easy for you. You had to cope with all kinds of new experiences, such as wearing a parachute and learning how to use it. I didn't envy you that. I actually felt sorry for you.'

'You were really sweet.'

'No,' he said, shaking his head dismissively, 'I've never been that.' He pulled into the side of the road. 'Here we are. The Chieftain.' He hurried round to her side and opened the door for her.

'I'm not used to this kind of treatment,' she said, nevertheless letting him help her out.

'Gentlemanly conduct is part of the training at Dartmouth.'

She wondered if it was a leg-pull, but decided not to pursue it. Instead, she waited for him to open the pub door.

'After you.'

'It just gets better.'

'No, there's a limit to my urbanity. I behave like an unmitigated cad after midnight, but I'll get you back on board before the hour is struck.' He led her into the ancient lounge, with its oak beams and stone-flagged floor. It was only half-full. 'What would you like to drink?'

'What are you going to drink? Beer seemed somehow inappropriate on a date.

'Gin. If they have any bitters, I'll make it a pink gin.'

'I'll join you with that, if I may.'

'You're more than welcome. Would you like to lay claim to a table while I get the drinks?'

Eileen found a table and took a seat, conscious of the scrutiny of the locals. Until the Americans arrived and caused a major social upheaval, women had rarely been seen in pubs, and she knew that many people resented the change. She was relieved when Reg returned with two pink gins and a jug of water. 'What an absolutely charming dress. I'm no expert, but turquoise and dark blue look perfect on you.'

'Thank you. It's one of the two I brought with me.'

'And well-chosen, too.'

'I feel awkward,' she said.

'Why's that?'

'I'm the only girl in the place.'

'It'll give the locals something to talk about. They've assured me they won't burn you at the stake. It's too cold for them to stand around watching that kind of thing.'

More as a diversion for herself than out of curiosity, she asked, 'What did your sister do at the department store?'

'She was a trainee buyer in Perfumes and Cosmetics. I expect she broke a few things, too. She's quite clumsy.'

'Don't be awful.' She tried a sip of her pink gin and found it quite pleasant.

'Okay,' he said, like someone calling a meeting to order, 'you know all about my family by now.'

'Not *all* about them.'

'But enough. Tell me about yours. I know your brother's a fireman, but that's all.'

'All right. He was a schoolmaster before the war and he taught English. I think he'll go back to that, because he was good at it.'

'Have you any other brothers and sisters?'

'No, there was a brother who died before I was born. Otherwise, there's just my parents.'

'Go on, spill the beans.' For some reason, it seemed important to him.

'My dad's a market gardener. I used to help him, usually by driving the lorry.'

Surprised, he asked, 'You drove a lorry?'

'Only a little one. Anyway, he wanted to take me on as an employee, so that I'd be in a reserved occupation and he'd have me working for him for the duration. Also, I'd continue to be Cinderella in my spare time, but I got my application into the Wrens before he could do anything. That was how I made myself unpopular with both of them.'

Intrigued, he asked, 'Why were you unpopular with your mother?'

'Ostensibly, it's because I used to do the greater share of the housework. As I said, I was a spare-time Cinderella, but my brother Ted thinks there's a darker reason. His theory is that my mum's never got over the loss of Joseph, the eldest, who died of rheumatic fever, and she can't forgive me for surviving when he didn't.' After brief reflection, she said, 'I don't know how I'd have managed without Ted. He always took my side, and he was always there for me to turn to.'

'Tell me more about him.'

'He's a big lad, as you can imagine, six-foot-two and powerfully built. He's very athletic, and he was devastated when the forces wouldn't take him because of his allergy to soya.'

Reg nodded. 'I can see how that would keep him out, but he's

21

serving his country just as surely as a fireman. My home's in London, and I'm full of admiration for firemen, wardens, the police, ambulance staff and everyone who saved the country from destruction.'

'I'm glad you see it that way.' As if it had just occurred to her, she said, 'You can be quite serious at times, can't you?'

'You've noticed. Incidentally, I gave Petty Officer Jackson an almighty bottle, partly for what he'd said, but mainly because he was hiding behind his rate, and that made him nothing more than a bully.'

'Thank you, Reg. I'm not really quick-tempered, but I wasn't going to let him say what he did about my brother.'

'Of course not.'

As a memory returned to her, she said, 'There's something I'll always remember about Ted.'

'Go on.'

'When I was little, I used to wash my hair and then sit in front of him beside the fire, and he'd dry it for me. He was ever so gentle, and it was a special, cosy thing between us. He did it again, shortly before he left for London with the AFS. Needless to say, my mum disapproved. She said he was spoiling me, but we didn't care.'

'A special memory, indeed.' Eyeing her appreciatively, he said, 'And your hair is quite exquisite.'

'Thank you, Of course, it's the first time you've seen it down, isn't it?'

'Oh yes, I'd have noticed it earlier if it hadn't been pinned up and under cover.' Looking at her glass, he said, 'The tide's out. Are you ready for another?'

She looked at him for an instant, uncomprehending, and then realised he was talking about her drink. 'Yes, please. I think I'll be all right with one more.' Almost apologetically, she said, 'I don't usually drink very much.'

'I won't let you get tight,' he promised. 'I'll be back shortly.' He took the empty glasses to the bar, leaving her to reflect on the evening so far. Reg really was a lovely chap, and he seemed genuinely interested in her background, which must be very different from his.

He returned after a few minutes, took his seat and asked, 'With no job to go back to, what will you do after the war, Eileen?'

'I'll go to university. That was the plan before the war changed things.'

'What will you do at university?'

'Probably languages, and maybe history. I became keen on those things when I was studying for Higher School Certificate.' She smiled apologetically and asked, 'Do I sound like an awful swot? I bet I do.'

'No, you don't. You're an intelligent girl, you've obviously had a good education, and you should go to university if that's what you want to do. I imagine there'll be some financial inducement from the government after the war – I believe there was after the last one – so you won't need to go cap in hand to your family.'

'What a horrible thought.' Then, feeling that the focus had been largely on her, she asked, 'Will you stay in the Navy, Reg?'

'If they'll keep me. It's the only job I know.'

'I can't believe that.'

'It's true. I was one of the first snotties to join the Fleet Air Arm when it was returned to its rightful owner. Prior to that, I'd been trained in gunnery, navigation and all the other things "proper" naval officers have to do.'

'What's a "snotty"?' After two-and-a-half years' service, there was naval slang that still defeated her.

'A midshipman. You know the three brass buttons on a chief petty officer's sleeve?'

'Yes.'

'They were once worn by midshipmen, the idea being to prevent the little horrors from wiping their noses on their cuffs, hence the name "snotties".'

'That's foul.'

He nodded. 'They're more civilised nowadays. I always was, of course.'

'Of course.'

'My father was very disappointed when I joined the Fleet Air Arm. He said it was no calling for a serious career officer.' He reflected momentarily and said, 'We never did resolve that argument.'

'Oh, Reg.' She reached for his hand and squeezed it in sympathy. Then, recollecting herself, said, 'I'm sorry.'

'Don't be. You're allowed to hold my hand if you want to.'

'I'm still getting over the shock of addressing an officer by his Christian name.'

'We're only flesh and blood.' An idea evidently came to him, and he asked, 'Why don't you join us?'

'I don't know.' At that moment, she genuinely didn't. 'I've never considered it.'

'It's worth it, if only for an easier life.'

'Okay, I'll think about it.'

'I know I shouldn't ask this question, but in case you do apply for officer training, how old are you?'

'Twenty.'

Encouraged, he asked, 'When's your birthday?'

'January.'

He shrugged. 'You'll be twenty-one by the time you're commissioned.'

It was quite a thought. She asked, 'What kind of thing would I have to learn?'

'Apparently, Wren and RNVR officer candidates have to do the "knife and fork course". I believe they have to go to the Royal Naval College in Greenwich for that. It's a splendid place, and you'll be able to visit your brother while you're there.'

'What is it about?'

'They'll need to know that you can behave like an officer and a lady.'

It sounded silly. 'What has that to do with cutlery?'

'They can't have an officer turn up at a wardroom dinner and hold her knife and fork the way Desperate Dan always does.' He demonstrated the vertical, hilt-down grip.

It was getting worse. 'Who is Desperate Dan?'

'That's an excellent question, Eileen. If you'd known who he was, that would have ruled you out immediately.'

'But you know who he is, always assuming you haven't just invented him.'

'He's a character in the *Dandy* comic, so my honorary nephews tell me, and I was a hopeless case from the start.'

She looked at her wristwatch and said, 'I'll be a hopeless case if I'm not back on board in the next half-hour or so.'

'You'll be okay if we leave now. It's almost "Last Orders", anyway.'

They stood up, beaming in response to the disapproving looks from locals in the bar. One man said very seriously to Reg, 'A public house has always been a man's preserve.'

'I agree,' said Reg, 'but I'm the sharing kind.'

As they walked out to the car, Eileen took his arm, grateful for his defence.

On the way back, she said, 'I can't help noticing the ribbon of the DSC on your jacket, and I know it's bad form to talk about these things, but I just wonder what kind of thing someone has to do to earn one.'

'You're quite right, Eileen, it's the worst kind of form, absolutely second-eleven behaviour. Just let me tell you that I got it for being in the right place at the wrong time.'

'I'm sorry, I shouldn't have asked. I'm just naturally inquisitive.'

'All right. What else are you inquisitive about?'

There was no harm in asking. All he could do was refuse to tell her. 'I've been wondering what it must be like, flying in pitch darkness.'

'Very risky.'

'Be sensible.'

'All right, we fly on instruments, which isn't as difficult as it sounds. If I'm honest, though, I prefer broad daylight, and I'd also prefer something more sophisticated than the Fulmar.'

'I thought it was a lovely aeroplane.'

He laughed. 'How like a woman.'

'What's wrong with it?'

'Not much, really. It's an excellent aircraft to fly and it has absolutely no vices. Some aircraft would kill you as soon as look at you, but the dear old Fulmar would never dream of it. Its only drawback is its performance. I shouldn't tell you this, but I'm sure the enemy have realised by now that it's too slow to catch a cold, never mind a Heinkel One-Eleven.'

'In that case, why do they use it?'

'Night fighting calls for a two-seater,' he explained patiently. 'The pilot flies it while the observer operates the radar and detects enemy aircraft. Now, some bright spark at the Admiralty, who'd never been higher than a conker tree and who'd struggle to start a lawnmower, evidently said, "Let's resurrect those old Fulmars. They're ideal for the job." '

'That's not fair, giving you aeroplanes that aren't up to the job.'

'Someone needs to tell them, Eileen. Get your commission, and you could be the one to do it.'

She imagined she might, if she ever got the opportunity, but it was a shame that the aeroplane in which she'd taken her first flight was less than she'd imagined. She asked, 'What other aeroplanes have you driven?'

'Flown.'

'Okay.'

'The Skua,' which was even slower. For six glorious months, we had the Sea Hurricane, but then Their Lordships decided they were spoiling us, and we were given back the Fulmar, now converted into a willing but sedate night fighter. Fortunately for Scapa Flow and the Fleet within it, Hitler seems to be concentrating his efforts on Russia.' He pulled up by the Main Gate. 'Can you find your paybook, Eileen?'

She obliged, and he showed both forms of identity to the sentry, who saluted and raised the barrier.

'What an OD,' observed Reg, 'saluting an officer at the wheel of a vehicle. Where do they find them? Never mind.' He drove on into the compound, where he parked.

'Thank you for a delightful evening, Reg,' said Eileen.

'Thank you for coming. I've enjoyed your company. Do you think we might do it again?'

'Yes, I'd like to.'

'I'm sure we'll see each other about the place.'

'We're bound to.' She inclined her cheek and accepted a kiss. 'Just to preserve the pretence,' she said, 'I'll leave you and walk back alone.'

'Good idea. Will you be all right?'

'As safe as houses. Goodnight.'

'Goodnight.'

She walked back to the Wrens' Quarters, surprisingly happy. It usually took a while for her to trust someone and truly like him, but Reg had won her confidence easily. He'd been good company, he didn't smoke, and he hadn't tried anything he shouldn't. That innocent kiss on her cheek had marked him out as a gentleman. As new relationships went, it was more than promising. She continued happily to the cabin she shared with two other girls.

4

Pledges and Favours

Two days later, Eileen was leaving the WT Office after the 'all-night-on', when she stopped in mid-yawn to greet Reg. As there were others around, she saluted him and spoke to him formally. 'Good morning, sir.'

'Good morning, Eileen. Are you just coming off watch?'

'Yes, sir.' She stifled another yawn.

He laughed easily. 'I shan't keep you. When's your next free evening?'

'Tonight, sir.'

'Will you join me again?'

'Of course. Nineteen hundred?'

'I'll be waiting. Sleep well.'

'I'm already half-asleep, sir.' She saluted him again.

'I'll see you later. 'Bye.'

''Bye, sir.'

'Lucky old you,' said Jane as Eileen caught up with her. 'He's really nice.'

'He's lovely,' agreed Eileen, 'and he'll seem even better when I've had seven hours' sleep.'

Bleary-eyed, she went into breakfast, the contents of her plate barely registering as she ate them. Then, after an illicit second mug of tea, she went to her messdeck, undressed and fell into her bunk.

Reg resumed his place in the driving seat and greeted her with a kiss on the cheek. He asked, 'Have you recovered from your twelve-hour watch?'

'Yes, thank you. An almost-tepid bath woke me up, and the rest was quite easy after that. Where are we going? "The Chieftain"?'

'No, pastures even newer. I heard someone in the Wardroom say he was heading for the "Chieftain" tonight, so I put my contingency plan into effect.'

'I'll wait and be surprised.' It was easier than getting a straight answer from Reg.

'We're going to St Mary's,' he said, surprising her. 'It's a very small place, a fishing village, but its appeal is that it's not likely to be populated by Wren officers.'

'How do you know all these places, Reg?'

'I've flown over them. That, and I hear talk in the Wardroom.'

She was thoughtful for a spell, and the silence prompted Reg to say, 'A penny for them.'

'I was only thinking that, when I joined, in 'forty-one, Wren officers weren't universally popular.' She added, 'Some of them, anyway, the silly, simpering ones.'

'Ah, the socialites.'

'Yes, that's a good name for them.'

'They were a minority, Eileen. Most Wren officers of that persuasion have gone, anyway.'

'Where have they gone?'

'Home to *mater* and *pater*. One thing they don't teach at Greenwich is how to have fun without baking a bun. You'll have to make your own arrangements in that respect.'

'What do you mean?' It was as if he were speaking a foreign language.

'Some of those who leap-frogged from the classroom to the wardroom via the bedroom,' he explained patiently, 'became unexpectedly and inconveniently pregnant as a result, and some of those who were successful fell into the same trap later through careless over-indulgence. Either way, they had "a bun in the oven".'

'Ah.' Now it made sense.

'How many wardroom socialites have you met, Eileen?'

'Very few, I'm happy to say. Of course, I don't know what goes on behind closed doors.'

'No, but be assured that most of the girls who get commissions nowadays are there for the right reasons. Jenny Blane is a case in point.'

That was a surprise. 'Third Officer Blane?'

'Yes, for a newly-commissioned officer, she's a marvel. She has everything at her fingertips and she works like a beaver.'

'She's certainly very efficient.' She thought she knew him well enough to say, 'When I was having the argument with Petty Officer Jackson, and you came out of Three-Oh Blane's office, I wondered for a moment if you and she were....'

He laughed. 'I don't think that kind of thing ever crosses her mind. She's married to her job.'

'I'm sorry. It was only a first impression.'

'I'd gone in there to return a book she'd lent me.'

'That was silly of me. I'm sorry.' She wished she hadn't mentioned it.

'Don't be. You're only human.'

It was distressingly true.

'We're just entering St Mary's.'

With no signs, she marvelled that he could be so sure, and it wasn't the only thing that impressed her. 'You don't waste time by worrying, do you?'

'You've noticed. Basically it's a route to self-destruction. Pilots who worry shorten their own lives and those of their crewmembers, and I don't intend to do that.' He got out to open her door and helped her out of the car. She took his arm and they went inside. At a first glance, it looked remarkably like the 'Chieftain' and the 'Jolly Fisherman'. She imagined there must be a kind of pattern on the island.

'What would you like?'

'A pink gin, if possible, please. I'll come with you to the bar. I'm not keen on being stared at by the locals.'

'It was always a pretty girl's burden.' He addressed the landlord. 'Have you any Angostura?'

'No bitters at all, sir, I'm afraid.'

'It's no matter. Have you any orange blossom cordial?'

'I do believe so, sir.' He gave Eileen a quick look, but elected to say nothing. 'I'll just have a wee look.'

'If he has,' he asked Eileen, 'will you be all right with an orange blossom cocktail?'

'What's that?'

'Gin and orange blossom cordial.'

'It sounds nice.'

The landlord reappeared with a bottle of the required beverage.

'Splendid. Two orange blossom cocktails, please.'

'With pleasure, sir.' He poured two gins and added the requisite quantity of orange blossom. 'I would advise you, sir,' he said discreetly, 'to take the lady into the Select Bar rather than the lounge. I'm thinking of the locals, you understand. If anybody says anything, I'll tell them you're a private party.' He indicated the bar with a subtle gesture.

'I appreciate your help and advice,' said Reg, and I'll do just that.' He paid for the drinks, adding a ten-shilling note. 'That's just right,' he said.

'I'm greatly obliged to you, sir.'

'And I to you.' Picking up the two drinks, Reg led the way into the small bar.

'I'm afraid I'm an embarrassment,' said Eileen.

'Perish the thought. Let me help you with your coat.' He eased it from her shoulders to reveal a dark-green dress with a yellow floral motif.

'You've seen the extent of my wardrobe, now,' she told him modestly.

'And I'm impressed beyond belief. You look wonderful.'

Eileen shook her head in bafflement. 'I've never known anyone like you,' she said, 'and the best thing is that you're so genuine.'

'I hope so. Genuine but fleeting, I'm afraid.'

'Why fleeting?'

'Ah well, I have something to tell you. I shan't beat about the bush. The fact is, I'm being posted.'

'Oh.' It was the last thing she wanted to hear. 'Where are you going?'

'I have to report with the rest of the squadron to the air station at Arbroath. I'll be there for a while, working up with the squadron, but thereafter, it's anyone's guess, and I wouldn't be allowed to tell you if I knew.' He took her hand between his and said, 'I don't know how to say this without sounding too big for my flying boots, but....' He paused.

'Just say it.' If it were something awful, she would just have to cope with it.

'I was going to say that it's naturally up to you whether or not you want us to keep in touch. I mean, we barely know each other, and you might easily meet someone else, but if you decided you wanted to write to me, I'd be very happy indeed.'

'Of course I'll write to you.' She had to say, 'But then, you might find someone else.'

'Not where I'm going.'

'Not at Arbroath?'

He shook his head. 'I shan't be there for very long, and I'll be very busy, learning about the new fighter – new to me, anyway – and then they'll send us to sea.' He added, 'That's all I can tell you, by the way. You deserve better, but that's security, I'm afraid.' He lifted her hand and kissed it gently by way of apology.

'I understand that well enough, Reg. Being a telegraphist, I live with security. Don't worry about it.' She forced herself to be positive. 'I'll make no bones about it, Reg. I'm going to miss you, even after such a short time, but you have to go wherever you're drafted.... I mean posted.' Grasping the nettle, she asked, 'When are you leaving?'

'At the end of this week.'

She thought about her watch bill, and said miserably, 'I'm on watch until twenty-hundred tomorrow, and then I've got another all-night-on.'

'I'll be gone after that, but I'll write to you as soon as I arrive at Arbroath. My address is easy enough. It's *HMS Condor*, Arbroath, Angus.'

She realised he was still holding her hand, a gesture that spoke for itself. She also realised that he was more serious than she'd known him in their brief association. 'We hardly know each other, Reg, and I'd never have expected it, but I'm going to miss you terribly.'

'Don't jump out of the window when I say this,' he said awkwardly, 'but I've got a feeling about you and me, which is why I'm so keen to keep in touch.'

'I know what you mean, Reg. I have a feeling, too. Maybe we're both being downright daft, but there are some things that defy explanation.'

Suddenly, he smiled and said, 'This is all very intense. If I let go of your hand, you'll be able to pick up your glass and have a drink.'

'I don't want you to let go of me at all, but I know what you mean.' She took her glass and tried its contents. 'This is very nice,' she said. 'You're leading me astray, Lieutenant Underwood.'

'Oonderwood? I've been meaning to ask you where your home is. I can't quite place the accent.'

'That's because it's had its corners rubbed off by the posh grammar school I attended. I'm from the West Riding.'

'I'd never have known it, but I've led a sheltered life.'

'Do you find my accent amusing?'

'No,' he said, taking her hand again, 'I find everything about you as fresh and appealing as ever.'

'You're a lovely man, Reg. It was a rotten time for the Admiralty to choose, but I shan't go on about it.' Having said that, she wondered quite how to avoid the subject. In the end, she asked, 'Are you allowed to tell me about your new fighter?'

'I'm afraid not.' He shook his head apologetically. 'I'm sorry. All I can tell you is that it's a single-seater and quite a lot faster than the Fulmar.'

'I'll never forget the Fulmar and your Cook's tour of Scapa Flow. I still marvel that it ever happened.'

'It was fun,' he agreed, 'but I'm relieved to be getting a fighter that's capable of overhauling and shooting down enemy bombers.'

'Does that give you satisfaction?' She'd never really considered it, largely because it was difficult for her to think of him doing something so aggressive.

'Only the satisfaction of knowing that I'm protecting a convoy. I'm a defensive kind of person, you see, not remotely aggressive. When I was flying a Skua and I had to drop bombs, I closed my eyes while I was doing it and pretended it wasn't happening.'

'You're an idiot sometimes.' She added soberly, 'It's one of the things I'll miss.'

'Would you like another drink?'

'Yes, please.' She saw off the remainder of her cocktail and put the glass down. 'Lead me astray.'

'That's the best offer I've ever had,' he said, taking the two glasses back to the bar. 'I'll be back in a minute.'

She mused about the sudden downturn in her fortunes, in fact, in both their fortunes. Earlier, she'd been happy and full of optimism about their blossoming relationship, as he apparently had, and now, fate had decreed that they must part. She brooded further, hoping she wouldn't do something awful, like crying. That would be too dreadful for words. She was twenty years old, for goodness' sake, and that was quite old enough for her to be able to control herself in the face of disappointment.

The door opened, and Reg came in bearing two orange blossom cocktails. It wasn't at all the kind of drink Eileen associated with a man, but what did she know? For all she knew, he might have settled for it just to keep her company. It was the kind of thing he would do.

'There was a man out there, complaining about this bar being out of bounds,' he said, 'so I explained the circumstances. He was very sympathetic.'

'You're amazing.'

'It was just common sense, really, and life's always better without ill-feeling.' Sensitive to her downcast expression, he said, 'What's the betting we find each other at a later date, and this business becomes nothing more than an inconvenient hiccup?'

'Have you always believed in fairy stories?'

'Yes, I have, if a myth qualifies as a fairy story, that is.'

'There's not much difference, is there?'

'I don't think so.' He took a draught to fortify himself, and said, 'There was one I learned long ago, in a Classics lesson at school, that I've never forgotten. It was about the people who were complete in every way. Do you know it?'

'I don't think so. Tell me about them.' Any distraction was welcome.

'All right. There was once a race of people who had two heads, four arms, four legs and presumably, both male and female... characteristics... a truly remarkable race, who became inordinately proud of their completeness. In doing so, they committed the heinous

33

offence of hubris, for which Nemesis would normally have taught them a salutary lesson by giving them a good old ducking in the River Styx. Unfortunately, their crime was discovered on her day off, which meant that Zeus had to punish them himself. In one of his more jaundiced moments, most likely on a Monday morning when he was feeling ill-disposed toward the whole of mankind, he divided them into halves, each half having one head, two arms, two legs and either male or female... characteristics, and scattered them to the four corners of the earth. Since that time, each half has roamed the planet, searching for his or her other half in a bid to form the perfect union of man and woman.'

'It's a good story,' she admitted, and it had been an effective, if temporary, distraction.

'But, if we keep in touch, so that we're acquainted with each other's movements, who knows? We might yet put one over on that jealous, irascible old tyrant Zeus.'

She let him take her hand again, and said, 'Certainly, if we don't make the effort, we can't expect anything to happen.'

Eventually, they made the journey back to Hatston, both quiet and subdued. Reg showed their identity to the sentry and proceeded to the car compound.

Eileen took out her diary and turned to one of the blank pages at the back. 'Have you a pencil handy, Reg?'

He felt in his inside pocket and said, ''Fraid not. I never have one when I need one.'

'It's all right, I've found one.' She took the pencil from her bag, wrote her full name and official number on a back page of her diary, tore it out, and gave it to Reg. 'I know your address,' she said.

He held out his arms to her, and she buried her face in the folds of his greatcoat, desperate not to cry like a silly little girl. He held her, stroking her hair, and she eventually lifted her head, ashamed to feel tears forming. She accepted the handkerchief he offered her.

'I'll send it to you washed and ironed,' she promised, controlling herself again.

'No, hold on to it. It'll be like a lady in medieval times giving a knight her favour to make sure he returned.'

'But it's the wrong way round,' she protested.

'This is the twentieth century, a time of enlightenment. We do things differently.'

'You're just full of ancient....' She never finished the sentence, because his lips touched hers, lightly at first, and then, taking control, he kissed her in a way she'd never experienced. She'd kissed with boyfriends, notably David, and then Geoffrey, the boys who lived next door in Cullington, but their kisses, whilst sincere, were artless compared with what was happening now. Reg's kisses were lingering and sensitive as well as sensuous, because he was unfailingly gentle. Excitement made some men clumsy, but Reg's attentions made her wish they would never end.

Unfortunately, it had to stop, however, when Reg looked at his watch and said, 'I'm afraid it's time you were getting back to the Wrennery.'

There was no arguing with that. Eileen felt in her bag for one of her small, embroidered handkerchiefs, one of her parents' token Christmas presents, and pushed it into his hand. 'Fair exchange,' she said. 'That's my favour. Now you have to come back to me.'

'If it's at all possible, I will. I'll write as well.'

'So will I.'

He kissed her again, and she let herself out of the car to make the short journey to her quarters.

5

Time to be Grown-Up

The wardroom steward appeared, bearing two gins on a tray.
'Thank you, Bennett.' Reg signed the mess chit and took the drinks.

'Thank you, Reg,' said Guy Davidson. 'How did the girl take it when you broke the news about your imminent departure?'

'Quite well, at first. The whole thing rather crowded in on her towards the end of the evening, and I have to say I'm not feeling exactly sprightly about it, either.'

'Do you mean parting with her?'

'Yes.'

Lieutenant Davidson considered the information. 'After just two dates, that's powerful medicine.'

'Heap powerful medicine,' agreed Reg, momentarily entertained, as he often was, by Guy's allusions to the tribes of North America. He needed amusement, although, on reflection, the memory of Eileen's distraught face demanded rather more than that.

'Are you going to correspond?'

'Of course. I hope you don't take me for a fly-by-night philanderer.'

'Hopefully, none of us will have to fly by night again. I must say, I'm looking forward to getting my hands on that Martlet. I know it's no faster than the Sea Hurricane, but it can still do the job, and those point-five Brownings will make all the difference.'

That was the answer. Reg had to concentrate on the job in hand. He inevitably would, but he needed to begin immediately.

Guy had another interest, however, and he hailed the passing steward to ask, 'What's for lunch, Bennett?'

'Fish, sir.'

'Any particular breed?'

'From what I can gather, it's a lucky dip, sir, quite literally, because it was created by a chance explosion at sea. A minesweeper apparently brought in more than its crew could eat.'

'Those minesweepers get all the excitement,' said Reg irreverently. It wasn't uncommon for a floating mine to be detonated accidentally by rifle-fire, when the object was to perforate its casing so that it filled with water and sank. However, such an accident was usually followed by an abundance of freshly-killed fish, a welcome bonus with food rationed and in short supply. Reg wondered what Eileen would be having for lunch.

***

'Fish,' said Jane Stead, 'anonymous fish. They say a minesweeper brought it in after detonating a mine.'

'I think they do it on purpose,' said Eileen, 'just to alleviate the boredom.'

The two Wrens took their places and waited for the cooks of the mess to serve the meal.

'So he's been drafted to Arbroath,' said Jane.

'Temporarily, before joining an aircraft carrier.'

'Okay, you've been on two dates with him—'

'And flown with him.'

'All right, but you've got to keep a sense of proportion. How well do you know him?'

Eileen pondered the question and said, 'There's a lot I don't know about his previous life, but I know *him* very well indeed.'

'But how?'

Eileen could only repeat what she'd said to Reg the previous evening. 'Some things defy explanation.'

'You say he kissed you, but did he try anything more than that?'

'No, he was a perfect gentleman.'

Jane looked doubtful. 'Something doesn't ring true.'

'You do enjoy playing devil's advocate, Jane, don't you?'

'Playing what?'

'Putting the opposite case.'

'No, but we're oppos, and I don't want to see you hurt.'

'We all get hurt sometime, Jane.'

The cooks of the mess arrived and began serving up. First the fish, then the mashed potato, then the cabbage went on to the plates.

Eileen stared at the combination. 'Whoever serves cabbage with fish?'

'The cooks in the Junior Ratings' Mess at Hatston,' said Jane. 'They know how to introduce a new... whatsit.'

'Initiative,' prompted Eileen. 'Don't worry, the cabbage will have been boiled to death, so it won't taste of anything.'

Plates were passed down the line, and Eileen and Jane received theirs.

'You were almost right,' said Jane, 'it's been boiled to within an inch of its life.'

'The fish isn't bad,' said Eileen, laying a bone on the side of her plate, 'although they might have filleted it.'

They worked their way stoically through the course and waited to see what the pudding was.

'Jam roly-poly,' guessed Jane, peering carefully, 'made with bread again, you can bet. It's anybody's guess what's gone into the custard this time.'

Eileen was inclined to be philosophical. 'Whatever it is, it can't be as bad as the cabbage.'

She was proved right. The improvised custard was slightly better than the cabbage, but they were both glad when they could escape from the mess.

They were heading for their quarters for the last twenty minutes before going on watch, when PO Wren Stubbs called out, 'Wren Dewhirst, Second Officer Clarke wants to see you in her office. Don't be adrift for your watch.'

'That will depend on Two-Oh Clarke,' said Eileen under her breath. Then, at normal volume, she said, 'Right-oh, PO.' She said to Jane, 'I wonder what she wants.'

'You'd better go and find out.'

Eileen retraced her journey along the passageway until she came to the door marked *2/O M. A. Clarke*. She knocked and waited.

'Come.'

Eileen pushed open the door and came to attention. 'You sent for me, ma'am.'

'Yes, Wren Dewhirst. Come in and take a seat.'

So far so good, thought Eileen. Had a bottle been in the offing, there would have been no offer of a seat. Obediently, she took the chair opposite her divisional officer's desk.

'Now, Wren Dewhirst, I've been looking at your service record, and an excellent one it is.'

'Thank you, ma'am.'

She turned a page. 'You also matriculated and you have an excellent Higher School Certificate.'

'Yes, ma'am.'

'You've been in the service now almost three years. Tell me, have you ever considered applying for officer training?'

That was a surprise as well as a remarkable coincidence. 'Yes, ma'am, in fact, I had it in mind to ask to see you about it tomorrow.'

'Really? Why tomorrow, particularly?'

'I'm on the twelve 'til twenty-hundred today, ma'am, but tomorrow, I'm free all day because I'm on the all-night-on.'

'I see. What do you consider to be the qualities required of an officer in the Wrens?'

'Leadership, example, fairness, and the ability to inspire trust, ma'am.'

'An excellent answer.' Miss Clarke sat back in her chair as if in surprise. 'What, would you say, are the elements of leadership?'

'Clear and decisive thinking, ma'am, plus example, fairness and the ability to inspire trust.'

'You really have thought about this, haven't you?'

'Yes, ma'am.' Actually, she hadn't given it a moment's consideration until then. Her replies were the result of quick thinking. She could usually think on the spot.

'Do you know what's involved in officer training?'

'Yes, ma'am, the "knife and fork course" at Greenwich.'

Miss Clarke smiled at her answer. 'There's rather more to it than that, Wren Dewhirst, but you're on the right track. How did you know about Greenwich?'

'One of the naval officers told me, ma'am. I had to install a transmitter in an aircraft and test it in flight. The pilot asked me if I'd thought of becoming an officer, and he told me about Greenwich.' It was basically the truth.

'Who was this officer?'

'Lieutenant Underwood, ma'am.'

'I see.' She perused Eileen's record further and said, 'Yes, you acquitted yourself well on that task. I'll speak to Lieutenant Underwood before he... when I can. It's always good to have a recommendation from a naval officer.'

'Thank you, ma'am.' Eileen would have liked to see Reg again, too, but that really was an officer's perk.

'There shouldn't be a problem, Wren Dewhirst. When you're called to Greenwich, though, it's likely to be at short notice.'

'That's all right, ma'am.' The sooner the better, as far as Eileen was concerned. With Reg gone, Orkney had little to offer her.

Second Officer Clarke found Reg in the Wardroom after lunch. 'Reg,' have you a moment?'

'I have several, now that I'm batting out time, May. Feel free to choose one. They're all available.'

'You recently took one of the Wren telegraphists up to test a transmitter.'

'That was all I did, May. My actions were those of an officer and a gentleman.' If she wanted to hold him to account for consorting with a Wren rating, she'd left it a little late. 'By the way,' he prevaricated, 'would you care for a post-prandial drink?'

'Not just now, thank you. She tells me that, whilst airborne, you asked her if she'd ever considered becoming an officer.'

Reg tried not to smile. So that was what it was about. Eileen was obviously boxing crafty when she told her that. 'Yes, I did. It's surprising what you can learn about some people in the briefest of meetings, and I thought she really had the makings of an officer.'

'I'm delighted to hear it. Have you any objection to my quoting you?'

'None whatsoever. Wren Dewhirst has my fullest recommendation.'

Miss Clarke blinked and said, 'She must have made quite an impression on you, for you to remember her name after so brief a meeting.'

'She made a lasting impression on me, May.' It was truer than he was prepared to say.

***

'Would you call it love at first sight? I mean, it does happen, and it can cause all kinds of problems.' Jane asked the question as they left the WT Office at the end of the watch.

'No, the first time I saw him, if you remember, was when he intervened between that horrible petty officer and me, and I just thought he looked nice, and he seemed to be on my side. The second time was when I installed the transmitter in his aeroplane, and he said he'd buy me a drink. I didn't believe him at the time.'

'What about when we were at the pub?' Jane seemed not to have noticed her argument weakening.

'That was when my knees began to wobble,' admitted Eileen.

'And then when he took you for a drink?'

'I was nervous at first, but then I decided I really wanted it to happen. Apparently, we both did.' She opened her locker and took out a folder of photographer's proofs. Ted had paid for them when she was at Whitehall Wireless Station, just before she was drafted to Orkney, because he particularly wanted a photo of her as he'd always known her, in civvies. As a rule, she wasn't keen on being photographed, but these had turned out all right. She was wearing the green dress she'd worn on her second date with Reg, not that its colour made a scrap of difference in a black-and-white photo. It simply made her look as he would hopefully remember her.

'Are you going to give him a photo?'

'Yes, this one.'

Jane nodded her approval. 'A good choice. You look really pretty in that dress.'

'Thanks. That's what he said.' Unscrewing the cap of her pen, she wrote on the back, '*To Reg. Be careful and come safe home. Lots of love, Eileen XXX.* Then, leaving it photo side down to let the ink dry, she opened her notepad and wrote:

Dear Reg,
I hope this photograph will help you remember me.
Thank you for two evenings and a flight I'll never forget. Let's see if we can, as you said, put one over on Zeus.
Bon voyage *and keep safe.*
Lots of love,
Eileen XXX.

She put the note and the photo in an envelope and sealed it, ready for morning.

Eileen arrived at the Wardroom the next morning, nervous but resolute. She was about to knock on the door, when it opened, and Third Officer Blane appeared in the doorway.

'Wren Dewhirst,' she said, 'are you looking for someone?'

'No, ma'am, I only want to leave a letter for Lieutenant Underwood.'

'Oh?' It was only natural that she should be surprised.

'He was very kind to me, ma'am, and I want to thank him before he leaves the station.'

'Of course.' Realisation became evident on Miss Blane's features. 'I remember now. It was the incident with the petty officer, wasn't it? Well, you've just caught him in time, as it happens, but how did you know he was leaving the station?'

Eileen thought quickly and said, 'It was just a "buzz", ma'am.'

'How these buzzes start baffles me, but I'll give Lieutenant Underwood your note.'

'Thank you, ma'am. That's very kind of you.'

'Not at all. I hear you're a candidate for officer training.'

'That's right, ma'am.'

'Well, good luck.'

'Thank you, ma'am.'

As the door closed, Eileen heard her say, 'Oh, Reg, a Wren just left a note for you.'

She was relieved that the note had reached him, but sick at the thought that he was only feet away, but beyond her reach. It was time for her to be grown-up about things.

6

November

Appointments and Diversions

Eileen occasionally received mail from home, and more often, from Ted, but the latest letter caught her eye and caused a ripple of excitement. She didn't recognise the handwriting, but the envelope was postmarked *Arbroath*. She was about to go on watch, so she tucked it into her shoulder bag to read later, when she could enjoy it in peace.

After what seemed far too long, she was allowed a stand-easy, and she took a mug of tea to a quiet corner and opened the envelope to find a visiting card, a letter and a photograph. He looked very handsome in what she imagined to be his best uniform, and she was reminded of his warm, expressive eyes. He'd written a message on the back, just as she had.

I had this taken as soon as I arrived here. The petty officer in the photography section was very obliging. I think it flatters me. Don't you agree?
Take care.
Lots of love, Reg XXX

She put the photograph safely in her bag and unfolded the letter.

Dear Eileen,
Thank you lots and lots for your note and the photograph. You look exquisite, just as I remember you.
We're hard at work here, as I expect you will be soon. Have you

heard anything, yet, about Greenwich? I told May Clarke it stood out a mile that you were wardroom material. She was very impressed with my lightning ability to recognise potential.

As soon as I know where I'm going, I'll give you the Postal Section details, but I suspect they'll give us a brief period of leave before that. Wouldn't it be marvellous if we were to find ourselves in London at the same time? At the risk of tempting Providence, and in case we do, I've enclosed a card with my home address and phone number. Don't be shy – my mother growls occasionally, but she doesn't bite.

I've just had a thought – it happens from time to time – in case we find ourselves in town together, do you enjoy dancing?

Please write soon.

Lots of love,

Reg XXX

Unaccountably tearful again, she put the letter and the card safely in her bag with the photograph.

Jane found her and sat beside her. 'Are you all right, Eileen?'

'Mm.' Eileen nodded happily. 'I've got a letter and a photo from Reg.'

'Have you? Can I see the photo?'

'All right.' She took it out of her bag.

Jane studied the photograph. 'You're just jammy, Eileen. I'd forgotten how good-looking he was, and now I hear wedding bells.'

'Make up your mind, Jane. Not long ago, you thought I was being daft.'

'That was before he wrote to you.'

At the end of the watch, Eileen returned to her quarters to reply to Reg's letter. She thought about it briefly and began.

Dear Reg,

Thank you for your letter and the lovely photograph. It's not at all flattering, but absolutely faithful to reality. I'm going to frame it and keep it safe in my locker, taking it out from time to time to remind myself of how lucky I am to have met you.

My application has gone in, but I've heard nothing as yet. 2/O Clarke told me I'd probably get very little notice, but I don't care.

I love dancing – my favourite dances are the foxtrot and the waltz – and it would be amazing if we did get leave in London at the same time. In case you should need it, you'll find my brother's address and phone number at the end of this letter.

Have you a favourite dance band/leader? Mine is Lew Stone and his Orchestra. I also used to love Al Bowlly's singing, and I was heartbroken when he was killed in the Blitz.

Do you have much time for reading? You said you'd borrowed a book from 3/O Blane. I read whenever I can. One of my favourite authors is P. G. Wodehouse.

Do write again, and I'll tell you just as soon as I hear from Greenwich.

Take care.

Lots of love,

Eileen XXX

She had not long to wait. The next morning, Second Officer Clarke handed her a draft notice, movement order and railway warrant. In the time left to her before her departure, she had time to open her letter to Reg, inserting a post script with her news, to dash off a quick note to Ted and also to her parents, and to break the news to Jane Stead. Theirs had been a solid friendship in the short time Eileen had been at Hatston, and they both vowed to keep in touch. The following morning, Eileen would catch the 0700 sailing from Stromness, but for the present, Second Officer Clarke wanted to speak to her.

Eileen knocked on her door, confident on this occasion that she had nothing to fear.

'Come.'

Eileen pushed open the door and came to attention.

'Don't stand on ceremony, Wren Dewhirst. Take a seat.'

'Thank you, ma'am.'

Miss Clarke smiled in a friendly way that came as quite a surprise to Eileen, and asked, 'Are you ready to leave?'

'Almost, ma'am. It won't take me long to pack.'

'Good.' She appeared to study her briefly before saying, 'It took you a while to make the decision, didn't it?'

'Yes, ma'am.' She had to be honest. 'When I first joined the service, ma'am, there was a type of officer candidate that, frankly, alienated me, so that I had no interest in taking that route. I'm referring to the socialites I met during training, who simpered at the instructors and courted the company of naval officers in order to get a leg-up the ladder.'

Miss Clarke eyed her sternly and said, 'I'm aware of the type of candidate you mean, and I can assure you that very few of them, if any, remain.'

'I gather so, ma'am. That's what Lieutenant Underwood told me, and I'm glad of it.'

'That was a long conversation you had with Lieutenant Underwood.'

'Yes, ma'am, it was.' She had a feeling she might have been caught out, and the officer's next words confirmed her suspicion.

'You know we have to read all outgoing correspondence, don't you?'

'Yes, ma'am.' In her excitement, the fact had slipped her mind. She braced herself.

'Duty must always come first, Wren Dewhirst. I think you're sensible enough not to let your attachment to Lieutenant Underwood distract you from that duty, but I thought a reminder would not go amiss.'

'Thank you, ma'am. I'll remember that.'

Less than two hundred miles away, as the crow flies, Reg was more interested in learning how the Grumman F4F Martlet flew. He signed both engine and airframe logs, waved the chocks away, and waited patiently for permission to take off.

After a minute or so, a green Very light soared from the Control

Tower, the signal for the squadron to taxi and take off. He watched the squadron commander go, followed by the other five aircraft that made up the flight, and then it was the turn of Reg's flight. The aircraft gathered speed, promptly demonstrating their superior performance over the Fulmar. The two-seater had addressed a pressing need at a desperate time, but it had always been a half-hearted gesture by the Air Ministry towards the end of its between-wars tenure.

Only the lightest touch on the controls was needed, and Reg eased back the joystick and took to the air, changing hands on the joystick so that he could wind the undercarriage retraction gear as he went.

At the requisite altitude, the whole squadron formed up in line ahead, and the squadron commander put them through various manoeuvres, including starboard echelon, port echelon and close 'V' formation.

It was a happy squadron that returned to the briefing room that morning. The Martlet, or 'Wildcat', as the Americans called it, had already been superseded in the US Navy by the faster and larger Hellcat, but, far from being a crumb from the rich man's table, it was manna from Heaven for the long-neglected Fleet Air Arm.

Commander (Flying) Edwards called them to order and addressed them.

'By this time, I imagine you're all madly in love with the Martlet, and that's as it should be. I hardly need to remind you that it's the first fighter of any quality that we've had since the Sea Hurricane, and that's in short supply.' He glanced down at his notes and continued. 'I'm sure you're wondering about your deployment, so I'll end the suspense now. You're each going to join one of two escort carriers. We don't know, as yet, where you'll be going, but I think we can safely narrow it down to two destinations.'

His observation prompted ironic laughter. The likelihood all along had been that they would join either Western Approaches or the North Russian convoys. The escort carriers, much smaller versions of the large, fleet carriers, were a relatively recent addition to the fleet and an essential part of any convoy's escort.

' "A" Flight, commanded by Lieutenant Commander Hughes, will join *HMS Seamer*, whilst "B" Flight, led by Lieutenant Underwood, will join *HMS Yorker*. The Tarpon dive-bombers that you see around you will be divided three to each ship so that three Fulmars can be assigned also. Their crews have already been informed. The Fulmars will form part of the fighter group in each ship. The remaining hangar space will, not surprisingly, accommodate a sub-flight of three Swordfish.' As the commander had said, that came as no surprise. The Swordfish biplane, slow and obsolete though it was, had proved itself repeatedly in anti-submarine warfare. It could also fly in weather conditions that prohibited more sophisticated aircraft, as it had demonstrated when taking off during gale-force conditions to carry out a successful torpedo attack on the battleship Bismarck.

One of the younger pilots, an RNVR sub-lieutenant, asked, ' "Yorker" and "Seamer" are cricketing terms, aren't they, sir?'

'Yes, they are. I imagine the Admiralty had run out of the kind of names they'd been giving the "*Attacker*" Class, and they started another series. Does that present you with a problem, Sub?'

'Well, sir, only that cricket's not a particularly warlike pursuit, is it?'

Patiently, the Commander (F) said, 'Ask any batsman who's faced Harold Larwood and, if he can stop shaking long enough, he'll tell you how warlike cricket can be.' As the others convulsed with laughter, he looked at the bulkhead clock. 'Any further questions?' Eyeing the unfortunate sub-lieutenant, he added, 'Sensible ones?'

There were none, so Commander Edwards dismissed the squadron, and Guy Davidson immediately sought Reg's company on the way out. 'So you're Big Chief Underwood, now,' he said.

'Still only a flight commander, Guy.'

'But as good as a squadron commander,' he insisted. 'You'll be leading the show without interference from the big tepee.'

'You can never rule that out, but one thing that hasn't changed is that you're still my wingman.'

'You can depend on me, Reg. Think of me as Doc Holiday to your Wyatt Earp.'

'I hope not. He was never sober.'

Guy stopped suddenly, and Reg asked, 'What's the matter?'

'I knew there was something I was going to do, and you've just reminded me.'

'You know I do all your thinking for you.'

'So you do. Come to the Wardroom and I'll buy you a drink.'

After two changes, Eileen arrived eventually in Edinburgh to find that she had a two-hour wait before the London train was due to depart. It was the kind of thing she'd come to expect in wartime, so she decided to pass some of the time in the station buffet.

As ever, the place was full of smoke. Nearly everyone smoked, even though they said cigarettes and tobacco were in short supply. She was glad that neither she nor Reg smoked. It was funny, the way she'd begun to think of them as a couple, and she hoped she wasn't tempting fate.

The buffet assistant finished serving someone and turned to Eileen to ask, 'What would be your pleasure, miss?'

'Just a cup of tea, please, with milk.' It was as well that the sandwiches didn't look very tempting, because she'd been given a bag meal at Hatston. She wanted to save that for later, though, working on the principle that the earlier she ate, the sooner she would be hungry again.

The assistant put the tea in front of her and indicated the large baking bowl that contained sugar. Here and there were wet, brown lumps where a wet spoon had been returned to the bowl. 'Only two per person,' she informed her.

'Thanks, but I don't take sugar.'

A voice on her left said unexpectedly, 'I expect you're sweet enough, aren't you darlin'?'

Eileen turned to see that the voice belonged to a corporal in the RAF. She made no response. Instead, she thanked the buffet assistant before taking her tea to an empty table, where she took her book, *Three Men in a Boat*, from her bag.

A few minutes later, the corporal reappeared to ask, 'Mind if I sit here?' he indicated one of the chairs opposite Eileen.

'I don't own the place. It's up to you.' She returned her attention to her book.

The corporal took that as encouragement and sat down. 'Where you headin', then?'

'London.'

'Whereabouts in London?'

'I'm not allowed to say.' It was always a convenient let-out, although the corporal was proving difficult to shake off.

'What you readin', then?'

Eileen was surprised at the number of people who asked that question without being remotely interested in the answer. It was just an approach. '*The Decline and Fall of the Roman Empire*,' she told him.

'Good, is it?'

'Riveting. I'm keen to find out how it ends.'

He seemed to give that some thought, and then said, 'Don't you fink the title sort o' gives it away?'

Eileen peered at the top of the page and then closed her eyes in a gesture of disappointment. 'Oh, dear,' she said, 'now you've spoiled the surprise for me.'

'I didn't mean to. I just fort you might have worked that out for yourself. You seem like a brainy sort o' gel.'

She closed the book and gave him a weary look.

He peered at the title. ''Ere,' he said, 'that ain't what you said it was. It's about free geezers and a boat.'

'Whatever it's about, I can't concentrate on it when someone insists on talking to me.'

He continued undeterred. 'You got a fella, then?'

'Yes.'

'What's he do, then, this fella?'

'He's a fighter pilot.'

'Officer?'

'Yes.'

The corporal got up, leaving his empty cup on the table. 'Have a nice journey,' he said.

7

Unwelcome News

In preparation for its deployment in the escort carriers, 844 Squadron was required to practise deck landings on the old aircraft carrier *HMS Argus*. For Reg and Guy, the only RN officers in Reg's flight, it was hardly necessary, but the more junior pilots had received only the most basic training in deck landing and take-off, having spent their active service operating from Hatston. That training, known as Assisted Dummy Deck Landing, or ADDL, had been carried out on dry land and with no arrester wires to stop them.

For much of the first morning, Reg and Owen Hughes watched their inexperienced pilots try to land, some managing to hook an arrester wire the first time, whilst others made circuit after circuit without success. By the end of the day, however, all pilots were able to land and take off confidently. Even so, the training continued on the basis that no degree of preparation was ever sufficient.

At the end of the week, the squadron bade farewell to the hard-working officers and aircraft handlers of *HMS Argus*, and returned to Arbroath to resume air combat practice.

'It's like running a kindergarten,' remarked Guy when they were back in the Wardroom.

'Everyone has to grow up,' Reg reminded him. 'I was at their stage by the end of 'thirty-nine, and just as clueless. That was almost four years ago.'

'Three for me,' admitted Guy. He reflected for a moment and said, 'Four years is a long time.'

'I've been operational for just three of them. Are you saying I should have been grounded by this time?' Because of the stress involved in operational flying, it was common for a veteran pilot to be given a non-flying appointment after a few years.

'Let's say that a lesser man might have been.'

'A cushy time at Hatston prolonged my flying career, Guy.' He looked hopefully at his glass.

Guy took the hint. 'My round, I think.' He signalled the Wardroom steward and ordered two pink gins.

'Most generous of you, Guy.'

'Not at all.'

'Going back to the VRs, give them time, Guy. They'll get there, just as you and I did. Do you remember looking down at the flight deck of a carrier for the first time?'

'Yes, it looked to be about the size of a postage stamp.' He gave up. 'Fair enough, it's not easy, and they coped very well.'

'Yes, they did.'

'Nothing ever worries you, does it?'

'If it's not worth the worry, Guy, why take the trouble?' He remembered Eileen also commenting on his customary carefree attitude, and he wondered how she was coping with the course at Greenwich.

'In short, ladies,' said the instructing officer, 'male ratings will not be required to salute you, just as junior naval officers are not required to salute senior Wren officers. It's one of the frustrating facts of life, and we must accept it. Maybe, one day, when the male population of the Senior Service suffers an attack of conscience... but don't hold your breath.' She waited until the ironic laughter had waned, and said, 'Thank you, ladies. Fall out.'

It was the weekend, and dispensation to sleep out made it more special than ever. After a brief word with some of her fellow candidates, Eileen picked up her valise, signed out, and left the college.

A little over half-an-hour later, she arrived at Ted's and Lorna's flat in Hoxton and let herself in with the spare key. She put her valise where it wasn't likely to be an obstacle, and went into the kitchen, where she found a note. It read: *Eileen, help yourself to tea. We'll be home by 6:00. Love, Lorna X (Ted as well, but he's shaving).*

Eileen glanced at her watch. It was almost six, so she put the kettle on for all of them and wasn't surprised when she heard the outer door open and close.

First, Ted hugged and kissed her, and then, in celebration, he lifted her almost to the ceiling.

'Careful,' she warned, 'you'll put your back out.'

'No, I won't. I lift people for a living.' He lowered her in front of Lorna, who greeted her warmly, if less spectacularly.

'The kettle's boiled,' said Eileen, tidying herself after her brother's exuberant greeting.

'That uniform was made for you,' said Lorna.

'That's just what I was going to say,' said Ted. 'We must have another photograph of you.'

'Why not wait until I get my third officer's uniform?'

'Why didn't I think of that? I know why. My brain's flagging for lack of tea.'

'I've just scalded it,' Lorna told him, 'so your brain will have to wait for it to brew.'

'Anyway,' said Eileen, 'thank you both for the compliment.'

Lorna brought the tea into the sitting room and gave it a stir. She asked, 'What have you been up to since we last saw you, apart from getting promoted?'

'I'm not promoted yet, not until the end of the course.' She could barely contain herself. 'I've got a fella!' She felt in her bag and took out the photograph of Reg to show them.

'He's a good-looking chap,' said Lorna.

'Let me look.' Ted held out his hand and took the picture. 'He looks honest enough. How did you meet him?'

Eileen told them about her argument with the petty officer and then her surprise flight in the Fulmar and Reg's promise of a drink on the strength of it. 'Then he asked me out. We went for a drink, and he told off one of the locals who'd objected to a girl going into the pub, except he did it in a nice way, the way he does everything.'

'Did he behave himself afterwards?'

'Yes,' she told her brother emphatically, 'he's a perfect gentleman.'

Lorna asked, 'Did he take you out again?'

'Yes, and that was when he told me he was being posted. He's gone to an air station near Arbroath, and he'll soon have to join an aircraft carrier, but he may get Christmas leave. His home's in London.'

'You've only just met him, so you can't know him all that well,' said Ted warily.

'We don't know very much about each other,' Eileen conceded, 'but we know each other intimately.'

'Intimately?'

'You know what I mean, Ted. Not in that way – I told you he's a gentleman – I mean that we understand each other... deeply.'

Clearly, Ted was struggling. 'But how, after such a short time?'

'I think I know what Eileen means,' said Lorna.

'I'm glad you do, darling, because I'm in the dark. I'm concerned because I've had to nurse her broken heart in the past.'

'Only once,' objected Eileen. 'It was David, next door, and I was only fifteen at the time.' To further her cause, she said, 'If he gets Christmas leave, you can meet him, and then you'll see for yourself why he means so much to me.'

'Two things you have to accept, Ted,' said Lorna, 'is that there's no point in arguing with Eileen's feelings – anyone's feelings, in fact – because you can't change them, and the other thing is that you can't change the future. It could all end in tears, but equally, Eileen and Reg may just live happily ever after. Does that make sense?'

Faced with incontrovertible logic, Ted had no alternative but to agree with Lorna. 'In that case,' he said, 'I'll look forward to meeting him at Christmas.'

'If he gets Christmas leave,' said Eileen.

Commander (F) Edwards mustered 844 Squadron again in the briefing room to say, 'Flight deck practice went particularly well, so I congratulate you all on that achievement.' He paused before delivering the next piece of information. ' "A" Flight will join *HMS Seamer* on the twenty-second of December preparatory to deployment as a convoy escort. "B" Flight will join *HMS Yorker* one day later, on the twenty-third, preparatory to similar deployment.' He ignored the scarcely-audible murmur of disappointment for the moment, and continued. 'For reasons of security, I can't give you any further details.' Then, in a more conciliatory tone, he said, 'I know you were hoping for Christmas leave, and I do sympathise, but convoys are a fact of life that we can't ignore and, to coin a phrase, there is a war on. I'm sorry, gentlemen. I shall see you all before you leave. Dismiss.'

Reg went to his cabin to write to his mother, and then to Eileen.

Dear Eileen,

I hope the course is going well. I imagine that when I hear from you again, you'll be Third Officer Dewhirst.

I'll come straight to the bad news, which is that there will be no Christmas leave for us. Instead, we're to be deployed before then. My service address from 23rd December is at the end of this letter.

Because we can't be together, I'm sending you a little something I found that I think you'll like. I would ask, though, that you don't open it until Christmas Day, and then, when you do, I want you to think of me. Wherever I am, I'll be thinking of you.

I'm sorry to be the bearer of bad news, but there's nothing I can do to change it. All I can do is wish you the happiest Christmas possible and say that one day, we'll see each other and put Zeus's nose out of joint.

Yours with all good wishes and lots of love,
Reg XXX

―――――

Eileen received the letter three days later, shortly before she was due to be examined in naval history, which made the examination a test of her concentration.

The second officer examining her asked, 'Who commanded the German cruiser squadron at the Battle of the Falkland Islands?'

Eileen forced herself to think. Reg's letter had driven everything else from her mind.

'Do you understand the question, Wren Dewhirst?'

'Yes, ma'am. I'm sorry, I've just received some bad news, but I'm trying to concentrate in spite of it.'

'Well then, do you remember the question?'

'Yes, ma'am, it was Admiral Maximilian von Spee.'

'Excellent.' The second officer adjusted her spectacles on her nose and asked, 'Who commanded the Battlecruiser Fleet at Jutland?'

Again, Eileen made herself concentrate. 'The British Battlecruiser Fleet was commanded by Vice-Admiral David Beatty, ma'am. Admiral Sir John Jellicoe commanded the Grand Fleet. Admiral Reinhardt Scheer masterminded the attack on the Grand Fleet, and Admiral Franz Hipper commanded the battlecruiser fleet sent to draw it out.'

The second officer gave her a straight look. 'You've just answered my next three questions without my asking them, Wren Dewhirst.'

'I'm sorry, ma'am. I offered the information while the Battle of Jutland was fresh in my mind.' She had an awful feeling that she'd put up a black as far as the exam was concerned.

'I can see you're struggling to concentrate, Wren Dewhirst, but it's greatly to your credit that you succeeded in answering all the questions correctly. Is your problem one we can help you with?'

'No, thank you, ma'am. It's just one of those things that happen in wartime.' She added, 'I don't want it to affect my performance in the exams.'

Quite unexpectedly, the officer smiled and said, 'On the contrary, you've just proved that you can rise above personal problems and concentrate on your duty.' She smiled again. 'Off you go.'

8

Reprieve and Reunion

On the day "A" Flight flew on to *HMS Seamer*, the pilots of "B" Flight were called to the briefing room.

Unusually, Commander Edwards was smiling. 'It's an ill wind, gentlemen,' he said, looking more cheerful by the second. '*HMS Yorker* is in dock with a damaged and leaking stern gland, which means that leave passes and rail warrants are being prepared for you as I speak. You're each being given a week's leave, which is about the time it'll take the dockyard to fit a new stern gland. Report back here by twenty-three fifty-nine on the twenty-ninth. Have a happy Christmas, all of you. Dismiss.'

The flight responded jubilantly.

Reg's first call was at the Post Office in Arbroath, where he sent two telegrams: one to his mother in London and, because he had no other address for Eileen, he sent the other to her brother, hoping he would be at home to receive it.

Ted was waiting when Eileen arrived at the flat. She was beaming, despite her earlier disappointment.

'I passed,' she said triumphantly. 'I'm now Third Officer Dewhirst. I'll collect my uniform when the outfitters reopen after Christmas, and I have to report to Whitehall Wireless Station on the twenty-eighth.'

'Congratulations!' Ted hugged her.

'Don't pick me up.' she begged. 'I'm an officer and a lady now.'

'And I'm proud of you.' Then, pretending he'd only just remembered, he said, 'Oh, yes. A telegram came today. You'd better read it.'

She frowned. 'A telegram?'

'Here.' He handed it to her in its envelope.

She opened it and read with growing incredulity:

DEAR MR DEWHIRST STOP PLEASE TELL EILEEN I HAVE LEAVE AFTER ALL STOP TRAVELLING TO LONDON TODAY STOP MANY THANKS STOP REG UNDERWOOD.

'He must think a lot about you to spend a fortune on a telegram,' said Ted.

'I don't believe it!' Eileen was almost dancing with joy.

'What's happened?' The query came from Lorna, who had just returned from shopping.

'Reg is coming home on leave,' sang Eileen, still euphoric.

'That,' said Ted, 'and the fact that she's passed the course, and I haven't to pick her up, because it ain't ladylike.'

'Congratulations,' said Lorna, 'and felicitations about Reg's leave.'

'If he's coming down from Arbroath,' said Ted, 'he won't get much change out of today. If I were you, Eileen, I'd leave phoning him until tomorrow.'

'All right, I'll phone his mother in the morning. She growls, apparently, but she doesn't bite.' Suddenly thoughtful, she asked, 'Does either of you know where there's a pawnbroker close by?'

'The East End's full of them,' Ted assured her. 'Do you need to pop your watch already?'

'No,' she said impatiently, 'I want to buy a present for Reg and I can't afford anything new. He's sent me something in a little box. I don't know what it is, but it'll be nice, if I know him.'

'I'd better come with you,' said Ted.

'Why? It's broad daylight.'

'It's not that, but I've never been shopping with an officer. You will be sure to behave like a lady, won't you?'

Reg was fortunate in catching the London train from Edinburgh in what little time the journey from Arbroath left him, but the train was crowded, and it seemed to stop at every station and halt along the line. He was also pestered for part of the journey by a civilian, who insisted on asking him about the war at sea.

'I really don't know,' he said. 'I haven't been to sea for some time. In any case, even if I knew anything, I wouldn't be allowed to tell you about it.'

'You're a pilot, aren't you?' The man pointed unnecessarily to the wings on Reg's sleeve.

'That's just it, you see. I don't know what's happening at sea, because I spend all my time in the air.'

The man was insistent. 'You must know how things stand,' he said.

'All right, this is how they stand. Rommel has been kicked out of Africa, the Allies have invaded Sicily, and the butter ration has fallen to two ounces per person per week. That's all I know, so will you please let me finish the ziz I was trying to have?'

The man grunted. 'Well, if that's how it is, I suppose there's nothing more to be said.'

'Thank goodness,' added Reg, feigning drowsiness, but privately evoking for himself the welcome image of Eileen as he remembered her and as she was in her photograph. She would surely phone him at home, probably in the morning. Before long, tiredness overtook him and he felt himself falling asleep.

Eileen looked despairingly at the object of her fancy, knowing it was beyond her pocket.

'That is the very best price I can do,' said the pawnbroker. 'If I took less than that, I should be robbing myself.'

Ted gave him a sceptical look and asked Eileen, 'What are you short of?'

'Realistically, twelve and six.'

'Well,' said Ted, 'it is Christmas.' He opened his wallet and took out a ten shilling note, placing it on the counter and adding a half-crown piece. 'There's your twelve and six,' he said.

'Oh, Ted, you're truly wonderful.'

The pawnbroker looked wistful, no doubt wishing he'd held out for more.

'Now,' said Ted, 'will you provide a gift box at no extra charge?'

'I should rob myself?' The pawnbroker asked the question of no one in particular, but reached beneath the counter for a small, plain cardboard box.

'Is that all you've got?'

With a deep sigh, the pawnbroker found a slim gift box and placed it on the counter in a way that made the pain of separation all too evident.

Eileen handed over her part of the purchase price to complete the transaction.

'You're wonderful, Ted,' she said, taking his arm as they left the shop.

'I know. That's what you keep telling me.'

'That's because you are.' They walked a little further, and then she said, 'I can't help thinking about the people who have to pawn their possessions with someone like him. I bet he gives them next to nothing for them.'

'It's a safe bet. I've seen a great deal of poverty since I came to the East End. Wherever there's need, you'll always find someone who's ready to benefit from it.'

They walked back to the flat, where they found Lorna at work in the kitchen. She asked, 'Did you find what you wanted?'

'Yes, thanks. Can I help?'

'Would you mind peeling some potatoes?'

'It'll be a pleasure. Where's your peeler?'

'In that drawer, behind you.' Lorna pointed to the kitchen cutlery drawer.

Eileen got to work on the potatoes.

'You don't waste any time,' remarked Lorna, watching her peel with familiar ease.

'No, these are the practised hands of the skivvy. I've been doing it all my life.'

'I know. Ted told me.'

As if answering to his name, Ted appeared in the doorway and said, 'I bet they're missing you in Cullington, Eileen.'

'No takers, Ted, and I haven't a scrap of sympathy for them.'

Half in fun, Lorna said, 'I feel guilty, now, asking you to peel the potatoes.'

'Don't, Lorna. It's a pleasure to do it for you.'

Ted remained for a while in the doorway, watching the two most important people in his life. He was a happy man.

At nine-thirty on the morning of Christmas Eve, Eileen could wait no longer. She hurried to the nearest telephone kiosk and dialled the number Reg had given her. The telephone rang for several seconds, and then a woman's voice came on the line. 'Hello?'

'Good morning. Am I speaking to Mrs Underwood?'

'Yes.'

'May I speak to Reg, please?'

'It's a little early for him, but I'll see if he's awake. It was almost three when he arrived home. Who shall I say is calling?'

'Will you please tell him it's Eileen?'

'Ah, Eileen. Of course.' There was a gentle bump as she put the receiver down, and Eileen waited, anxious not to lose valuable calling time, although Reg had all her sympathy. She knew how precious sleep could be.

She heard a voice emerge from its slumbers to say, 'Hello?'

'Reg, it's Eileen, also known as Third Officer Dewhirst. I'm sorry if I got you out of bed.'

'Eileen! How marvellous!' He sounded fully awake, now. 'I came down on a slow train that stopped at every available opportunity. It's wonderful to hear your voice.'

'Yours, too.'

'So, you passed, and with flying colours, I'll bet. Congratulations, and welcome to the wardroom!'

'Thank you.' She was conscious that time was ticking away. 'When can we meet?'

'Have you anything organised for this evening?'

'Nothing binding.'

'I'll call for you at seven. Okay?'

'Okay, but what are we going to do?' She needed to know that so that she could decide on what to wear, not that she had a great deal of choice.

'We'll have a drink and then have dinner at a place I know in Soho. After that, if you like, we can go on to somewhere else and dance the night away.'

'Oh Reg, you're amazing. I've really been looking forward to this, and it's going to be wonderful, I know.'

'It will be.' He sounded confident.

'Our six minutes are almost up.'

'Before you go, Eileen....'

'What?' She didn't want to put the phone down, but there was no arguing with wartime restrictions.

'That present I sent you. I asked you to open it on Christmas Day, didn't I?'

'Yes, it's still in its wrapping.'

'Will you open it and wear it tonight?'

'I don't know what it is, but yes, I will.'

'Until tonight, Eileen.'

'Until tonight, Reg.'

Happy and excited, she returned to the flat, where Lorna was waiting with a questioning look.

'He's calling for me tonight. We're going out to dinner and then we're going dancing. I can barely wait.'

'What are you going to wear?'

Ted came into the room, but retreated when he heard the last sentence and realised that the conversation was going to be conducted in girl code.

'I don't know. I only have two decent frocks.'

Lorna cast a speculative eye over her and said, 'You're a bit taller than me, but we're otherwise about the same size. Just a minute.' She disappeared into the bedroom and returned with a dark-blue, *lamé*-trimmed gown with puffed sleeves.

'It's beautiful.'

'Try it on. If it fits, you can wear it tonight.'

Scarcely able to believe her luck, Eileen took the gown to her bedroom and laid it on the bed. Nervously, she removed her skirt and blouse, and stepped into Lorna's gown, drawing it up to her shoulders and taking a quick look at herself in the long mirror. So far, so good. Leaving it unfastened for the moment, she returned to the sitting room to show Lorna.

'Eileen, you put me to shame. Put your arms through, and I'll do you up.' When the task was complete, Lorna stood back and surveyed the overall effect. 'Ted,' she called, 'where are you?'

'I'm hiding in the kitchen. All that women's talk makes me nervous.'

'Come out, you silly man. Cinderella's going to the ball tonight, and you're allowed a preview before she changes again.'

Ted walked into the sitting room and stopped abruptly. In a reverential tone, he said, 'Any man who doesn't find you irresistible, Eileen, must turn out for the other side.'

'Ted, really!'

'I'm sorry, Lorna, but it's true. That dress has magical properties. If you remember, the moment I saw you in it, I was hooked.'

'In that case, I'll forgive you.'

Eileen asked, 'What do you mean by "the other side"?'

Lorna left Ted to explain. It would be a reminder that, grown-up though his sister had become, she was still innocent, and in some respects, unworldly.

9

A Binding Promise

Reg arrived shortly before seven, but Eileen was ready. His gift of a Royal Navy sweetheart's brooch complemented the dark-blue evening gown with its silver *lamé* trim beautifully, a detail he noticed as soon as she answered the door.

'It's perfect, Reg,' she said. 'Thank you.'

'It's enough for me to see you wearing it.'

'Come in and meet my brother and his wife before we go.' She stepped back to let him into the flat. 'Reg, I want you to meet my brother Ted and my sister-in-law Lorna.'

'I'm delighted to meet you both,' he said, shaking hands with them. 'Has Eileen to be back by any particular time?'

'No,' Ted assured him, 'we know she's in safe hands. Have a terrific evening together.'

'Thank you.' Reg took Eileen's coat from her and helped her on with it. 'You look wonderful in that gown,' he said. 'It's almost a shame to cover it up, however briefly, but it is quite nippy out there.'

'Thank you.' She buttoned up her coat and picked up her bag. ''Bye, you two. See you in the morning.'

They got into the taxi, and the driver asked, 'Where to, guv?'

'The Savoy Hotel, please.'

'Right you are, guv.'

Eileen's eyes had opened wide. 'The Savoy?'

'Of course. You're an officer, now. There'll be no more char and a wad at a mobile café for you.'

'I've never been to a mobile café.'

'Well, it's too late to rectify that now.'

'You're as daft as ever,' she said, reaching for his hand, but it's wonderful to see you again, just when I thought it wouldn't be possible.'

'There was a technical hitch,' he told her cryptically.

''Nough said.'

The driver half-turned his head and asked, 'All set for Christmas, then?'

'I should hope so,' Reg told him. 'As sure as fate, I'll have forgotten something.'

'If you ask me, guv, Christmas is all hard work and expense, an' then it's all over an' done wiv in no time at all.'

'Mr Scrooge, I presume? Or are we allowed to call you "Ebenezer"?'

'I might as well be. That geezer had a point, if you ask me.'

'In that case, we'll have to agree to differ. I'm like the kiddies, waiting for the sound of sleighbells, except I've already got what I wanted.' He squeezed Eileen's hand gently.

They continued in silence until the taxi drew up in the wide courtyard of the Savoy Hotel.

''Ere we are, guv.'

A doorman opened the door for Eileen to get out, and Reg followed her, paying the driver and mischievously wishing him a happy Christmas.

'Can I help you, sir?' The offer came from a member of the hotel staff.

'We're going to the American Bar,' Reg told him, nodding towards the short flight of steps.

'You know the way, then, sir.'

'Yes, but thanks anyway.' He led Eileen, who was staring around her with wonder, to the cocktail bar, and they found a table. 'Choose anything you like,' he said, offering her the drinks menu. 'You could have a pink gin, an orange blossom cocktail, or there's a new cocktail they've put together in honour of the Senior Service. It's called the "Eight Bells".'

'I'll try that, but if it's very strong, I can't promise I'll drink all of it.'

'You don't have to.'

The waiter came to them. 'Good evening, sir. Good evening, miss. What is your pleasure?'

'We'd both like an Eight Bells, please.'

'Two Eight Bells,' repeated the waiter. 'It will be a pleasure, sir.'

When he'd gone, Eileen asked, 'Why is it called the American Bar?'

'It was once the name given to most cocktail bars, simply because the cocktail was an American invention. They're allowed to invent the odd thing from time to time. It makes them feel useful and it keeps them on their toes.'

She peered beyond him and said, 'There are two bars.'

'That's right. The inner bar is for men only.'

She nodded slowly. There was a great deal of information to assimilate. She whispered, 'What is that man on your right? I don't recognise the uniform.'

'The Polish Brigade,' he told her, 'first-class chaps, by all accounts.'

Her sightseeing was momentarily interrupted when the waiter brought their drinks to the table.

'Thank you.' Reg looked at the bill and handed one of the glasses to Eileen, who sniffed it discreetly before taking a cautious sip.

'Okay?'

'It's very nice.' The pianist was playing 'White Christmas' by Irving Berlin, thereby creating the perfect cocktail ambience, or so it seemed to Eileen. With her other considerations, the number served to remind her that it was Christmas Eve. 'Oh,' she said suddenly.

'Is something the matter?'

'No, I just remembered that I have a present for you.' She felt in her bag and took out the box. 'I thought it was appropriate when I bought it, but I'm not sure, now.'

'Maybe I can help.' He opened the box. 'Oh,' he said, 'a magnifying glass. How beautifully made.'

'Pull the handle out,' she prompted. 'It just pulls out. You don't have to unscrew anything.'

He pulled gently and took out a propelling pencil.

'You said you never had a pencil when you needed one,' she prompted. 'It's only gold-plated, I'm afraid, but Wrens aren't exactly rolling in money—'

'Not another word,' he cautioned. 'It's a terrific present, and all the better for being highly appropriate. Thank you.' He threw her a kiss and said, 'I'll never be caught without a pencil again.' He inspected it closely and said, 'What was that about gold-plate? I've just found a hallmark.'

'Surely not.'

'Here, look.' He showed her.

'Your eyesight's better than mine,' she said. 'I'll take your word for it.' She tried focusing on it again, but gave up.

'Use the magnifying glass.'

She peered again and said, 'You're right. All the same, I'm glad the man who sold it to me missed it as well. I wonder what he gave for it.'

'It was a good buy, as well as being the perfect present.'

'It serves him right. He's "a squeezing, wrenching, grasping, scraping, clutching, covetous old sinner".'

'I gather you weren't keen on him. Do you often go in for catalogue name-calling?'

'No, I don't. It was actually a quotation from *A Christmas Carol*, by Charles Dickens.'

'I know.'

'Reg,' she said, sounding like a sorely-tried parent, 'if I had something soft and harmless, I'd throw it at you for teasing me.'

He extended his lower lip and made it tremble.

'And it's no use sulking.' Her stern look collapsed into a broad smile. She asked, 'Where are we going next?'

'To a restaurant I know. I think you'll like it. My parents used to take me there for a treat at the end of a school holiday.'

'And can you still bear to eat there after losing your father?'

'He'd turn in his grave if I stopped going there. "Brace up, me boy," he'd say. "Behave like a man".'

As usual, Eileen was unsure whether to take him seriously or regard it as one of his silly utterances. 'Did he really speak to you like that?'

'Only when he was skylarking. He could be enormous fun. He'd say things such as, "For the whole of today, we have to speak to each other like the characters in *Treasure Island*." My sister used to take part as well, but she wasn't a good pirate. Even so, we'd all drive my mother mad, aping Long John Silver and Ben Gunn, not to mention Cap'n Flint, the parrot.' He looked at his watch and said, 'It's time to weigh anchor and set sail, me hearty.'

Laughing, she stood up, and he helped her again with her coat.

'Right,' he said, leaving the money with the bill, 'helm a-lee, full and by.'

'What does that mean?'

'I haven't the foggiest idea. I think it's just something the ancient mariners used to say when they were making light conversation.'

They left the bar and walked into the lobby, where an alert member of staff asked, 'Can I get you a taxi, sir?'

'Yes, please.'

In a very short time, they were told that a taxi was available. They walked out of the hotel, and Reg spoke to the driver.

'Edouard's in Greek Street, please.'

'Right you are, guv.'

It seemed to Eileen that stock phrases and pro-words were something taxi drivers and signallers had in common, and that 'Right you are, guv' was only like saying, 'Roger, out'. It was a small world, now she thought of it.

'You're wearing that perfume again,' said Reg.

'It's the only one I've got.'

'Don't ever part with it.'

'Idiot.' Even so, she moved closer to him and let him take her hand.

Presently, the driver reported, 'Edouard's, guv.' Then, possibly feeling that his fare might be expecting the obligatory statement of opinion, he said, 'If you ask me, them foreigners need to learn how to spell. My little grandson can spell "Edward", and he's only eight.'

Reg could only shake his head in hopeless agreement as he paid the aggrieved driver.

Edouard himself met them at the door, with an effusive welcome, before leaving them in the care of Raoul, his elderly Head Waiter. Eileen wondered briefly what the taxi driver's grandson would have made of Raoul's spelling of his name.

He showed them to a table, and produced a menu, informing them of the items that were no longer available.

Reg asked, 'What have you got that's not on the menu?'

Raoul leaned forward, as if he were sharing a secret, which, in fact, he was. 'Roast pheasant, sir.'

'What do you think, Eileen?'

'I've never had pheasant, but I'm game, if you'll allow the pun.'

'We'd both like the pheasant,' said Reg.

'And to start, sir? Also off the menu, we have an excellent pigeon pâté.'

'Never in the whole of my life,' said Reg, 'have I eaten pigeon pâté, an omission I must remedy as soon as possible. How about you, Eileen?'

'I have, and I can recommend it. I'd like that, too, please.'

'It'll be a game-rich meal,' said Reg, 'but times are far from normal.' To the waiter, he said, 'we'd both like that, please.'

'An excellent choice, sir. Would you care to see the wine list?'

'Wine lists always make interesting reading in wartime. Yes, please.' He took the proffered list.

'I'll leave that to you,' said Eileen. 'You know how much I know about drinks.'

'I do, but have you really eaten pigeon pâté?'

'No, but I've eaten pigeon, and there has to be a limit to what they can do with it.' She added, 'At least it'll be free of shot.'

Reg ran his eye down the now-depleted wine list and said, 'Let's have a bottle of the thirty-three white Bordeaux before it disappears. Heaven only knows what will be left when the Germans have gone home.'

'If I may be permitted to reassure you, sir, no *patron* worthy of the title would make good wines available to the Boche.'

'But how….'

Raoul demonstrated with a finger against his nose the confidential nature of that information.

'Right enough, Raoul, and thank you for the reassurance.'

'It was my pleasure, sir.'

Looking around her, Eileen said, 'This is all new to me. I've never eaten out on this level.'

Reg looked over the balustrade at the diners below and nodded.

'I don't mean that. I was talking about posh restaurants.'

'As I told you not long ago, you have to be prepared for a new way of life as an officer. The rules of wardroom dining are like the laws of the Medes and the Persians.' He gave a half-shrug and said, 'That's until the bread-throwing begins.'

'I don't believe you,' she said. 'That's a Bertie Woosterism.'

'You like Wodehouse, don't you?'

'I love it.'

Reg tasted the wine and gave it his approval.

'Two years ago, Ted's first fiancée was killed in the Blitz.'

'Poor chap. How awful.'

'Yes, he came home on leave, and it was difficult to know what I could do for him. Then, I remembered how he used to read to me when I was ill with measles and chickenpox and that sort of thing, so I read to him. I read a story from *The Inimitable Jeeves*, and I'm convinced it gave him some temporary comfort.'

Reg reached across the table to take her hand. 'What a wonderful girl you are,' he said, 'and what an excellent idea it was to read to him. Which story did you read?'

'*The Pride of the Woosters is Wounded.*'

'The one in which young Bingo Little falls for the dubious charms of Honoria Glossop?'

'The musclebound girl who "probably boxed for the varsity." That's right.'

They chatted throughout dinner, learning more about each other, although, as Eileen had already said, they already knew each other well enough.

When the time came to leave, they thanked Raoul and Edouard for a memorable meal and boarded the taxi hailed for them.

'The Blue Lagoon, please,' said Reg, and, in the time-honoured custom, the driver confirmed the destination. 'The Blue Lagoon. Right you are, guv.'

After a short journey, the taxi pulled into the side of the road.

'The Blue Lagoon, guv,' reported the driver.

'Thank you.' Reg paid him, and they entered the club, where a man in short-jacket evening dress asked, 'Are you a member, sir?'

'I am.' Reg showed his membership card, and the man took their coats.

In less than a minute, a young woman in a dress that was only just respectable, joined them and led them through a red, baize-lined door and into the main part of the club, where tables and chairs were arranged tastefully apart, and a band, comprising piano, clarinet, alto saxophone, bass and drums, played beside a small dance floor. The place was quiet; it was not yet ten o' clock, and members would be arriving, as they just had, having eaten elsewhere.

'One of the alcoves, I think,' said Reg.

'With pleasure, sir. I'm afraid supper ended fifteen minutes ago.'

'That's all right. We've already eaten. I'd like to see the wine list, though.'

'By all means, sir.' She took them to a table in a secluded alcove and lit the candle on their table. 'I'll be with you in a moment, sir.'

'This is the first time I've been to a nightclub,' said Eileen.

'Get used to it, Third Officer. It's expected of you now.'

'Fiddlesticks.'

The hostess returned with a somewhat depleted wine list. It was no surprise that only the more expensive wines remained.

Reg examined it critically and said, 'A bottle of the 'thirty-five Lussac St Émilion, please.'

'Certainly, sir.'

When the hostess was gone, Eileen said, 'I hope the wine's not too expensive.'

'Not in the least.'

She suspected he was making light of it, but she knew he would never admit it, so she asked, 'Do people actually eat in nightclubs?'

'Some do, but it's usually very basic fare. Most members use them as places for late-night dancing.' The thought seemed to remind him of something, and he asked, 'Have you a favourite number you like to dance to?'

'I have lots, but there's a dearth of Christmas numbers, isn't there?'

'They're not plentiful,' he agreed.

'If I had to choose a Christmas foxtrot, it would be between "Winter Wonderland" and "Santa Sent Me You".'

He looked blankly at her. 'You've lost me with the second one,' he said.

'Ann Todd sang it quite beautifully in *Ships With Wings*,' she prompted. Then, seeing his expression change from enquiry to unequivocal distaste, she asked, 'Don't you like Ann Todd?'

'She's delightful as well as beautiful and talented, but I was distracted by the wretched film itself.'

'I enjoyed it.' Puzzled, she asked, 'What was wrong with it?'

In the manner of someone breaking bad news gently, he said, 'If you remember, they used Ark Royal and her aircraft for all the carrier and proper flying scenes.'

'Yes, I was sickened when I heard she'd been sunk.'

'As were those of us who experienced it. Anyway, they shot a great deal of excellent footage – you couldn't have known it at the time, of course, but it's just possible you saw me flying one of the Fulmars—'

'Were you there?' Suddenly, she was excited.

'I was one of several,' he told her modestly, but you have to blame someone else for dreaming up that ludicrous story about the admiral's daughter. As for the impossible achievements of one Swordfish and one Skua, not to mention John Clements landing a Fulmar on top of a bomber and riding it piggy-back into a dam….' It was clear that he found words inadequate to describe his disdain.

'That's a shame. I thought it was a lovely film, as I said, and I went through at least two hankies when the John Clements character was killed.'

'I'm sorry, Eileen.' He smiled and reached for her hand. 'It evidently meant something else to you, and if it gets me off the hook, let me tell you that we entertained John Clements, Ann Todd and quite a few of the cast in the Wardroom, and they turned out to be very charming people indeed.'

'That must have been wonderful.' She tried to imagine such a gathering, but without success. 'You're not on the hook,' she assured him. 'It's just a difference of… emphasis.'

Any residual disagreement was forgotten just then, because the hostess returned with a bottle of the Lussac St Émilion, which she showed to Reg, who nodded.

She drew the cork expertly and poured a little into his glass to taste.

'That's excellent,' he said, putting his glass down. 'Thank you.'

She filled both their glasses. 'Enjoy the wine,' she said as she left them.

He asked, 'What was the name of that song, again?'

' "Santa Sent Me You". I hope we're not going spend the rest of the evening arguing about it.'

'No, we're not. Will you excuse me for a few seconds?'

'Of course.' She saw him approach the band, who were taking a short break between numbers. There appeared to be a brief conversation and a nodding of heads, and then he returned to their table, where he gave no explanation for his excursion, but picked up his glass and touched hers with it, saying, 'Here's to us.'

There, they had total agreement, and they both drank the toast.

'Here's a request,' said the bandleader. 'It's for Eileen, and it's "Santa Sent Me You" from the film *Ships With Wings*.'

'Reg!' It was difficult to know what else to say.

'May I have the pleasure?'

'Of course.' She followed him to the dance floor and let him lead her into the dance. The floor was filling up as more members arrived, making it difficult to dance properly.

'It's always the same with these club dance floors,' he said. 'They make them tiny so that they can get more tables in. Let's just shuffle.'

'All right.' Holding each other close, literally cheek-to-cheek, was more than acceptable, and she shuffled happily with him. 'Thank you for the request. It was a lovely surprise.'

Turning his head, he kissed her cheek discreetly. Then, in a curious, clipped manner, he said, 'Simply being with you, my dear, brings out the best in me.'

'Who was that?'

'It was supposed to be John Clements.' He hesitated. 'Or, was it Charles Laughton? I'm always confusing those two.'

'Beast,' she laughed. 'Just be yourself.'

'All right.' The number reached its end. 'Let's thank the musicians,' he suggested. 'We owe them that much.'

They stopped by the band, thanked them for playing the request, and returned to their table.

Examining her very obviously in the light of the candle, he said, 'I can't get over how absolutely scrumptious you look in that gown.'

'You make it sound as if you want to eat me,' she laughed.

'I do, starting with your fingers, one at a time.' He took her hand and pretended to nibble.

'Don't be silly, but thank you for the compliment, all the same. Actually, it's not my gown.'

'Isn't it?'

'No, and before you ask me if I stole it out of Harrod's window, Lorna lent me it.'

He looked hurt. 'I wasn't going to say that about Harrod's.'

'Good.'

'I thought you'd pinched it from Chanel.' Before she could respond, he said, 'As well as demonstrating excellent taste, your sister-in-law is obviously a good hand to have around.'

Eileen laughed again. 'She's lovely,' she agreed. 'I used to think I'd resent whoever Ted married, just for taking him away, but Lorna and I are the best of friends.'

'You and she are very much alike, physically.'

'Oh, the hair? I suppose so.' With a mischievous look, she said, 'When you came to pick me up, I didn't realise you were casting your eye over my sister-in-law.'

'To coin a phrase, I only had eyes for you,' he assured her.

After a little thought, she said, 'I'm glad I'm going to Whitehall Wireless for my first appointment.'

'It couldn't be more convenient for you.'

'And you can't say where you're going, can you?'

'I'll let you know the address to write to,' he assured her.

She cocked her head. 'He's just announced "Winter Wonderland",' she said wistfully, but the floor's very crowded.'

'Let's dance, or shuffle, here,' he suggested.

'Is it allowed?'

He narrowed his eyes. 'It's pushing the bounds of acceptable behaviour,' he said, standing up and offering her his hand, 'but I don't think anyone will mind.'

'It's quite secluded here,' she said, watching him a little nervously as he extinguished the candle.

'That's why I asked for an alcove,' he admitted with a licentious chuckle.

They held each other very close and swayed to the familiar music. Now secure in the darkness of the alcove, Eileen closed her eyes in sheer bliss. After a while, she felt a soft kiss on her neck. No one had ever kissed her there, and it was lovely. She wished he would do it again, and she learned quite soon that wishes sometimes came true, because he repeated the gesture twice before moving to her parted lips.

Inexperienced though she was, she found herself responding, mirror-like, to his attentions and was conscious of a quickening of her breath. It was another new experience for her.

Their moment of intimacy was interrupted, however, when the bandleader said, 'In a few minutes, the bells will usher in Christmas Day, ladies and gentlemen, but before that, we have time for another number. It's that great Bing Crosby success, "I'll Be Home for Christmas".'

'I'd have said his biggest success was "White Christmas",' said Reg as they returned to their table.

'I can't help wondering if "I'll Be Home for Christmas" has left a few people feeling a bit raw.'

'Like "We'll Meet Again"? Songwriters never think, do they?'

'Even so,' said Eileen, standing up, 'let's not waste it.'

Again, they retreated into the darkness and swayed blissfully to the gentle beat.

In what seemed no time at all, the band came to the end of the number and, with immaculate timing, the leader announced, 'Merry Christmas, everybody!' The revellers returned his greeting, and he went on to say, 'Let's welcome Christmas nineteen forty-three with a truly great song: "White Christmas"!'

Reg leaned closer and kissed Eileen. 'Happy Christmas, darling,' he said.

No one had ever called her that, and she was quick to respond in her excitement. 'Happy Christmas, darling.'

They stood up to dance to 'White Christmas", but dancing was soon forgotten as they kissed again with undiminished enthusiasm.

The number drew to its close, and Reg asked, 'Do you remember the last time we met, and I said I had a feeling about us?'

She nodded. 'I still have.'

'So have I.'

In the seclusion of the alcove, they made their avowal and promised never to lose contact.

10

Moving On

The news that Eileen's twenty-first birthday would be on the nineteenth of January, long after the end of Reg's leave, eclipsed even the sinking of the battlecruiser Scharnhorst, at least, for the time being, and it involved him in some urgent shopping, after which, he presented her with a charm bracelet. To start her collection, he added a tiny, golden key to mark her majority, and a heart pierced by an arrow, which needed no explanation.

'I'm going to add to it each year,' he told her, 'hostilities permitting, of course.'

'It's wonderful, Reg. Thank you.' They were at the flat, Ted and Lorna having gone to the Plaza to see *For Whom the Bell Tolls*.

'I'm glad you like it.'

'I love you.' In the unlikely event of her trying to keep count of the number of times she'd told him that, she would have long since lost count. 'I'll send you a photo of me in my new uniform.'

'I'll look forward to that, although you look wonderful in everything. You're what my sister calls a "clothes horse". It's a compliment,' he assured her. It means that, being tall and slim, you'd look *chic* in a sack tied in the middle with parcel string.'

'Thank you. What's your sister's name?'

'Vera. She hates it, but it's an old family name, so she's saddled with it. I'd have introduced you, but they only gave her seventy-two hours for Christmas, so she's gone back to Faslane.'

'That was awful.'

'Well, it does mean that some of the family porcelain's still intact.' He patted her hand consolingly.

'Don't be awful.'

'Vera doesn't mind. She really is a smasher.'

'I can well imagine that.'

'I mean she smashes things. She's clumsy.'

Determined to find some quality worthy of commendation, Eileen asked, 'Is she a clothes horse, too?'

'She's quite slender, but she has to work at it.'

'So do I, but rationing helps.' She nestled more closely against him and said, 'No one's ever paid me compliments the way you do.'

'How do they usually do it?'

'With wolf-whistles and crude remarks. Window cleaners are the worst offenders.'

He nodded sympathetically. 'I blame George Formby for much of it.' Then, more seriously, he said, 'There hasn't been much love in your life, has there? It's no wonder Ted and you are so close. He must have been the sole provider, and there's a limit to what a brother or a sister can do.'

'That's true.' She was more interested in his background. 'Did you go to a posh boarding school, Reg?'

'I boarded at prep school and then at my public school, but the only thing that was posh was the fees.' Suddenly, he smiled broadly.

'What's the joke?'

'I just remembered something.'

'Well, go on. Tell me.'

Clearly enjoying the recollection, he said, 'My father received a letter from my headmaster, notifying him that the school fees would be increased by two-and-a-half percent.... Now, I'm sure he dictated, "*per annum*", but his secretary typed, "*per anum*". Anyway, my father replied, saying he could probably stump up the extra money, but asking if he could continue to pay as he always had, through the nose.'

'That's rude, but it's funny.' She allowed herself to laugh, despite the ribald reference.

'Lots of rude things are, and my father had a *risqué* sense of humour. It possibly came of being a career naval officer, so watch out.'

'Oh, I shall.' She took the opportunity to remark on something that had impressed her ever since he told her about his father's death. 'Isn't it good that you can remember all those happy times you had with your father?'

'Yes, it is. They were buried for some time. The news hit us all very hard, but the good times eventually began to shine through again. We shared a few this Christmas, especially when I had to stand in for him.'

'In what way?'

'My mother managed to find a capon – turkeys seem to have disappeared off the planet – and, in-keeping with my role as the surviving male member of the family, I had to carve the damned thing.'

'What's wrong with that?'

'Only that I haven't a clue about carving. I suppose I should take lessons from one of the stewards on board ship. It's worth a try. At all events,' he said, returning to his story, 'my mother had to take over, and she's not brilliant at it, either. In the end, we all had a good laugh. It was all we could do.'

'It was good that you could.' Eileen was reminded of something that had puzzled her in the past. 'I've eaten capon,' she said, 'and I know it's a kind of chicken, but what's so special about it?'

'Seriously?'

'Yes, I've always wondered.'

He gave it some thought. Finally, he said, 'You know that to produce a big, strong ox, it's necessary to separate a bull from its… reproductive parts, don't you?'

'No, I didn't know that, but I'll take your word for it.'

'The same applies to a capon. It's a chicken without its… egg-fertilising gear. It grows bigger without them.' He hesitated. 'I hope I haven't embarrassed you.'

'No, I'll survive.' She looked up at the clock and said, 'Ted and Lorna will be back soon.'

'And I have to pack my things.'

Eileen stood up with him. 'I'd come to the station,' she said, 'but I do think it's better if I respect your mother's right to do that.'

'Probably.' He took her in his arms. 'Take care and keep in touch. I love you.'

'You take care. I love you too.'

They kissed finally and then broke apart.

She watched him go. It had been the best Christmas ever. She could only hope for more, and that, like her future happiness, would depend on Reg's continued safety.

She managed to persuade Ted not to accompany her to the naval outfitters, as she didn't wish to be reminded embarrassingly of being kitted out for the girls' school when she was eleven. He agreed, but still insisted on her being photographed in her new uniform.

An assistant completed his transaction, waited until his customer, a lieutenant commander in the RNVR had taken his leave, and turned to Eileen. 'Can I help you, miss?'

'Yes, please. I'm Third Officer Dewhirst. You have some uniform for me.'

The assistant consulted a large book on the counter and said, 'Yes, Miss Dewhirst, we have. Please bear with me for a moment.' He went into a back room and returned with two substantial cardboard boxes. 'I'll put these in a changing room for you and ask a female assistant to come to you when you're ready.'

'I'm going to need stockings as well,' she told him.

'I'll inform the female assistant.'

Buoyed by the significance of the occasion, she closed the changing room door and removed her outer clothing and then her skirt.

The new number five uniform looked magnificent, and when she tried it on and looked in the mirror, it was evident that the tailor had done a superb job. She would have a best uniform made of doeskin when she could afford it, but that really would have to wait.

While she was admiring the tailor's skill, there was a discreet knock on the door. She opened it to find the female assistant carrying a raincoat, a greatcoat and a tricorne hat.

'Would you like to try these on, Miss Dewhirst?'

'Yes, please. She tried both garments and found, as she expected, that they fitted her perfectly. 'Excellent.'

'How many pairs of stockings would you like?'

'Just two, please. I can always buy replacements from "slops".' She corrected herself hastily. 'Rechargeable Stores, that is.' As Reg had reminded her more than once, she was a lady now.

'May I?' The assistant picked up her civilian blouse and nodded. 'I can usually tell shirt and collar sizes just by looking.'

'Four of them, I think. I still have the shirts and collars that were issued to me.'

'Of course.'

Eventually, two assistants carried Eileen's purchases to the waiting taxi. For convenience, she had changed back into civilian clothes, but she would make the necessary effort, later, for the photographer.

Reg arrived at Arbroath to learn that the new stern gland had been fitted to *HMS Yorker* and that the ship was 'in all respects ready for sea.' She would only be ready for war when her aircraft were embarked, an event that would take place in two days' time. He wrote and posted notes to his mother and then to Eileen at her brother's address, as there was every likelihood she would be allowed to sleep out, billets being usually at a premium.

Dearest Eileen,

This is just a quick note to give you my address, which is: HMS Yorker, BFPO Ships.

Good luck in your new appointment. I know you'll do well.

I'll never forget Christmas Eve and the other times we spent together. I only wish I could be with you for the New Year. Unfortunately, I can't, so I'll just wish you the happiest of New Years. Let's hope we get together again soon. I'll write more fully when I can.

Yours with all my love,

Reg XXX.

After a surprisingly easy journey, Eileen reported to the Old Admiralty Building, which housed Whitehall Wireless Station. Everything felt strange: the uniform, the deferential attitude of the Wren on the Quartermaster's desk, and even identifying herself as 'Third Officer Dewhirst'.

The Wren examined her temporary identity card and spoke to someone on the internal telephone, after which she said pleasantly, 'If you'd like to take a seat, ma'am, someone will be here shortly to take you down to the station.'

'Thank you.' She realised that it was the first time anyone had called her 'ma'am', and for some reason she was unable to fathom, it brought the whole experience into focus.

After only a few minutes, a Third Officer with dimpled cheeks and a friendly smile came to the desk and greeted her with a handshake. 'You must be Eileen Dewhirst. How d' you do? I'm Angela Crowthorne. I'm to take you on a Cook's tour of the station and then present you to the Paymaster Lieutenant Commander.' She led the way down a gently-sloping passageway, explaining as she went, 'Everything happens underground, you understand, basically where it's safe from bombing. She stopped at the intersection of two passages and pointed to the left. 'Through there is where the grown-up stuff happens, the Admiralty Operations Room and all that sort of thing. They say if you go far enough along that passageway, you end up in the cellar of Number Ten, Downing Street. Naturally, no one can get through the door without a special pass.' Taking the passage in the opposite direction, she said, 'Let's go to Message Handling first. You're not likely to see anything you haven't seen before, but those are my orders.' It was now apparent that Angela was a prolific chatterbox, and inevitably, she asked, 'Have you got a chap?'

'Yes.'

'It's just as well, because there's no one at all exciting here. What does your chap do?'

'He's a pilot. I met him on Orkney, but he's about to join an aircraft carrier.'

'Oh, bad luck. I hope you can get together before long.'

'We had some time together at Christmas.' Then, feeling that the interest had become one-sided, she asked, 'How about you? Have you got someone?'

'Yes, a chap in the Tank Corps, of all things. We're from the same village, so it's almost a childhood romance. Soppy, isn't it?'

'No, I think it's delightful.'

Angela stopped at the door marked *Message Handling*, to say, 'Remove your hat before going in there, Eileen, or you'll stand out as a novice.'

'Thanks for the tip.' Eileen removed her hat and held it under her arm. She still had much to learn.

Angela led her to the glass-fronted office, where she tapped on the door and opened it. 'Good morning, ma'am,' she said to the second officer behind the desk. 'This is Third Officer Dewhirst joining the station for the first time.' The triangular sign on her desk bore the name *2/O J. J. Curwen*.

'How d' you do, Miss Dewhirst?'

'How do you do, ma'am?'

'Where were you previously?'

'Before I went to Greenwich, I was at *HMS Sparrowhawk* on Orkney, ma'am.'

Miss Curwen smiled unexpectedly. 'At least, you'll find it warmer here.'

'I imagine so, ma'am.'

'So, you're newly-commissioned. You'll soon settle in. I wish you every success.' She offered her hand again, and it was clearly the signal for them to leave.

'Thank you, and good day to you, ma'am.'

Once they were outside the door, Angela said, 'Just keep your fingers crossed they don't put you in Message Handling. It's only slightly more fascinating than watching hair grow.'

'I was a telegraphist until I went to Greenwich. Do you think they'll take that into account?'

'I wouldn't bank on it.' She inclined her head forward and said, 'Come on, I have to take you to Coding and then W/T before lunch.'

11

January 1944

'Of Ships and Shoes and Sealing Wax....'

The aircraft were to join *HMS Yorker* at Loch Ewe. As Guy observed, the destination rather gave the game away, as Loch Ewe was the collection point for North Russian Convoys. The Swordfish and Tarpon dive-bombers took off from Arbroath at 0800, followed by the Fulmars and Martlets at 1000. The two-hour interval was dictated not so much by differences in speed, as the need to allow for any problems in landing-on.

Reg learned subsequently that there'd been no real hitches, although two of the Tarpon pilots had been obliged to have more than one attempt before making a successful deck landing. When he arrived with the fighter group, he elected to land first so that he could watch the rest of his flight from the Observation Platform.

The signal was made, giving him permission to land, and he lowered his arrester hook and made his approach, conscious of his responsibility as flight commander to set an example to his flight. As he approached from astern, he saw the Deck Landing Control Officer, or 'Batman', as he was known because his signalling apparatus resembled two perforated table tennis bats. He was holding them level, which meant that he was happy with Reg's trim and speed. He then gave the 'Come On' signal, beckoning with both bats at head height, so Reg descended and felt the reassuring 'grab' as the first arrester wire prevented his onward travel, and then the thump as his wheels touched the flight deck. The handlers released the wire from the hook, and Reg proceeded to the forward part of the flight deck, where the DLCO passed one finger across his throat, ordering him to cut his engine, and then gave him the hands-raised, fists-clenched signal to apply his brakes. Finally, he rewarded him with the thumbs-up sign, and the handlers came forward to fold the Martlet's wings prior to taking it down to the hangar.

He hurried up to the observation platform that was the domain of Commander (Flying), and introduced himself.

'Underwood, sir, in charge of the fighter group.'

'Welcome aboard, Underwood. My name's Stevenson.' He offered his hand. 'We seem to have avoided each other so far.'

'Unintentionally, I'm sure, sir.'

'Where have you been until now?'

'Orkney, and before that, Lee-on-Solent and *Ark Royal*, sir.'

The commander winced. 'Bad luck. I was fortunate enough to survive the sinking of *Courageous*. I went on to serve in the macship Audacity.'

'That's a wealth of experience in escort work, sir.' The macships, or merchant aircraft carriers, were converted grain or oil tankers with their superstructure removed to allow the addition of a flight deck. Before the advent of the escort carrier, they were invaluable in protecting convoys by air, particularly in the mid-Atlantic gap, which was beyond the range of land-based aircraft, but an easy hunting ground for U-boats.

'At all events, Underwood, that was a copybook landing.'

'Thank you, sir. If you've no objection, I'm rather keen to watch the others land.'

'None whatsoever.' Quite unnecessarily, Stevenson pointed to the huge glass screen.

Next to land was Guy.

'This is Davidson, sir, my wing man and an excellent pilot.'

The commander nodded and continued to watch. Happily, Guy did nothing to contradict Reg's description, and Stevenson nodded approvingly.

'The others are all RNVR, sir, keen and conscientious, all of them.'

'You're very loyal to your flight, Underwood. I like that.'

'Thank you, sir. This is Andrews. He's rather high, but I see the batman's on to him.' Andrews adjusted his altitude and descended, catching the second arrester wire.

'Very nice,' commented Stevenson.

Each Martlet pilot made his landing without embarrassing Reg, and then it was the turn of the Fulmars, which were to be deployed as night fighters and early warning aircraft.

The first made his approach far too high, and the batman waved him off to try again. On his third approach, he was able to make a good landing, catching the fourth wire. Happily, the second and third Fulmar pilots were each successful on their first attempt.

'That was a good showing, Underwood,' said the commander. 'What was the name of the first Fulmar pilot?'

'Carpenter, sir.'

'He'll be fine, given time. It's only a matter of practice and concentration.'

'He did well, landing on *Argus*, sir. I imagine nerves affected his performance today.'

'Oh well, if the last convoy I did in *Piper* was any indication, the routine will become second nature to him in no time at all.'

They were portentous words. 'I gather you were kept busy, sir.'

The commander looked up at the bulkhead clock and said, 'The Captain will broadcast in just over an hour's time, but you'll have gathered by now that we're engaged in carrying munitions to Murmansk. As you probably know, the war in Russia is going less well for the Nazis than they would prefer, so they're particularly keen to stop the convoys that are supplying the Russians.' He shrugged. 'In the mid-Atlantic gap, our Swordfish and Tarpons have the task of keeping the U-boats' heads down and, if possible, sinking them, and then, as soon as we come within range of land-based aircraft in Norway, the Luftwaffe raises its ugly head. That's where our Martlets and Fulmars come in.'

'I'm glad we're not going to be bored, sir.'

'Oh, you won't be, Underwood. I can assure you of that.'

Reg spent the next hour with his flight, making sure they had everything they needed, and reassuring Sub-Lieutenant Carpenter that neither he nor Commander Stevenson had been at all worried about his landing. 'Practice makes perfect,' he told him. 'Don't let it prey on your mind, and remember that I have complete confidence in your ability.'

At 1130, the Tannoy crackled. 'D' you hear, there? D' you hear, there? This is the Captain speaking. First, let me welcome our air group, who arrived within the last couple of hours. The rest of the ship's company have been kept busy, exercising without you, but you are our *raison d'être*, and your presence means that we are now "in all respects ready for sea and for war." Secondly, no one can have failed to work out that we are about to escort a convoy. That, after all, is our purpose. As soon as Convoy JW Thirty-Nine is assembled, we shall sail to our rendezvous in mid-Atlantic. There, we shall complete the exchange with our Canadian and American allies for Convoy RA Thirty-Nine. Our destination will then, on this occasion, be Archangel, rather than Murmansk. I wish I could tell you why, but our Russian allies regard most information as classified. On my last visit to Murmansk, I even found the location of lavatory paper to be a matter of the utmost secrecy. When I eventually found some, its lamentable quality convinced me that they'd been quite right to keep quiet about it. We hope to sail in two days' time. Good luck, all of you.'

It was good that the captain had a sense of humour, and with that thought, Reg went to his cabin to write to Eileen.

Six hundred and fifty miles away, in the flat, Eileen was reading Reg's earlier letter. It was unfortunate that, in wartime, there was so little they were allowed to write about. She knew the name of his ship, but she had no idea where he was going, and mail was going to be infrequent and sometimes erratic. She resolved to write to him often and regularly, even if her letters consisted of banal nonsense. She reasoned that, if he received several of them at once, he would know that she was as full of love for him as she'd ever been, and that was important. Only in keeping in touch would they 'put one over', as Reg had said, on that jealous old tyrant of a Greek deity. Determined, she took out her notepaper and wrote to him. Hopefully, her letter would arrive before he sailed.

'Last call for mail!' The message came through the Tannoy, prompting Reg to take his latest letters to the Regulating Office.

Having done that, he inspected his pigeon hole, and was surprised to find letters from his mother and Vera, and there was another addressed to him in Eileen's ill-formed but no less welcome handwriting. 'I'll take these now,' he told the Regulating Petty Officer. 'It'll save someone a journey.'

'You're right there, sir.' The RPO spoke into the Tannoy again. 'Last call, the very last call, for mail.'

'You spoil us to death, RPO.'

The hard-pressed RPO merely grinned and dropped Reg's letter in the mail bag.

Back in his cabin, he read his mother's and his sister's letters. It was good to hear from them both, but if he were honest, it was Eileen's letter that excited him most.

Dearest Reg,

I was on watch on New Year's Eve, but your wishes meant everything to me.

Naturally, I can't say anything about what I'm doing, so instead, I'm going to tell you what I'm thinking. Let me know if you find my musings boring.

I think about that wonderful Christmas Eve we spent in London, and then I can't think of a single reason why we shouldn't do it again. We could make it a regular event, albeit after the war. It could be an annual tryst. I think that's the right name for it, but I'm sure you know what I mean. It would be something special and meaningful to just you and me.

I also think about the Cook's tour you gave me, sightseeing from the air! I think aircraft have improved so much in the last few years, that people will travel by air much more after the war. Don't you think so? We could do that, and you could take a break from driving – sorry – flying, and let someone else do the hard work.

At times, I think of you in the future as a senior officer. You'll appear terribly grand to some people, especially junior officers and ratings, but I'll know the truth. Of course, I'll have to brush up my party manners before that happens, although I did get high marks on the 'knife and fork course'.

As I sit here alone – Ted and Lorna are both on watch at the fire station – I think about things that have happened in this war: awful things, of course, but good things as well. Lots of people have been brought together, not always as ideal partners, I have to admit, but Zeus is to blame for that. Anyway, who invented that silly law about hubris? If Zeus himself was responsible for it, I can only conclude that he was insecure and paranoid. Of course, I'm new to all this. I did Latin at school, but.... as for Greek mythology, well, it's all Greek to me!

You know, I wanted so much to wear my sweetheart's brooch all the time, and now I can. Lorna gave me a chain so that I can hang it round my neck, inside my uniform collar and shirt, and nobody has a clue it's there.

By this time, I've probably wittered on for far too long, so I'll close now. I have to press my uniform and polish my shoes for tomorrow. There are no stewards where I live.

Take special care.
Lots and lots of love,
Eileen XXX.

Reg read the letter twice before putting it away to enjoy again later. Eileen had given him cause to think. What could two people write about whilst observing strict security? Letters sometimes went astray in wartime, occasionally falling into enemy hands. Bearing that in mind, he thought Eileen's idea was an excellent one, although it should have been no surprise, as she was highly intelligent. As he thought more about her, he reminded himself that she was most likely innocent as well as nubile, two opposing influences his conscience could scarcely ignore. However, with Eileen in London, and he about to enter the North Atlantic, guilt could safely remain dormant for the time being.

As a distraction, and because it was highly necessary, he returned to the question of letter-writing, which he pursued almost until lunchtime. At that point, and unable to improve on Eileen's idea, he decided to follow her example.

Eileen found walking from the bus, along the south-eastern side of Trafalgar Square, to Whitehall Wireless Station an enjoyable experience, particularly in fine weather. In addition to the historic majesty of Nelson's Column, the famous Landseer lions were a pleasing sight as they peered from their sandbag shelters. It may have been a trick of her imagination, but they did seem rather less fierce than in their accustomed postcard presence.

Something else that pleased her was the number of friendly salutes she received. Foreign servicemen were ignorant of the fact that Wren officers were the poor relation of the Royal Navy, and on one morning alone, Eileen had collected salutes from two Polish and three Czech airmen, two Free-French soldiers, and numerous men in uniforms that were difficult to identify exactly, but whose cheery, 'Good morning, ma'am,' marked them out as American. She resolved to tell Reg about them in her next letter. She would also tell him about London in the winter sunshine, because it would please him to think of his home city in that way. Wherever he was going would be very different from London, or any other city, for that matter.

Everywhere she went, she found innocent things to write about in her letters. Somehow, a task that had once seemed almost impossible had become engaging and fun. She thought about that as she returned the salutes and friendly smiles of Britain's courteous allies.

12

Success and Innocence

Reg learned that the passage to the mid-Atlantic rendezvous was likely to be less exciting than the homeward stretch. Torpedoes were expensive, and it made more sense to the Kriegsmarine that they should sink ships when they were carrying munitions, than when they were yet to take on their cargo. The Luftwaffe, however, were less thrifty with their bombs, so it was as well that *Yorker* kept up an early-warning patrol, provided by Fulmars and Tarpons, the only aircraft equipped with radar.

The convoy had barely left Loch Ewe and put out to sea, when the Tannoy came live. 'D' you hear there? D' you hear there? Scramble the fighters! Scramble the fighters!'

Reg raced down into the hangar, where the handlers were already preparing the Martlets by moving them on to the lift. He found his aircraft and climbed into the cockpit, signing the logs as he went, after which he went through the cockpit drill. The rest of his flight were similarly occupied. When everyone signalled ready, he waved to the petty officer in charge of the handlers, and the lift ascended. Once on the flight deck, the chocks were removed, and Reg started his engine and taxied on to the steam catapult in the bows. At a signal from above, the catapult hurled his aircraft forward. Simultaneously, he opened the throttle wide. The Martlet dipped a little on leaving the flight deck, but then picked up speed.

He continued to climb in a wide spiral that enabled him to see each member of his flight take off. When the last aircraft was airborne, he switched on the intercom and ordered them to join him at fifteen thousand feet. Not surprisingly, the threat was reported to be approaching from the east, from one of the bases in occupied Norway, and he kept a careful look-out in that direction.

Within a very short time, Guy Davidson came on the intercom. 'Bogeys, Boss! Two o' clock down!'

'I see them. Sub Flight Baker, remain at this altitude and keep a look-out for fighters. Sub Flight Able, choose your targets and... break!' Peeling off, he led the other two into the formation of six Heinkel One-Elevens, thankful again for the performance of the Pratt and Whitney engine. With the nearest Heinkel in his gunsight, he flipped the guard off his trigger and opened fire. Such was the devastating effect of the six 0.5 calibre guns, his reward was immediate, and he saw the Heinkel leave the formation, trailing a long plume of black smoke. Others had also been hit; one was actually diving towards the sea with its tailplane and rudder shot away. The mayhem continued until all six bombers were accounted for.

'Well done, Sub-Flight Able! Sub-Flight Baker, is anything happening up top?'

'Negative, Boss,' reported Guy. 'You had all the excitement today.'

'Come and join us.' He waited until Guy's sub-flight came in sight, and ordered, 'Flight Two, form up on me, line ahead.'

The other five Martlets followed him back to *HMS Yorker*, where Commander Stevenson had news for them as well as approval.

'Well done, all of you,' he said, joining them in the briefing room. 'Six HE One-Elevens is an excellent start. I expect they were rather surprised.' There was a chuckle, and he continued. 'A decision of great moment was made this morning; at least, that's when it was announced. I'll read the signal to you.' He referred to a signal form on his desk and read, ' "From Admiralty to all Fleet Air Arm units." Message begins. "To facilitate seamless co-operation between the Fleet Air Arm and the US Navy Air Force, the Grumman Martlet will become known universally, and from the date of this signal, as the 'Wildcat' ".' He shook his head and smiled. 'Clearly,' he said, 'someone at the Admiralty has too much time on his hands.'

Guy said, 'But the Yanks never use names, sir. As far as they're concerned, it's the F-Four-F. It always was.'

'My point exactly, Davidson.' Picking up the signal again, he said, 'You're not alone in this. The Tarpon is reverting to its original name, and will be known from henceforth, as the "Avenger". I imagine it will still be the TBF to our allies.' He laughed shortly and said, 'As far as I'm concerned the Americans can call it whatever they like. It's their property, after all.' He picked up the signal forms, still shaking his head at the absurdity, and said, 'Well done again. Dismiss.'

In the Coding Room at Whitehall, Eileen was still unable to see why changing the names of two aircraft was going to facilitate seamless co-operation with anyone. She'd taken particular notice of the signal because it was to do with the Fleet Air Arm, and that was where her interest lay, but it seemed meaningless. She wondered, however, if Reg's new fighter happened to be either of those affected. She would never know, at least, as long as the war continued, but she couldn't help wondering.

The matter was driven from her mind at lunchtime, when Angela Crowthorne said, 'You're free tomorrow night, aren't you?'

'Yes. Why do you ask?'

'I am, too. Shall we go to the Odeon to see *Fanny By Gaslight*? I've heard it's good.'

Eileen wondered. Angela seemed to live her life in a state of enthusiasm. She asked, 'Who's in it?'

'Jean Kent, James Mason, Phyllis Calvert... lots of people.'

An RN lieutenant asked, 'What are you going to see, ladies?'

'*Fanny By Gaslight*,' Angela told him.

'That should be interesting.' Catching the eye of a fellow officer, he said, 'They're going to see *Fanny By Gaslight*, old man.'

'Really? I suppose there's nothing like seeing things in a different light, is there?'

'Maybe not,' but I do feel that some things are best left to the imagination.'

'Better to feel your way, rather than see it in stark realism,' his friend agreed.

They both laughed.

'You two,' said Angela, 'have minds like sewers.'

As hard as she tried, Eileen could make no sense of the men's conversation, neither could she understand Angela's objection to it. When they'd left the table, she asked, 'What was all that about?'

Angela looked faintly surprised. 'D' you mean you really don't know?'

'That's why I'm asking. Why did you say what you did, just then?'

'About them having dirty minds?'

Eileen looked around to see if anyone was within earshot, and said, 'Yes.'

'Have you never heard it called that?'

The mystery was becoming more involved all the time. 'Have I never heard what called what?'

Angela leaned over and whispered in her ear, causing Eileen's eyes to open wide. 'It's one of many pet names,' she said. 'My chap calls it "Paradise", although I suppose most men would agree with that. It's so important to them that it makes them do all kinds of silly things.' Leaning sideways confidentially again, she said, 'My brother says that it takes one woman twenty-one years to make a man of her son, and it takes another no time at all to make a fool of him. He's a bit of a wag, my brother.'

Eileen was still speechless.

'Think of me as your guide and mentor,' said Angela generously. 'You obviously need one.'

Sub-lieutenant Bellamy, the young man who had questioned the naming of the new carriers, had identified another anomaly, at least, as he saw it. He was in conversation with a fellow sub-lieutenant, and the subject turned out to be the decision to operate Fulmars from *Yorker*'s already overcrowded hangar. 'Frankly,' he was saying, 'they should be in a museum. They're outclassed by any enemy aircraft you care to mention.'

It was unfortunate for him that Reg overheard the conversation.

'Bellamy,' he said quietly, 'a word in your ear. The dry, outward-facing side, that is. It may interest you to know that, in nineteen-forty and forty-one. Lieutenant Davidson and I flew the Fulmar in the Mediterranean against aircraft of both the Regia Aeronautica and the Luftwaffe. It was at a particularly crucial time in the war, when we had to get fighters to Malta or lose the island altogether.'

'I realise that, sir. I simply—'

'Be quiet and listen, Bellamy. The Fulmar was all we had, and it did the job remarkably well. By skilful deployment on the part of the Fighter Direction Team and some desperate and determined work on our part, we made that task possible. It's true that the Fulmar is slow, but it has other, excellent qualities, and it doesn't deserve to be derided by someone who has little or no knowledge of its history.'

Bellamy's face glowed red. 'I'm awfully sorry, sir. I spoke out of turn.' His last sentence was hardly more than a whisper.

'But now you know the truth, so you're unlikely to repeat the mistake. Let me buy you a drink, and we'll put it behind us.' He held up his hand to beckon the steward. 'What would you like?'

'That's awfully kind of you, sir. A glass of beer, please, if that's all right.'

The steward waited. 'Sir?'

'A glass of beer and two pink gins, please, Roberts.'

'Aye, aye, sir.'

The drinks arrived very quickly, and Bellamy retired, still embarrassed.

'That,' said Guy, 'was the most lenient of all bottles, and possibly the gentlest since Leonardo said to Mona Lisa, "I didn't fart for your amusement, so kindly stop grinning when I'm trying to paint your portrait." You're the very model of clemency, Reg.'

'I just saw it as a friendly piece of advice. It didn't call for a full-scale bottle. In any case, I want him to be able to look to me for advice and encouragement, not just the heavy hand.'

'I wonder what James Mason is really like,' said Eileen. They were at Angela's flat, having returned from the cinema. 'He always comes over as sinister.'

'He wasn't sinister in *The Bells Go Down*,' said Angela. 'I thought he was quite appealing, actually.'

'Mm. There was one thing I didn't understand, and I still don't. What was the place John Laurie owned that was so awful?'

'A brothel. Apparently, they were common in London in the last century.' She studied Eileen's mystified features and explained. 'It was a place where men could pay for intimacy with women, and I'm talking about men who couldn't find it any other way.'

'Why couldn't they?'

'Oh, well.' Angela had to think about that. 'They might have been too old to appeal to women, or they might have been too shy.'

It sounded awful to Eileen. She asked, 'Weren't they against the law?'

'I'm not sure. I'll ask my brother when I see him. If it's on the subject of you-know-what, you can be sure he'll know the answer.' After a little more thought, she said, 'One thing I do know is that it's dangerous.'

'Is it?'

'It's possible to catch diseases in those places.'

Eileen was reminded of her early days in the WRNS. 'A surgeon lieutenant gave us a lecture about that at *HMS Pembroke*,' she said, 'shortly before we left for *Cabbala*. No one can call me stupid, but I found him difficult to follow.'

'He might have been the same one we had. The trouble with doctors is that they speak their own language and expect everyone else to be fluent in it.'

Eileen wasn't used to discussing matters of intimacy, but it was somehow easier with Angela. 'He showed us a box and said it was a safeguard against disease. Like all pusser's property, there was an anchor on it, but he never showed us what was in the box, and he didn't say how it worked.'

'Yes, the medical profession does like to deal in mystery, but don't worry, because I can help you with that.'

Yorker's fighters were scrambled twice more before the rendezvous with the homeward-bound convoy, and each attempted strike proved expensive for the enemy. It also demonstrated the value of early-warning patrols.

Commander Stevenson told Reg, 'You've had just a sample of how the enemy feels about Russian convoys. Keep your fingers crossed for a drop of roughers between here and Archangel. It'll keep the U-boats' heads down and the Luftwaffe will be grounded. Otherwise, we'll be kept very busy indeed.'

As it happened, the Air Group's next brush with the enemy involved a U-boat. Reg was on the bridge when the signal came through.

The Captain read it, and a huge smile spread across his face. 'Good news, gentlemen,' he said, 'Swordfish 3F has just sunk a U-boat that was shadowing the convoy. Good old "Stringbag"!'

The officers on the bridge joined in the celebration. Yet again, the obsolete Swordfish had proved itself invaluable.

Commander Stevenson looked at his watch and said, 'It should return within the next ten minutes.'

Everyone waited for the return of the successful aircraft, all eager to congratulate the crew as soon as they landed. Soon, a speck in the clear sky grew larger and became a Swordfish biplane.

The captain gave the helm order that would turn the ship into the wind to facilitate the Swordfish's landing, and said to the senior rating on the signalling lamp, 'Yeoman, make to Senior Officer, "Your attention is drawn to the Fleet Hymnal…."' He took the book from the bridge counter and referred to the index of first lines. 'Hymn four five two, verse eight.' As the lamp clattered, he handed the hymn book to Reg, who stood nearest him.

'Thank you, sir.' Reg read for everyone's benefit:

'O happy band of pilgrims,
Look upward to the skies,
Where such a light affliction
Shall win you such a prize!'

It was a special moment, and one that was shared by the whole ship's company.

13

Wise Counsel – and an Important Question

One of Eileen's new duties was that of Divisional Officer. Each rating had to know the identity of his or her DO, because it was that officer to whom those problems were taken that couldn't be addressed by a senior rating. It wasn't long before her services were in demand.

'Wren Donaldson,' she said, opening her door, 'come in and take a seat.' The girl entered diffidently, and Eileen waited for her to sit down. 'Now,' she asked, 'what can I do for you?'

'I don't know, ma'am.' Her face crumpled, and she began to sob uncontrollably.

'Have you got a hanky? If not, I have one somewhere.' Eileen rummaged through the disorganised contents of her bag and found one just as Wren Donaldson located hers.

Presently, the girl's sobs grew less frequent.

'Blow your nose,' advised Eileen. Then, noticing the waterlogged state of the unfortunate girl's handkerchief, she said, 'Here, use mine, and then take your time and tell me about your problem.' Strictly speaking, she was off-watch, but she was happy to give the Wren the time she needed.

After several blows, Wren Donaldson said, 'I want to... leave the... Wrens, ma'am.' Her voice was interrupted by tiny shudders in a way that Eileen remembered from her own past woes.

'That's rather drastic after all your training, isn't it?'

'Yes, ma'am.'

'You must have a very good reason for wanting to leave, and I have to say that what you want is by no means easy to achieve.' An uncomfortable thought occurred to her, and she asked, 'Are you pregnant?'

'No, ma'am, it's... nothing like that.' Happily, the shudders seemed to be subsiding.

'Well, tell me your reason.'

She appeared to brace herself, and then she spoke. 'On my last leave, my boyfriend and I got engaged, ma'am.'

'Lovely. Congratulations, Wren Donaldson.' Eileen had already noticed the engagement ring. 'But what's so awful about that? I'd have expected you to be brimming over with happiness.'

'It's just that my fiancé is in Scotland, and I'm here in London, ma'am.'

'Is he in the armed forces?'

'No, ma'am, he's a farm worker. It's a reserved occupation.'

'I see, and you're missing each other.'

'Yes, ma'am.'

'Hm.' Eileen forced herself to be compassionate. 'The man in my life is serving in an aircraft carrier, goodness knows where, and I don't know when I'm likely to see him again, so I can sympathise with you, but that's not a lot of use, is it?'

'No, ma'am.'

'Let's look at the possibilities, shall we? I don't suppose you want to rush into marriage and start a family?'

'Not so soon, ma'am.'

'Well, that's sensible of you, at least. Let's consider what would happen if your request were approved. I imagine you'd be sent to work in a factory, maybe in Birmingham or Sheffield, so you'd be back to square one.'

The girl gaped. 'Would they really do that, ma'am?'

'Yes, they would. The National Service Act requires young women who have no children to perform some kind of war service. Of course, they might direct you into the Women's Land Army, but chances of finding yourself on the same farm as your fiancé would be similar to those of landing on the moon with a return ticket.' She shrugged. 'I'm sorry, Wren Donaldson, you're left with only one other option.'

'What's that, ma'am?'

'Let's take stock of the situation. Your fiancé is in Scotland, and he's not likely to be moved, so you'll always know where he is – I could envy you that – and you'll always be able to spend your leaves with him.' She consulted the file in front of her and said, 'You're doing a useful job in Message Handling, and you might think of that as "doing your bit", as people insist on calling it, but you can do much more than that.' She could see she had the girl's complete attention, and she went on. 'Women all over the country are doing what they have to do whilst their husbands, fiancés and boyfriends serve in Italy, Burma, at sea and in many other places. Many of those men won't come home until the war's over.' Although she could hardly bear to think of it, she had to say, 'Some will never come home.' Leaving the thought to register for a moment, she asked, 'Don't you consider yourself luckier than those women?'

The girl bit her lip. 'I suppose I am, ma'am.'

'You'll get another leave before long, and you'll see him again. Meanwhile, just remember that part of your war effort consists of getting on with your duties and coping with what is no more than temporary separation.' She added mischievously, 'You will meet again, and what's more, Vera Lynn agrees with me.'

Now more in charge of herself, the girl said, 'I see what you mean, ma'am, about all those other women. I feel guilty, now.'

'Feeling guilty does no good whatsoever, Wren Donaldson. Turn that feeling into a force for good. Write to your fiancé, tell him how much you love him, and then return to your duties resolved to play your part in winning this war.' She stood up to indicate that the interview had ended.

'Aye, aye, ma'am. Thank you, ma'am.'

'It was no trouble.'

———

It was a new experience for Eileen, and one she shared with Angela at her next opportunity, which came that evening. They were at Angela's bedsitter.

'So there I was, playing Dutch aunt to a girl marginally younger than I was.'

'It's all in a day's work for a divisional officer,' said Angela. 'Mind you, it's not a good idea for an officer to mention her private life to a Wren. You're best keeping that under wraps.'

'I thought she needed to know she wasn't the only one in that situation.'

Angela considered the argument and said, 'On the whole, I think you did well, but try to keep it neutral in future.'

Eileen felt justifiably pleased with her efforts, and the incident had given her an idea for her next letter to Reg.

Dearest Reg,

How I miss you and long for our next leave together, whenever that may be. It's as well we both have plenty with which to occupy ourselves. Let me tell you about something that happened here recently. I was called on to hear about the troubles of a junior Wren in my division. She's twenty, just a year younger than me, but I felt somehow much older than my twenty-one years. I think it was the effect of the sudden responsibility that caused it. Anyway, the wretched girl wanted to leave the WRNS because she's recently become engaged and she's missing her fiancé. Well, I'll admit that I felt quite dismissive at first, and especially when I discovered that her fiancé is a farm worker in a reserved occupation, but I had to give her a fair hearing, and I persuaded her that she would be serving her country just as well by coping with the situation, as well as performing her duties with a degree of enthusiasm. What a hard-hearted person I've become! Not really, of course.

On a cheerier note, you know, of course, how Wren officers seldom receive salutes, but did you know that a great many of our allies are ignorant of the fact? You'd be surprised if you saw me walking through Trafalgar Square, returning salutes from Americans, Canadians, Dutchmen, Free Frenchmen, South Africans, Rhodesians, Czechs and Poles. They really know how to treat a lady!

I hope everything is well with you. I think about you most of the time. One day....

Keep smiling. I love you tons, hundredweights and quarters, rods, poles and perches.

Eileen XXX

She was surprised to receive a letter from him the next day. It was three weeks old, which wasn't at all bad.

Dearest Eileen,

No less a person than the Commander (Flying) admired your photograph, today. I thought he might compliment me on my immaculate taste, but he just said I was a lucky so-and-so, which I am. I can't deny it.

I'm writing this with some difficulty, as I'm obliged to wedge myself into my bunk. We're currently battling with a storm force ten and, happily, so are the other side. I find it occasionally therapeutic to think of Nazis helpless with seasickness. What makes them think they have any right to be at sea, anyway? I thought they'd learned that lesson at Jutland... but pleasanter thoughts beckon.

I've been thinking about your idea of an annual tryst, and yes, I've consulted the Wardroom Dictionary, also known as the Paymaster Commander, and he says it's the right word, all right. It's an excellent idea – yours always are, damn it – but I fear it may be necessary to make it a movable feast, as Their Lordships are never too keen on all their officers being granted Christmas leave, and there may well be times when I'm left holding the fort, so to speak. Now, that brings me neatly to another question, which I shall address when this ship recovers from its present gyration. Wait... that's better. You see, it's all very well to talk of trysts in the possibly distant future, but don't you think we're signalling a six to the scorer before the batsman's played his stroke? We haven't yet asked and answered the important question, but there's no time like the present. You'll have to imagine, just for the nonce, that instead of being jammed in my bunk, I'm down on one knee in earnest supplication, holding the ring that I fully intend to buy when we're next on leave together. There, I've committed myself. Eileen, will you be mine for evermore and, forsaking all others, put up with my vagaries and shortcomings for the rest of our lives? I mean it, honestly.

After that broadside, I can't think of anything else to say, so I'll just tell you that I'm yours, with love by the bucketful,

Reg XXX

To say that ongoing togetherness was something Eileen had been taking almost as read, Reg's proposal had come as a huge and wonderful surprise, and her reaction invited immediate comment.

Lorna asked, 'Is everything all right, Eileen?'

'Yes,' she said jubilantly, 'things couldn't be better. I've just received a proposal of marriage!'

'Wonderful!' Lorna extended a cautionary hand to Ted, who seemed unsure how to react.

'I only want my little sister to be happy,' he said with studied innocence and a wary eye on Lorna, 'but I hope she's not going to make a lightning decision.'

'And I couldn't be happier! All this time, we've been talking about doing things after the war's over, and Reg has just reminded me of the one conversation we never had. That was until now.'

<hr />

She enjoyed telling the story again, when she and Angela were alone in the Wardroom anteroom.

Angela waited until the steward was gone, and said, 'You're looking pleased about something, Eileen.'

'I had a letter from Reg yesterday, and he popped the question.'

'Wonderful! You must be ecstatic!'

'I am.' She demonstrated the fact by almost knocking her coffee over and spilling it.

'The only time my chap gets around to asking a question, it's usually something like, "Can we do it with the light on?" He's not the most romantic of souls.'

'But you'll get married, won't you?'

'That's the general idea.'

103

'Reg signed off with, "Yours, with love by the bucketful." I don't think that's very romantic, either, but I'll forgive him after his proposal.'

Angela wrinkled her nose in thought and said, 'It must be quite difficult, waxing romantic when he's at sea with everything going on around him.'

Eileen preferred not to think of it.

14

Surprises

After a final skirmish with enemy aircraft that ended with the remaining two Nazi aeroplanes breaking off the engagement and heading for their base in Norway, *HMS Yorker* negotiated the Kola Inlet and led the convoy into the port of Archangel.

'I must confess,' said Guy when the ship was at anchor, 'I'm not in a hurry to go ashore this time.'

'I found the warmth of the welcome less than overwhelming,' agreed Reg. 'Let's resist the temptation and stay on board.'

It had been a gruelling convoy, although losses had been few. Unfortunately, however, to arrive in Archangel or Murmansk with fewer than the original number of ships was to prompt the indignation of their demanding and ungrateful allies, which meant that neither port was a favourite with British naval personnel.

'Let's have a drink,' said Guy. 'It's your turn to pay.'

'I paid for the last round.'

'I'm sure you're mistaken.'

'Not in the least, but look here, instead of arguing about it, why don't we do the grown-up thing and "zob" for it?'

'All right.' Guy turned his chair to face Reg's. 'Stone, paper, scissors or tiger, man, gun?'

'We used stone, paper, scissors last time, and I lost,' said Reg.

With a condescending look, Guy said, 'If you think it'll make the slightest difference, we'll use tiger, man, gun. The best of three lurks, okay?'

They sat facing each other with poker-straight expressions, and Reg counted, 'One, two.' Both of them clapped their hands on their knees twice and made their first bid. Reg folded his arms, as a proud man of the Empire, whilst Guy curled his fingers to impersonate the claws of a tiger.

'Tiger eats man,' he said.

Again, they clapped and made their bid. This time, Guy chose the tiger again, but Reg held an imaginary rifle. 'Gun shoots tiger,' he said, not without satisfaction.

'Last time,' said Guy. For his final bid, he chose the rifle, whereas Reg reverted to the man. 'Man holds gun,' he said. 'I win, you pay.'

'The usual three fingers?'

Reg nodded. 'Three fingers' was Guy's adopted measure, not of raw whiskey, as in the Wild West, but the home-produced luxury of pink gin.

As the wardroom steward approached, Commander Dodds, the Engineer Officer entered the wardroom, so Guy bought him a drink as well.

'Thanks, Davidson.' When the drinks arrived, Commander Dodds said, 'I need this. Do you chaps mind if I join you?'

'We'd be honoured, sir,' said Reg.

'I don't believe you.'

'Well, you'd be very welcome, sir.'

'That's right, Underwood. It's better not to be too extravagant.'

Guy said, 'I gather all is not well, sir.'

'You're quite right, Davidson. I'm experiencing a problem again with the stern gland.'

Both junior officers knew better than to make a ribald comment. Instead, they waited for the commander to go on.

'This ship seems to go through them. I suspect that the problem is the prop shaft rather than the gland, but that can only be ascertained in dock.'

'That's a shame, sir,' said Reg, whose heart was dancing a jig. A dockyard job had to generate leave.

The commander laughed shortly. 'I suppose you two poodle-fakers can't wait to go on leave.'

'Lieutenant Underwood is now a respectable man, sir,' Guy informed him with mock-seriousness. 'He's semi-betrothed.'

'How the devil can you be half-betrothed, Underwood? Either you are or you're not.'

'I proposed marriage in a letter, sir. I've yet to receive the lady's reply, but I'm quite confident.'

'In that case,' said the Engineer Commander, beckoning the steward, 'I was going to buy you both a drink, so let's drink to the happiness of you and your fiancée-to-be, Underwood.'

'I'll drink to that, sir.'

Once again, *Yorker* ran the gauntlet of the Luftwaffe on leaving the Kola inlet, and the fighter group fought off each attack successfully, but not without loss. Sub-Lieutenant Bellamy, the officer whose judgement of the Fulmar Reg had been obliged to correct, was shot down off Hammerfest. He failed to bale out and was therefore posted 'killed in action'. Reg wrote what words of comfort he could find to Bellamy's next-of-kin, knowing that his efforts would do no good whatsoever.

A distraction came in the form of a 'pipe' from the Captain.

'D' you hear, there? D' you hear, there? This is the Captain speaking. *HMS Yorker* has been ordered to Chatham Dockyard for repairs. You're probably wondering why Chatham has been chosen, and I can only conclude that the shipyards are too busy building ships to be bothered with the likes of us, and a repair yard is the obvious choice. Leave will naturally be granted. I should like to take this opportunity to thank you for your hard work and dedication on this deployment. That is all.'

The distraction didn't end there, at least for Reg and Guy, who were summoned to the office of Commander (F).

'Come in and take a seat, both of you,' he said, 'and I'll tell you about your next adventure.'

They sat in silence, both eager to hear more.

'After a period of leave, you're going to cross the pond. Yes, you're going to Quonset Point, Rhode Island, to train on the new fighter.' He added, 'New to us, anyway. It's been in service with the US Marines for some time, and it's earned itself a fearsome reputation.'

Reg asked, 'What's this new fighter, sir?'

'The Chance Vought Corsair.'

They'd heard of it, but neither of them had ever seen one..

'You'll then form a new squadron, mainly Wavy Navy, as it

happens. Actually, the squadron will be all RNVR apart from you two. Underwood, you will ship an extra half-ring and be appointed squadron commander. You, Davidson, will have to wait your turn, but you'll be a flight commander, so it's only a matter of time.'

When they docked in Chatham, they learned that they were to sail from Liverpool in ten days' time. It was better than Reg had hoped. He took the train to London, where he spent some time with his mother, and then made his way over to Whitehall Wireless Station.

The Wren on the Quartermaster's desk looked at him and his civilian suit in surprise. She asked, 'Can I help you, sir?'

'I'm sure you can.' He took out his Naval Identity Card to show her. 'I want to leave a note for Third Officer Dewhirst. Can I leave it with you?'

'Of course, sir.' She took the envelope and passed it to a Wren who presumably performed the role of messenger, because she set off immediately down the sloping corridor.

'Thank you,' he said to the girl on the desk. 'Carry on.'

'Aye, aye, sir.'

He had to visit Gieves, the naval tailors and outfitters in Savile Row, and his business there kept him occupied for much of the morning. When he arrived at his mother's address, she had a message for him from Eileen, simply asking him to call on her at her brother's flat after six. He spent the rest of the day with his mother, who was naturally delighted to see him. She was also excited because his sister Vera was due to arrive home the next day.

'But why are you in civvies, dear? I was going to ask you this morning, but you left so quickly, I never got a chance.'

'I'm sorry, Mother. My uniform, in its various formats, is at Gieves for alteration. I'll pick it up tomorrow.'

She examined him critically and asked, 'Have you lost weight or something?'

'Quite the reverse, I should think. I'd have thought a naval wife would have suspected a better reason for uniform alterations. I've been promoted.'

Her expression changed immediately to one of joy. 'That's wonderful, darling.' She kissed him in celebration. 'I didn't expect it to happen so soon.'

'Things do happen quickly in wartime, and Gieves have to sew on the half-ring.'

His mother held out her arms to him, and he joined her in a rare hug. When he was free again, he said, 'There's more.'

'Oh?'

'I'm engaged to be married. At least, I'm fairly sure I am.'

His mother sat down, apparently in need of support. 'Why are you less than sure?'

'I proposed to her by letter, so I shan't receive her reply until this evening.'

'I take it your intended is the Eileen I've spoken with on the phone. I must say, you're full of surprises, but I'm sure you know what you're doing.' She fanned herself with her hand, and said, 'Tell me you've no more surprises, Reg.'

'None that I can think of. I'll bring Eileen to meet you and Vera as soon as she can get leave.'

'That will be wonderful, Reg. Your father would have loved all this. He was a great one for spontaneity, and it seems the apple hasn't fallen far from the tree.'

Reg's civilian suit evoked surprise again when he called for Eileen, but not before she'd greeted him ecstatically on the doorstep. 'Oh, Reg,' she said, 'it's wonderful to see you, and the answer's "yes", by the way!' Performing a double-take, she asked, 'Why are you in civvies?'

'Let me in, and I'll tell you.'

She stood aside for him to enter the flat, where Ted and Lorna greeted him.

'We're about to go on watch,' Lorna told him, 'but we must congratulate you before we go.'

'We must,' agreed Ted, 'but do end the suspense and tell us why you're out of uniform.'

'It's being altered. I've been promoted.'

Further congratulations followed before Eileen gave further voice to her thoughts. Sounding like a stern mother, she said, 'I hope you haven't been doing dangerous things while we've been parted.'

'Very dangerous things,' he admitted. 'A heavy sea threw me out of my bunk last week.' He rubbed his head sorrowfully. 'Those decks are very unyielding.'

'You're impossible, Reg.'

'Don't be too hard on him,' said Ted, kissing her and shaking Reg's hand. 'Have a good time, you two.'

Lorna also took her leave of them, and they left for the fire station.

'I couldn't believe it when I read your last letter,' said Eileen.

'Was that the last one to arrive?'

'Yes, but it was no less special. How many of mine have you received?'

'Just the one about Greek mythology being all Greek to you. I suppose our letters will follow us around. I'm going to America next, so it'll be even harder for your letters to find me. Keep writing, though, because they're bound to catch up with me eventually.'

'Why are they sending you to America?'

Alerted by the sound of an engine outside, he said, 'I'll tell you what I can over dinner, but the taxi's waiting outside, so we'd better make tracks.'

The taxi took them to Edouard's of recent memory, where Raoul welcomed them as if they were regular diners, which they naturally hoped to become.

Once again, there were better things off the menu than the advertised fare, game apparently being a regular feature, and they chose the game pie.

'I've got four days' leave from Saturday,' said Eileen.

'Good. We'll go to Bravington's on Saturday, and then I'll introduce you to my mother and sister. After that, I suppose I'd better ask your father for your hand in marriage. That's how it's done, isn't it?'

'If you insist. My dad will be so embarrassed, he'll be tongue-tied, and my mother will probably tell you she's well rid of me.' Performing one of her delayed double-takes, she asked, 'What's Bravington's?'

'A jeweller's of sheer excellence. That's where we'll buy the ring.'

'Reg, I feel spoiled to death.'

'Quite right,' he told her soothingly, 'and I do feel it would be right to visit your parents.'

After the waiter had brought the wine, and Reg had tried it, Eileen said, 'You're right. It makes perfect sense.' When the waiter was out of earshot, she gave way to excitement again and said, 'We're actually engaged. It's too wonderful for words!'

'It is,' he agreed, taking her hand and kissing it. It was as intimate as they could be in the crowded restaurant.

'You haven't told me why you're going to America.'

'That's because I haven't had a chance until now. Two of us, my best chum and I, are being posted to a US Navy airbase, as they call them over there, to be trained on the new fighter they're sending us. When we've done that, we're going to form a new squadron. I'll be the boss, and Guy will be a flight commander.'

'Another new fighter?'

He nodded. 'Even better than the old one, but I can't tell you more than that.' Mischievously, he said, 'What I can tell you is that I'll have access to some of the things you're missing, such as stockings, make-up and perfume, so just wait until I come home.'

'I can hardly wait, but mainly because I'll see you again.'

Later, at the Blue Lagoon, they forsook the crowded dance floor, just as they had at Christmas, and moved almost imperceptibly in their alcove. The music was soft, and lighting was minimal, but those two elements were as nothing, because all that mattered to them was that they were together again.

After a while, Eileen asked, 'Are you going to blow the candle out? It seems a shame to waste it in wartime.'

'I take it you have an ulterior motive.' He nevertheless bent over the table to blow out the candle before taking her again in his arms. Secure in the darkness, they kissed and renewed their pledge.

15

They All Say the Same Thing

The shop window in Pentonville Road was filled with the kind of luxuries of which Eileen had previously only dreamt. There were brooches, pendants, necklaces, earrings, cufflinks, tie pins, shirt studs, engagement rings, wedding rings, signet rings, napkin rings, clocks and watches. It was an Aladdin's Cave.

Reg opened the door, and Eileen walked in, feeling almost as if she were trespassing.

The assistant looked up when he heard the bell. Good morning, sir. Good morning, Miss. How may I be of assistance?'

'We're looking for an engagement ring,' Reg told him.

'You're both very welcome. May I offer my warmest congratulations?'

'Thank you,' said Reg. 'You're very kind.'

'May I ask what kind of price you have in mind, sir?'

'You may ask, but I'd prefer just to see a selection of rings.'

The assistant left the counter to return with three trays of engagement rings, and Eileen had to remind herself that this was reality; in fact, one glance at the prices seemed to suggest a cruel kind of reality, but Reg was clearly unfazed.

'Look at these, darling,' he said, 'but take your time over it.'

'They're all beautiful,' she protested, 'but they're very expensive.'

'Don't worry about that. Engagements don't happen every day,' he said, adding with a sly look at the assistant, 'unless you're a jeweller.' Turning to Eileen again, he asked, 'Have you seen anything yet, darling?'

Eileen shook her head. 'I hardly like to at these prices.'

'As I said, don't worry about that.' He pushed one tray towards her and asked, 'Do any of these appeal to you?'

'Are you sure?'

'Absolutely.'

Still hesitating, but looking from one fabulous ring to the next, Eileen pointed to what looked like a sapphire surrounded by tiny diamonds. 'If you're really sure, I like this one best of all.'

'Is it your final choice?'

'Yes, as long as—'

'Then that's the one you shall have. Would you like to try it on and see how it looks?'

The assistant took it from its slot and placed it gently on her finger. 'Do you know your ring size, miss?'

'I'm afraid not.' The question had never arisen.

'Well, it doesn't matter, now, because the ring fits your finger perfectly.'

'It might have been made for you,' said Reg. 'Does it feel comfortable?'

'It's perfect. Thank you, Reg.' She felt tears pricking her eyes and she blinked to dispel them. 'Thank you. It's wonderful.'

Reg took out his cheque book and opened it, asking, 'Is a cheque acceptable?'

Recognising the banker's name printed on the cheque, the assistant said with easy confidence, 'A cheque drawn on Coutts' Bank is always acceptable, sir.'

Reg opened the large, heavy door and invited Eileen into the house. She was still in the entrance hall when she heard the sounds of affectionate greeting, and Reg said, 'Vera, meet Eileen. Eileen, this is my sister Vera.'

Eileen closed the door behind her and looked around, unsure what to expect. She found herself facing an attractive, fair-haired Wren second officer. 'How do you do, ma'am,' she said.

'Oh, let's not worry about that, Eileen. I'm Vera, for my sins, and I gather that, for yours, you're engaged to my brother.' They shook hands as an older woman came down the staircase.

Reg introduced Eileen to his mother, and when the formalities were complete, Mrs Underwood looked at the huge longcase clock and said, 'It's still coffee time, I see. Are you happy with coffee, Eileen, or would you prefer something else?'

'No, coffee would be wonderful, thank you, Mrs Underwood.'

'Good. Let's all go into the morning room.' She led the way and pulled on a bell-pull. 'Now, before we do anything else, let's congratulate Eileen and Reg, and ask Eileen to show us the ring.'

Their celebration was interrupted when a maid of mature years appeared at the door.

'Elsie,' said Mrs Underwood, 'coffee for four, please. By the way, this is Miss…. What is your surname, Eileen?'

'Dewhirst.'

'This is Miss Dewhirst, Mr Reg's fiancée. I know you'll want to see the ring, so have a look now before you make coffee.'

Still dazed, Eileen showed her new ring to the maid, who was predictably impressed.

'Now, sit down, everyone. I want to hear Eileen's life story.'

'There's hardly anything to tell,' said Eileen. 'I went to school, I left school, I joined the Wrens and I met Reg.'

'And, as usual, you can't say anything about what you do in the Wrens. I'm used to that.'

'I'm at Faslane,' Vera told her, in signals, the same as you, and just as reticent.'

'Eileen's father's a market gardener,' Reg told them, 'and she used to drive a lorry for him.'

'How game of you, Eileen,' said Mrs Underwood.

'And clever, I'd say,' said Vera.

'It was only a small lorry,' protested Eileen.

'Now, Eileen,' said Vera seriously, 'your standing in this household was considerable until the moment you undermined it with that remark. In fact, we'll all pretend we didn't hear it, and hail you as the only female lorry driver we know.'

'You don't know what this means to me,' said Eileen, 'being accepted in this way.'

'We're delighted to have you on board,' said Vera, 'and I'm going to have a whale of a time telling everyone that my brother is engaged to a lorry driver.'

'Don't you dare.' Her mother wagged the finger of good taste. 'I'm sure Eileen has lots of other qualities and skills.'

'She's an excellent cook, apparently,' said Reg.

Eileen looked at him in surprise. 'How did you know that?'

'Your brother told me.'

'Well,' said Vera, 'that's something neither of us can claim, isn't it, Mother?'

'I'm afraid so. How do your parents feel about your engagement, Eileen?'

'I haven't told them yet.' As she spoke, she felt awkward, but Reg came to her rescue.

'Eileen's relationship with her parents lacks the warmth it might have,' he explained. 'We're going to visit them because it's only right. If they make the experience less than comfortable, it will be their fault, but if we didn't tell them about our engagement and it were to cause ill-feeling, the fault would be ours.'

'Quite right, Reg.' His mother was unequivocal in her support.

'Maybe they'll be as pleased as we are, and everything will go swimmingly.' Vera floated the possibility in good faith, and Eileen smiled gratefully whilst remaining unconvinced.

'But you have an excellent relationship with your brother, I believe,' said Mrs Underwood. 'Reg told me that.'

'Yes, we're very close, and I also count my sister-in-law as a close friend.'

'What does your brother do, Eileen?'

'He's a schoolmaster in peacetime, but he's currently serving as an auxiliary fireman. He managed to get a draft to London just as the Blitz was starting.'

'Oh, how brave,' said Vera, and it was clear that the sentiment was genuine.

'Yes,' said Mrs Underwood, 'one of the unsung heroes of the Blitz.'

'Ted maintains he's not a hero, just a fireman doing his duty.'

'Well,' said Vera, 'we remain highly impressed. We lived through the Blitz. At least, Mother lived through it. I did a bunk partway through, and joined the Wrens.'

Elsie opened the door and walked in with a tray of coffee things.

'Thank you, Elsie,' said Mrs Underwood. 'I'll pour it.'

'Very good, ma'am.' She had another quick look at Eileen's ring and showed her pleasure again. As she left the room, Eileen gained the impression that even the maid in that household was on her side. It was a glorious feeling.

On leaving the house, Eileen said, 'You once told me your mother growled, and she couldn't have been more charming or welcoming.'

'She only growls when I upset her. Vera usually throws things at me.'

'I like Vera, too, and I don't believe you.' Changing the subject abruptly, she asked, 'What are we going to do now? Ted and Lorna won't be home until six.'

'Let's invite them out to dinner, and then our departure tomorrow won't seem so abrupt.'

'That's a good idea.' On immediate reflection, she said, 'It's going to be an expensive day for you.'

'But an enjoyable one. As for this afternoon, shall we book our tickets to…? Where's our destination?'

'Cullington. Our best plan is to stay at a hotel in Bradford, and then we have somewhere to escape to.'

'How exciting.' He raised his right arm to hail a taxi, which drew up alongside them. 'King's Cross Station, please.'

Dining out was an unusual event for Ted and Lorna, so they were naturally excited, especially in view of the reason for the celebration.

'It's the most beautiful ring,' said Lorna for possibly the third time, and admiring it across the table.

'It is,' agreed Eileen, 'and I love it, although, when you think about it, engagement rings all say the same thing, don't they?'

'That's right.' Reg was quick to agree. 'They say, "Hands off, this one's spoken for." '

'Beast.' Eileen punched him playfully. 'Is there no poetry in your soul?' Suddenly contrite, she said, 'Credit where it's due, though, a proposal of marriage made by a man wedging himself in his bunk during a force nine gale is romance indeed.'

'Storm force ten,' he corrected her.

Ted was impressed. 'You're clearly a man for a grand occasion,' he said.

'Much depends on the nature of the occasion.'

'You're modest, as well,' said Lorna, 'and that's worth riches.' Moving the conversation on rather than embarrass him, she said, 'Eileen tells us you're going to America, Reg.'

'I am, but I can't say much about it, except that we're going to be trained on a new fighter.'

'It seems a long way to go for training,' said Ted. 'Why can't they do it here?'

'I suppose because it's a highly-sophisticated piece of equipment, and the Yankee marines have been operating it in the Pacific, so they know all about it.' He shrugged. 'The only other thing I can tell you about it is that the Japanese have dubbed it "Whistling Death", and that's quite an accolade.'

Eileen asked, 'Why does it whistle?'

'I expect it doesn't know the words in Japanese.'

'Oh, Eileen,' said Ted, 'you walked into that one.'

'Seriously,' said Reg, 'That's as much as I can tell you, but I don't think I'll be over there for long.'

Eileen said thoughtfully, 'For now, let's just enjoy this leave.'

'Yes,' said Ted, 'good luck in Cullington, and then enjoy your leave.'

16

A Day of 'Firsts'

Eileen sank into the cushioned seat and said, 'This is the first time I've travelled First Class.'

'Oh, tut-tut, and you're an officer and a lady.'

'This is the first time I've travelled by train since I was commissioned,' she reminded him.

'It's a day of "firsts" for you, isn't it?'

'It'll be the first time I'll tell my parents I'm engaged,' she said grimly.

'And hopefully the last.'

'Don't joke about it, Reg. I'm not looking forward to it.'

Squeezing her hand, he asked her, 'What's the worst that can happen?'

After a few moments' thought, she said, 'My mother could make it highly embarrassing for both of us.'

'Honestly, darling, don't worry about me. I've been snarled at by drill instructors at Dartmouth, by first lieutenants at sea, and by petulant, ungrateful and unmannerly Soviet commissars in Archangel and Murmansk. When it comes to winning the prize for embarrassing me, your mother has stiff competition, believe me.'

His catalogue had amused her until he came to the last item, and she asked, 'What were you doing in Russia?'

'Now that I'm back, I can tell you. Those were the ports where the surviving ships of the convoy delivered their cargoes to the undeserving.'

'Don't you like Russians?'

'Not much.'

'I don't think I've ever met one.'

'You'd know if you did.'

'How?'

'They'd have snow on their boots.'

'Oh, you....' She left the indictment unspoken. Then, after a while, she asked, 'Did you see *Goodbye, Mr Chips*?'

'Oh, yes.'

Eyeing him suspiciously, she asked, 'You're not going to be rude about it, the way you were about *Ships With Wings*, are you?'

'No, it was an excellent film, and much more true to life than *Ships With Wings*. Mind you, the same could be said of *Snow White*.'

'Beast.'

'No, fair's fair. The headmaster who caned a whole year of boys for ragging Mr Chips at the beginning of the film was almost a carbon copy of my housemaster. He was just as brutal; in fact, I only joined the Navy to get away from him and his cane.'

Disbelievingly, she nevertheless asked, 'Was it worth the effort?'

'I'm afraid not. For the least misdemeanour, the First Lieutenant would bend a snotty across the gun room table and beat him with his sword scabbard.'

Now aware that two elderly women were listening to his account, she said, 'What nonsense.'

'It's true, I tell you.' He shifted uncomfortably in his seat and said, 'I bear the marks on my posterior to this day, although I'm not going to show them to you in this crowded compartment. You'll have to take my word for it.'

The two women attended immediately to their own business, leaving Eileen to laugh silently, which she did with some difficulty.

They left the station, and before long, Reg spotted the Midland Hotel. He said, 'This is the hotel you mentioned, isn't it? I haven't booked rooms. I thought we'd take pot luck.'

'Yes. Listen, Reg, before we go in, there's something I have to ask.'

'Don't worry. I'll ask for two single rooms.'

'That's just what I need to talk to you about. The thing is….' Now that she'd raised the subject, she felt terribly embarrassed.

Moving their bags out of the way of passing pedestrians, he said, 'Tell me what's on your mind, darling. I'm human, after all.'

'That's the trouble. So am I.' Having got so far, she had to go on. 'The thing is, if you'd rather we took a double room, I'd be more than happy to do that.' The words rather tumbled out, thankfully, in the right order.

Taken momentarily by surprise, he asked, 'Are you absolutely sure?'

'Yes,' she whispered, fearful of being overheard by passers-by, 'I've been to the clinic and everything.'

'Good heavens. Well, if your mind's made up….' He took the signet ring from his little finger and slipped it on to her ring finger. 'Just keep my initials out of sight and you'll pass for a married woman,' he told her.

They crossed the road and entered the Midland Hotel, where Reg spoke to a receptionist while Eileen stood to one side and a little further back, wondering if she looked as guilty as she felt.

'We'd like a double room for two nights, please,' he told the receptionist.

'With pleasure, sir. We have a double room on the second floor, overlooking Forster Square.'

'It's my first time in Bradford, but that sounds perfect, doesn't it, darling?'

Realising somewhat belatedly that he was addressing her, Eileen said, 'Absolutely.'

Reg signed the register and showed the receptionist his Naval Identity Card and Eileen's, explaining that they were recently married, and that Eileen's married name had yet to appear on hers.

'Well, sir, we can't be expected to do everything all at once, can we?'

'Not when more important matters require our attention,' he agreed.

'Shall I get the porter to take your luggage up, sir?'

'No, thank you. It's no trouble.'

She took a key from the board behind her and gave it to him, saying, 'Room two-oh-four, sir. I hope you enjoy your stay with us. The lift is on your left.'

'Thank you.' He lifted the bags and smiled at Eileen, who joined him, thankful she was no longer under the gaze of the receptionist.

They took the lift to the second floor and followed the signs to Room 204. Once inside, Reg went to the window and asked, 'What's this square-thing the receptionist mentioned?'

'Forster Square. William Edward Forster's statue is down there,' Eileen told him.

'What did he do?'

'He was responsible for the Education Act of eighteen-seventy, that made education free, universal and compulsory.'

'He was a sadist, and they erected a statue in his memory?'

Laughing at his naivete, she said, 'He freed a lot of little children from hard work, and sent them to school instead.'

'Oh, well, that puts a different complexion on it, I suppose.' He held out his arms to gather her up. Kissing her, he said, 'Don't worry, nothing's going to happen yet.'

'I'm not worried.'

'It just came as a surprise. I thought you were a....'

'To all intents and purposes, I am, but circumstances are far from normal.'

He kissed her again. 'I love you.'

'And I love you. Let's unpack and then we can go to Cullington and beard the dragon.' She spoke without enthusiasm.

As it was Sunday, the market garden was closed, but Eileen pointed it out to Reg as they passed it in the taxi.

'My word,' he said, 'that looks like a lot of hard work.'

'Yes, I remember it well, and so does Ted. My dad has a girl working for him now, a land girl, and what's the betting she can't get anything right, either?'

'This war's put a lot of people into jobs that are completely new to them. I think about that when I hear officers and senior ratings complain about the Wavy Navy. It's quite unfair.'

'You must be the fairest man I know.'

'I'm actually a martinet, feared and avoided throughout the service.'

'Bunkum.' Turning to the driver, she said, 'Anywhere here will be fine, thank you.'

'Right you are, love.' The driver pulled in and Reg paid him.

'About five o' clock, you said?'

'That's right. Thank you.' He helped Eileen out of the taxi and closed the door.

'Prepare to meet your doom,' she warned, opening the garden gate.

As they reached the end of the path, the door opened, and Eileen's mother greeted them.

'Mother, this is Reg.'

'How d' you do, Reg. Come inside.'

'How d' you do, Mrs Dewhirst. Thank you.'

He entered the house ahead of Eileen, and she heard her mother say, 'This is Eileen's dad. Wilfred, this is Reg, our Eileen's young man.'

When the introductions were complete, Eileen greeted her father with a kiss.

Mrs Dewhirst called upstairs, 'Joyce, put the kettle on, will you? We have visitors.'

Eileen asked, 'Is Joyce the land girl?'

'Aye,' said her father, 'for what use she is.'

Eileen closed her eyes in silent sympathy for the wretched girl.

'We heard you'd got some kind of promotion.'

'I got a commission.'

'So why aren't you in your uniform?'

'Wrens don't have to wear uniform when we're off-watch.'

'Well I never. So,' said her mother, pointing to Eileen's left hand, 'let's have a look, then.'

Eileen extended her hand to show them her ring, having temporarily removed Reg's signet ring.

'By heck, Reg,' said her mother, 'you must have more brass nor sense.'

'It must have been expensive,' translated Eileen, blushing with embarrassment.

'Not very,' he told her. 'In any case, a special occasion calls for something appropriate.'

'That's a very fair ring,' commented Eileen's father, inadequate as ever.

'I don't know if Eileen's told you, Reg, but she's a good cook. I can tell you that because I taught her.'

'Actually, Ted told me, and it's good news, because I doubt we'll be able to keep a cook after the war. I think the days of servants are numbered, don't you?'

Mrs Dewhirst looked at him in shock. 'Have you got servants at home?'

'My mother has, yes. Only a cook and a maid, nowadays, I have to say.'

Her surprise was interrupted when a young woman came into the room with a tray of tea things that, it seemed, failed to win Mrs Dewhirst's approval. 'Bring out the best tea service, you stupid girl. Can't you see we've got polite company?'

'Well, you should 'ave said.' She was about to return to the kitchen when Eileen said, 'You must be Joyce. I'm Eileen. You'll have heard horrible things about me, and this is Reg, my fiancé.'

'Glad to meet you bof.' Her accent was unmistakably Cockney, and Eileen warmed to her for her defiant attitude. She was also more generous-natured than her mother, because she said, 'What a beautiful ring! You're ever so lucky.'

'Don't let her keep you, Joyce,' said Mrs Dewhirst. 'We're waiting for that tea.' When the girl was out of the room, she said, 'She's the third land girl we've had, and she's no better than the others.'

Mr Dewhirst, who had been characteristically quiet, suddenly pointed and asked, 'What's that thing on your arm, Reg?'

Reg looked at his sleeve, wondering if a bird had paid its respects, and then he realised what his future father-in-law was referring to. 'Oh, the wings. They're to show I'm a pilot.'

'RAF pilots wear 'em on their chests.'

'Only because they don't know any better.'

'Well, I never.'

Mrs Dewhirst asked, 'What will you do after the war?'

'Hopefully, the same as I'm doing now, only without the unpleasantness from across the Channel.'

'Reg is a professional naval officer,' explained Eileen. 'That's what he does for a living.'

It was another surprise for Mrs Dewhirst, although her husband was more inclined to air his curiosity. 'If you wanted to fly,' he asked, 'why didn't you join the Air Force?'

'My family have served in the Royal Navy for the past five generations, all except for one, who was an all-round waste of space. My great-great-great-grandfather served under Lord Nelson at Trafalgar, so you see, I never considered either of the other services.'

'Well, I never.'

Joyce walked in again with the tea tray, this time stacked with what Eileen recognised as the best tea service, the one that was only ever used when they entertained special guests.

'About time, too,' said Mrs Dewhirst. 'I'll pour it. You'd most likely spill it or break somethin'.'

'Please yourself.' It was gratifyingly evident that Joyce was in no way cowed by Mrs Dewhirst's unpleasantness.

'An' we'll have a bit of respect round here, particularly when we have company.'

Eileen wondered when her mother would do something to earn that respect. She wasn't hopeful. Meanwhile, Joyce had provided a measure of light relief, however unwittingly.

Happily, the time passed, and the taxi appeared outside. Their goodbyes were mercifully brief, although Eileen and Reg both made a point of speaking to Joyce before they left.

Outside, in the taxi, Eileen simply hung her head.

'Chin up, darling. You warned me, and you didn't exaggerate.'

'What a pair, though. My dad's bad enough, but my mother could feature in a pantomime as the wicked witch, and she wouldn't even need to learn the lines.'

'You once told me you were Cinderella, which makes me Prince Charming, and he was never impressed by the wicked stepmother and the ugly sisters. He was just delighted with his bride-to-be, and so am I.'

Eileen came out of the bathroom, and Reg kissed her. 'I love the taste of toothpaste,' he said, so much that it takes me several minutes to brush my teeth.'

Reading gratefully between the lines, she undressed while he was in the bathroom.

He gave her a full five minutes before opening the bathroom door and asking, 'Are you decent?'

'Yes. Are you?'

'There's nothing decent about me.' He left the bathroom, hung his uniform neatly in the wardrobe, and turned out the main light, leaving only the light from a dim table lamp. Then, removing the rest of his clothes, he slipped beneath the bedclothes beside her. 'There,' he said, 'that was quite painless, wasn't it?'

'You're very considerate.'

He took her in his arms, kissing her and relishing the softness of her body through the thin fabric of her nightgown. Feeling that he should deal with a prosaic but no less important matter, he asked, 'What did they give you at the clinic?'

'Something to keep me from getting pregnant. I fitted it when I was in the bathroom.'

'Good girl.' He kissed her again.

'Would you rather I took off my nightie? I will if you like.'

'You even read my thoughts.'

'Being a newcomer to this, I didn't know.' She hauled up the lower part of her nightgown and sat upright to pull it over her head. As she did so, she treated him inadvertently to the unveiling of her flawless breasts.

'I think I've just died and gone to Heaven,' he said, taking her in his arms again and kissing her with great feeling, sharing his kisses with her lips, her neck and then her breasts. He felt her stiffen when he touched one nipple with his lips, but then she became more relaxed, responding to the attention he was giving to the parts of her body that had remained concealed since childhood.

He retraced his path via her neck to her lips, and she moaned softly, mirroring his kisses, clearly ecstatic and stiffening only a little when he explored further. He felt an eyelash flicker against his cheek in surprise and delight, and her murmurings grew louder and more insistent.

Joining her in an ecstasy of kisses, he moved into the space she created for him, and she gave a welcoming gasp.

Prompted by nature alone, she moved against him, wrapping her legs around him as if to prevent his unlikely escape, and moaned at the thrill it gave her. Soon, her breath quickened and the sounds she uttered had no meaning, yet they carried the simplest of messages. Then she cried out, grasping him with her arms and legs until the urgency receded.

'Please don't move yet,' she whispered.

'I shan't.'

She lay still for a minute or so, and then asked, 'Have we finished?'

'Not unless you want us to.'

Still whispering, she said, 'You have to remember that I'm new to all this, but I don't ever want it to stop.'

'It's a lot to ask, but I'll do my best.' He kissed her as if to seal the arrangement.

'I meant within reason.'

He began to shake involuntarily.

'Reg, you mustn't laugh. It's not my fault I'm a beginner.'

'You've taken to it like a three-badge hand, darling. I was laughing because you negotiate so politely.' To discourage further argument, he began to move again, prompting consensus and mutual ecstasy.

17

Back to Work – And a Touch of Glamour

After a day in Ilkley, tea at the celebrated Betty's Café, and another night of bliss, it was time to return to London, so that Eileen could resume her duties at Whitehall. They would meet once more before Reg had to embark for the USA, but not before Vera Underwood had tested Eileen with Chanel Number Five.

'It was kind of Vera to do that,' said Eileen when Reg called for her, 'but it's one thing to know that a perfume works on me, and quite another to be in a position to buy the stuff, even if it's available.'

Reg inhaled the celebrated scent with unashamed self-indulgence as he opened the taxi door for her. 'Arturo's in Greek Street, please.'

'Arturo's. Right you are, guv.'

Settling back in his seat, Reg said, 'I'll see if I can find you some in New York or wherever the ship docks. Is that lipstick you're wearing your favourite, too?'

'Battle Red? Yes. Don't you like it?'

'Of course I do. I'll try to find you some make-up as well.'

'That would be wonderful, but don't forget your official reason for being there, will you?'

'That would be difficult.'

Predictably, the driver couldn't keep quiet for long. He asked, 'Just back from the sea, are you, guv?'

'Yes.'

'Been anywhere interesting?'

'I really couldn't say.'

'Secret, eh?'

'That's right.'

'If you want my opinion, there's too many secrets and too many jacks-in-office inventing them.'

Leaning forward confidentially, Reg said, 'You should write to the Prime Minister. Politicians want to know these things. That's why they have people keeping diaries.'

'Right enough, but what do you think of that fella Churchill? If you ask me—'

'I won't hear a word said against my great-uncle, and that's final.'

'Oh, no offence, I'm sure.' The driver lapsed into embarrassed silence until they reached their destination, when he reported meekly, 'Arturo's, guv.'

'Thank you.' He paid the driver and helped Eileen on to the pavement.

'Oh, good grief,' she said, watching the taxi depart. 'I nearly laughed aloud when you told him Mr Churchill was your great-uncle.'

'What's funny about that?'

'Oh, he's not, is he?' She covered her mouth as if to prevent a further *faux pas*.

'No, but he might have been.'

'You horror.' She took his arm and they entered Arturo's Club and Restaurant.

The doorman asked, 'Are you a member, sir?'

'Yes.' Reg produced his membership card. 'I have a reservation.'

A waiter appeared, looked at Reg's card and said, 'Commander Underwood, I believe?'

'Lieutenant Commander, actually, but give me time and an unblemished record, and who can say what might happen?'

'May I take your coats, sir?'

'Thank you.' He helped Eileen with hers, handing it to the waiter, and then removed his coat and cap.

The waiter hung them on a stand and said, 'If you care to follow me, I'll show you to your table.'

They took their seats. The band was playing 'As Time Goes By.'

'I'm afraid the loin of pork is no longer available, sir,' the waiter told him as he handed the menu to them both.

'What's not on the menu?'

The waiter lowered his voice to say, 'We have a few excellent turbot, sir, and a mackerel pâté.'

Reg looked at Eileen, whose expression suggested enthusiasm. 'We'll start with the pâté,' he said, 'and have the turbot as a main course.'

'An excellent choice, sir, if I may say so. Would you care to consult the wine list?'

'Yes, please.'

'Very good, sir. I'll speak to the wine waiter.'

'Reg,' said Eileen when they were alone, 'I thought you said that the food in night clubs was very basic.'

'It usually is, but Arturo's became a restaurant as well as a club shortly before the war.'

'How many clubs are you a member of?'

'Only a few.' He considered the question and said, 'Four, counting this one.'

That revelation was spared comment when the wine waiter came to the table.

'Thank you,' said Reg, scanning the French dry white wines and noticing that the cupboard was almost bare. 'A bottle of the St Emilion white, please.'

'Very good, sir.' The wine waiter left them.

'Some of the officers at Whitehall are downright abrupt in their dealings with the stewards,' said Eileen, 'but you're not like that, are you?'

'My parents were always keen on *noblesse oblige* and that kind of thing, my father in particular. It was one of his characteristics that commanded loyalty and respect from officers and ratings alike.'

'Oh, darling, I've reminded you of your father again.' She squeezed his hand in apology.

'I'm not likely to forget him. In any case, it's good to remember the things he did for us.'

Releasing his hand, she said, 'From what you've told me about him and things I've noticed about you, it seems to me that the apple hasn't fallen far from the tree.'

He laughed. 'My mother said that only last week.'

The wine waiter arrived with a wine cooler and a bottle. He showed the latter to Reg.

'That's the one,' he confirmed.

'A wise choice, sir.' He cut the foil and drew the cork deftly, pouring a little for Reg to taste.

'That's excellent. Thank you.'

'Thank you, sir.' He poured wine into both their glasses and returned the bottle to the wine cooler.

Listening to the band, Reg remarked, 'They could have been more tactful in their choice.' They were playing 'Coming In On a Wing And a Prayer', a favourite with many from the previous year.

'Songwriters are an insensitive lot, as I think we've already agreed.'

They heard the number out and were rewarded when the band followed it with 'That Old Black Magic.'

'Shall we?' Reg offered her his hand and led her on to the floor, which had yet to become crowded.

They danced together closely in the subdued light of the dance floor, neither of them speaking, simply content to be together. At the end of the number, Reg kissed her softly beneath her ear and whispered the time-honoured salutation before applauding the band.

Back at the table, he raised his glass. 'Here's to us, and confusion to Zeus.'

She repeated the toast. 'Actually,' she said, 'we've defied him so far.'

'Hush,' he warned. 'Nemesis might hear you, and she's not the most forgiving soul on Mount Olympus. Not by a long chalk.'

The mackerel pâté arrived, thus providing a distraction. It was also very good.

Eileen asked, 'Have you still got the handkerchief I gave you?'

'Of course. Do you need it?'

'No,' she laughed, 'I just like to think of it tucked into your suit of armour.'

'We have armoured seats,' he confided. 'Suits are considered unnecessary.'

'How odd.'

'If you like to know,' he said, looking around the room to make sure they weren't overheard, 'they're to protect the head, the back, the bottom and the naughty bits.'

'I don't like to think of you in action, but it's some comfort to know that your various parts are protected.' More seriously, she said, 'It's an awful shame we can't... be together... tonight.' In spite of her blissful introduction to the act of love, she was still shy when referring to it.

Taking her hand, he said, 'I shan't be in America for long, and as soon as I'm back on British soil, I'll be at your disposal.'

'That sounds too utilitarian for words.'

'And "be together" sounds shy and inhibited. Let's save the euphemisms for letters that have to be censored.'

'Yes,' she agreed, 'I couldn't bear the idea of someone reading our most intimate secrets.'

'Let's dance instead. They're playing "There Are Such Things". It's an excuse for a song, but it makes no reference to forced landings, and it's very danceable.' He led her on to the dance floor, which was a little busier than before. 'For the remainder of the evening,' he told her, 'we have to speak in the clipped and precisely-articulated manner of stage actors.'

'It's a tale. What made you think of that?'

'*Ships With Wings*,' he told her in a fair imitation of John Clements.

'You're teasing again.'

'I thought you'd like it.' He kissed her cheek and steered her into the line of dance.

'Not if you're going to poke fun.'

'I've got something from that little episode that you may like.'

'Don't tease.'

'All right.'

On the due date, Reg and Guy embarked in the *RMS Duchess of Fife* at the Prince's Landing Stage in Liverpool. It was a crowded ship, and they were obliged to share a cabin, which was no hardship, as they'd been friends for three years, and that counted as a lifetime in war. Also, the voyage would take little more than a week, as the ship would be steaming at full speed as a precaution against U-boats.

On the same day, Eileen received a letter from Reg. Enclosed with it were signed photographs of Michael Wilding, Ann Todd and, most importantly, John Clements. Reg hadn't been teasing her, after all.

18

Taming the Beast

After a voyage that was uneventful apart from the surprise announcement that the invasion of Europe had begun, the *Duchess of Fife* docked in New York. June wasn't the healthiest month to be in that crowded city, as the heat and humidity were, if not at their most intense, at least at a level that took British visitors unpleasantly by surprise, although Reg was happy, shopping in Bloomingdale's air-conditioned department store. He took his time, finding gifts for Eileen, his mother and Vera; in any case, he was completely unaccustomed to shopping for such feminine mysteries as stockings and perfume, and he found it necessary to enlist the help of the obliging assistants.

He found one such member of staff in the hosiery department, who showed him an array of nylon stockings in various shades. It was like being led through a maze, until he said, 'Those stockings you're wearing look rather good. What's the colour called?'

'Why, thank you, sir,' said the girl, hitching her skirt up a little way to give him a fuller effect. 'These are Dark Beige. As a matter of fact, Betty Grable wore them in the movie *Man About Town*.'

'Really? How generous of her to let you have them.'

'No, sir, you misunderstand. When I say she wore them, I mean she wore stockings of this make and colour.'

'I see.'

Distracted for the moment, she said, 'If you don't mind me saying so, sir, I find your uniform very appealing, but I don't recognise it.'

'Royal Navy,' he explained.

'Oh, are you people still involved in the war?'

'Just here and there. You haven't beaten us yet.' Returning to the original subject, he said, 'What's good enough for Betty Grable is good enough for the ladies in my life. I'll settle for Dark Beige in that, er... fine...mesh, I suppose.'

'Fifteen denier,' she prompted. 'An excellent choice, sir.' Unable to harness her curiosity, she asked, 'Are there many ladies in your life?'

He cocked his head, as if carrying out a mental count, and said, 'For the purpose of this shopping trip, I've narrowed them down to four.'

'Really, sir?'

'Absolutely. My mother, my sister, my fiancée and her sister-in-law. She's a sport, so I can't leave her out.'

'You do like to tease, sir.' The fact had apparently dawned on her. 'I think your ladies will be delighted with these gifts. I understand stockings are in short supply in England.'

'Almost impossible to find,' he confirmed, 'which is why I crossed the Atlantic.'

'Is that a fact, sir?' Then, realisation dawned again, and she said, 'Okay, sir, I know when I'm being strung along.' It was reassuring to know that she wasn't completely gullible.

Angela returned from an enjoyable and hectic leave, but she seemed more interested in Eileen's experience.

'Did you see your parents?'

'Yes, we got that hurdle out of the way. As I'd anticipated, they weren't terribly interested, but they were impressed with Reg.'

'Were they?'

'They were bound to be. Just imagine it. They've lived all their lives in the rugged north, working hard for a living and taking nothing for granted, and suddenly, they found that their wayward daughter was engaged to an umpteenth-generation naval officer whose family kept servants.'

Angela blinked. 'Do they?'

'Just a cook and a maid nowadays. Times aren't what they were, and economies have to be made.'

'Now I'm impressed.'

'Actually,' said Eileen thoughtfully, 'I'm wondering quite how I'm going to fit into the family.'

'You've met them, though. Did you find the experience difficult?'

'Not in the least. They're lovely people, both his mother and his sister, but they're used to their way of life, and I'm not.'

Angela frowned. 'No, I don't follow you.'

Eileen tried to explain. 'As well as his naval pay, Reg has what he calls a small private income, although his "small" probably differs greatly from my understanding of the word.'

'No, try as I will, I still can't see your problem.'

'Never mind.'

'No, never mind any of that,' said Angela impatiently. 'Where did you stay when you went to see your parents? I don't suppose you stayed with them.'

'No, that would have been too awful for words. Also, they've got a land girl living there, poor thing. No, we stayed at the Midland Hotel in Bradford.'

'And?' Angela's eyes were bright with anticipation.

'Nowhere else, just the Midland Hotel.'

'I didn't mean that, silly. I meant, did you and he *do it*?'

Eileen looked around the Wardroom nervously and decided that there was no one within earshot. 'If you really want to know, yes, we did.' It wasn't a thing Eileen found easy to discuss, but Angela had, after all, been her mentor in that respect.

'Well? How was it?'

'What do you mean?'

'To coin a phrase, how was it for you, let's say, on a scale of "I don't know why people take the trouble to do this" to "all my life, I've been waiting for this to happen"?'

'If you must know,' she said, savouring her friend's eager curiosity, 'it was absolutely wonderful.'

The train journey to Rhode Island took several hours, stopping at Newhaven in Connecticut and Providence in Rhode Island. They completed the final part of the journey to Quonset Point by motor coach, where a party of officers greeted them warmly, whisking them off immediately to dispense hospitality.

'Isn't it odd,' remarked Guy in a private moment, 'that they couldn't get rid of us quickly enough two hundred years ago, and now they're treating us as if we're long-lost friends?'

It was true. The Americans were offering them everything from sight-seeing trips to female companionship, and everything, it seemed, came with an unlimited supply of alcohol. American ships, they were told, were strictly dry, so their crews found compensation ashore wherever they could.

After a night spent in what appeared to them to be palatial accommodation, they reported for instruction. They had already seen a Corsair parked in front of a hangar, and its unusual shape and conformation had caused them some disquiet.

'Gentlemen,' said their instructor, a lieutenant commander with a lugubrious Texan accent, 'let me introduce you. This,' he said, indicating the Corsair behind him, 'is the Chance Vought F-Four-U Corsair Mark Two. It has two other names. The Japanese call it "Whistling Death", and we know it simply as "the Bent-Wing Bastard from Connecticut". It will be yours for the duration of World War Two, and let me tell you, gentlemen, you are welcome to the goddamned thing.'

At first sight, it looked ungainly, with the largest propellor ever fitted to a fighter, and the 2000 horsepower engine and the large fuel tank it necessitated explained the unusual distance between the cockpit and the propellor. Because of that huge propellor, it stood on long undercarriage legs, and further clearance was made possible by wings that swept downward for four feet or so in the inverted-gull pattern, before adopting a more traditional rake.

'The F-Four-U was ordered as a replacement for the F-Four-F, or "Wildcat", as you know it,' their instructor told them, 'but it proved so problematic in deck landing that the Navy switched to the F-Six-F "Hellcat", an airplane that has far superior flight deck manners. The F-Four-U was given to the US Marines, who don't know what a flight deck is, being the landlubbers they are, but they have achieved notable success with it in the Pacific, hence its Japanese nickname. I will instruct you in the flying of it, but deck landing will be a problem for you to solve.'

As introductions went, it was far from encouraging, but the Fleet Air Arm's only alternatives were the relatively slow Wildcat and Sea Hurricane, and the Seafire, which was the seagoing equivalent of the Spitfire. Both the Hurricane and the Spitfire were highly successful land-based fighters, but they were woefully unsuitable at sea, with their short range and flimsy undercarriage unsuited to landing on a pitching flight deck. However, times were desperate and, starved as it had been of first-class aircraft during the inter-war years, the Royal Navy simply had somehow to make the Corsair work at sea.

Training began in the classroom, where the British pilots, handlers, armourers and mechanics learned about the aircraft in minute detail before they were even allowed to touch their machines. Then, when they progressed on to the tarmac, pilots were required to sit in their cockpits, familiarising themselves with the instruments, of which there were many. When they had done that to Lieutenant Commander Kincaid's satisfaction, they were allowed to take a short flight.

'You may already have been told this,' he said, 'but you must never, on any account, put this airplane into a spin, because the cold, hard truth is that it will not recover from it, and you will exchange the joystick for a harp, if you're lucky, because I've heard that the great aircraft carrier in the sky is getting kinda full-up with naval aviators.' Having delivered his characteristic warning, he said, 'Right, I want to see you all back here fifteen minutes from now.'

More than a little apprehensive, Reg started the engine, running it up until the signal came to take off. Then, he led the squadron down the runway, feeling the huge power of the two thousand horsepower engine and the familiar thrill of becoming airborne.

Once everyone was up and circling the airfield, he spoke to the squadron. 'Able Squadron, this is Able Leader, form up on me in Victor formation. Over.'

He was relieved when all eleven pilots receipted his command, and he took them on a brief tour of Rhode Island's extensive coastline, which was well worth seeing. He was mindful not to test the Corsair's famed speed. That would happen during a later flight.

At the appointed time, he ordered the squadron to follow him back to Quonset Point. 'Remember you can't see a damned thing below the nose of the aircraft, so you'll have to fly in a wide arc on your approach, but don't get too ambitious.'

He made his approach, steering a gentle arc until he touched down, and then he steered a straight course to the end of the runway. Lieutenant Commander Kincaid was waiting for him.

'Everything okay?'

'Perfect. I just want to watch my squadron land.'

'Your chicks, yes.' Watching the first make his approach, he said, 'I see they've gotten the hang of approaching their landing in an arc. It's the long nose that makes the F Four U such a sonofabitch to land on a flight deck.'

'I rather got that impression.'

They watched as each member of the squadron made his landing, and Reg felt a wave of relief.

'I'm glad that was successful,' said Kincaid, 'because you're all going to practise like hell for seven days, and then you're going on to ADDLs. That's Assisted Dummy Deck Landings.'

'I know. I believe the system was designed at the Royal Aircraft Establishment at Farnborough.'

'You don't say. I thought it was a good old American invention.'

Reg wasn't surprised.

During that week, he became better acquainted with his squadron, and he found some of its members more memorable than others. There was Sandy McGregor, a tall Canadian, who seemed unfazed by service protocol, and who clearly had no use for the word 'sir'. Instead, he greeted Reg as 'Boss', both in the air and on the ground. It was all the same to Reg, who took a pragmatic line, as usual. As long as McGregor was obedient and behaved sensibly, he didn't care.

Another character who stood out from the rest was Daniel Fisher, a native of Sussex with a polished accent and, it seemed, the intention of pleasuring as many American girls as he could during his short stay.

His reputation was such that when one pilot was struggling with the *New York Times* crossword, and he read aloud, 'The male equivalent of a nymphomaniac....' there was a chorus of, 'Fisher!'

Preparations were not without mishap, however, and Reg was saddened, on the third day, to lose one of the squadron. Sub-Lieutenant Andrew Byrne allowed his aircraft to be caught in the slipstream of a Hellcat, which resulted in the dreaded spin. As Kincaid had predicted, the aircraft failed to recover, and Byrne did not survive the crash.

After a week of ADDLs, 1846 squadron was ready to practise the real thing aboard its new home, *HMS Invincible*, a recently-commissioned carrier now at anchor with her escort of destroyers in Narragansett Bay, ready to weigh anchor and steam into the wind for the benefit of the fighters about to join her.

When the time came, Reg made the first landing, as usual, approaching in an arc and finally picking up the second arrester wire. He left the aircraft with the handlers and made his way up to the observation deck to introduce himself to the Commander (F), whose name was Turnbull.

'I'm glad to meet you, Underwood. That was a nice landing. Let's see what the others can do.'

They watched together as the rest of 'A' Flight came in, one of them rather too high, so that he had to make a second attempt, at which he picked up the third wire.

Not surprisingly, Guy landed safely, and the rest followed, two of them making a second approach before landing.

In the lull before the next event, Reg reported to the captain, who approved of his insistence on watching the squadron land before carrying out the usual protocol. Reg thought it probably helped that the captain was a relatively young man.

For the rest of the week, deck landing and take-off exercises went fairly smoothly, given the Corsair's peculiarities, until the squadron suffered its second casualty.

Sub-Lieutenant Paul Thorganby made his approach too high, but when the 'batman' waved him away to go round again and make another attempt, he tried to correct his altitude and make a landing. The result was a nosedive, after which the Corsair cartwheeled across the flight deck and fell into the sea. By the time one of the escorting destroyers reached the scene, there was no trace of the pilot or the aircraft, and Reg found himself writing a second next-of-kin letter. The incident had been caused purely by pilot error, but Reg naturally made no mention of that, describing it as simply 'a tragic flying accident'. It was a sad end to the squadron's stay in America.

During the crossing, the Corsairs continued to exercise with the Firefly strike aircraft and the Avenger dive-bombers, only stopping occasionally to wonder if leave would be granted before the ship's first deployment.

As they reached the approaches to Portsmouth and the aircraft were flown off temporarily to Lee-on-Solent and Worthy Down, leave was announced. As soon as he was ashore, Reg telephoned Eileen at Whitehall to tell her he was on his way to London.

19

A Flying Visit

Not surprisingly, Reg's presents of perfume, make-up and stockings were well received. Vera was at Faslane, and she would get hers later, but his mother, Eileen and a surprised Lorna were delighted with them. The make-up had been guesswork on his part, but he seemed to have guessed right, and Ted was just as pleased with his silk tie, an item he would never have found at home, and an extravagance he might never have considered, either.

On Eileen's next evening off-watch, they went to a different night club from those they'd visited earlier. It was called 'The Glass Slipper'.

'The food is fairly basic,' he reminded her on the way there, 'but it's a good place for a short leave.'

'I don't like to ask about that.'

'I have to report to Lee-on-Solent on Monday,' he told her with some regret.

'Maybe it's just as well I got a stand-down for tomorrow night.'

'Good girl. Let's talk about it when we get to the club.'

Happily, they arrived at their destination without too much chat from the driver, and Reg paid him off.

He showed his card to the doorman, who allowed them to enter.

'We're very quiet tonight, sir,' said the man who greeted them and took their coats. 'Things will no doubt liven up later.'

'I've no doubt they will,' agreed Reg. 'We'd like an alcove, please.'

'Take your pick, sir. I'll bring the menu to you.'

'And the wine list, if you will.'

'Of course, sir. I should tell you, sir, that everything on the menu is available.'

Reg looked at the brief and somewhat basic menu and asked, 'What have you got that's not on the menu?'

'Hare, sir, casseroled in red wine.'

He asked Eileen, 'Have you tried hare, darling?'

'I did, years ago. I rather liked it. I thought it was like rabbit, but much gamier.'

'All right, we'll have the hare.'

'Of course, sir.' He handed Reg the wine list.

The task was easy, as the war had emptied so many shelves. Finally, he said, 'A bottle of the Louis Jadot Beaune, please.'

'Very good, sir.'

When they were alone, Eileen said, 'All these wines that you order must be expensive. I mean, everything else has disappeared.'

'But we're left with the quality, and that's important.'

'I'm not used to this, Reg,' she said, shaking her head in bewilderment.

'You'll get the idea.'

She gave up.

'What would you like to do tomorrow evening?'

Illogically, she looked around her, but they were completely alone. 'I'd like us to be together properly before you leave, as we were in Bradford.'

'Ah, you want us to spend the night together. I must say the thought appeals to me, but how will you cover it at home?'

'I'll say I want to see you off at the end of your leave, and I'll probably have to spend the night in a hotel. It has the advantage of being truthful as well as cryptic.'

He nodded appreciatively. 'You've sold it to me. Let's celebrate on the dance floor.' The band had just begun 'Silver Wings in the Moonlight'. 'I don't fly at night nowadays,' he said, 'so this one's all right.' He led her past the band, where they had the floor to themselves for the entire number.

As they returned to their table, Eileen asked, 'What was it like in America? Is it just like the pictures?'

'I thought so, except everything's in colour, and not just partway through, like *The Wizard of Oz*.'

'Silly. Tell me about the people.'

They took their places at the table. 'They're the most generous and welcoming people I've ever met. If I have to find a fault, it's that they like to think they invented everything, and nothing can possibly happen without their being at the forefront.' He shrugged. 'That's nothing, though. They were hospitality itself. Even the sales staff in Bloomingdale's were friendly and remarkably helpful.'

'What's Bloomingdale's?'

'The department store where I bought your stuff.' He paused when the steward arrived with the wine.

Reg tasted it and declared it excellent. When the steward had gone, he continued. 'Believe it or not, Betty Grable wore stockings just like yours in a film called, *Man About Town*.'

She pulled a face and said, 'That's a lot to live up to.'

'Now, I won't have you belittling yourself. You're extremely well-favoured in that respect as well as in others.'

'Thank you. You do wonders for my self-esteem.' She lifted her glass and asked, 'What shall we drink to this time?'

'I think we should adopt "Confusion to Zeus" as our regular toast. Don't you?'

'All right.' Together, they drank to 'Confusion to Zeus,' and then Eileen said, 'I don't suppose you're allowed to tell me where you're going.'

'I'm afraid not. I don't know yet.' He'd actually seen a quantity of tropical uniform come on board, but that didn't necessarily mean anything. It was the kind of thing that prompted 'buzzes', and they were almost invariably misleading. 'I think,' he said, 'you should prepare yourself for a long separation, and then enjoy the surprise if it turns out to be shorter than you think.' On brief reflection, he added, 'Try not to be too frustrated when mail takes a long time to come through. I'll write frequently, but it sometimes takes longer than we would like.'

The band was playing 'You'll Never Know', and Eileen said, 'Let's dance while we can.'

They moved to the slow, gentle beat of the music, happy to be together once more, but guarded about the future.

Within minutes of their returning to their table, the hare arrived, providing a welcome distraction.

When the tables were cleared and supper was officially over, the lights came down, and members began to arrive, having eaten elsewhere. The dance floor became crowded, so it seemed only sensible for Reg and Eileen to use their alcove for dancing, or shuffling, as a purist might have described the activity. In fact, they spent the remainder of the evening moving to the music whilst taking hardly a step.

Eventually, however, the time came for Reg to see Eileen home, which he did, knowing he would see her again the following evening before travelling to Portsmouth to join his ship.

They booked into a hotel in Waterloo, as it was convenient for them both, and ate there. Unfortunately, the band was less than inspiring, which was an added reason for an early night, and they went to their room.

Eileen asked, 'Why did you bring the wine up?'

'It saves wasting it, and we can have a drink in between.' He closed the curtains to hide the blackout. 'There,' he said, 'that's almost civilised. One day, there will be no blackout, and life will return to normal.'

Eileen was still wondering about his reference to 'in between', then realisation came, and she could only say, 'Oh, how decadent.'

'It's the kind of thing Bonaparte and Josephine used to do on the eve of a campaign. At least, I can only imagine they did, because I'm not sure that they were ever indiscreet about their love-life.'

'Oh, don't. I'd rather not think about the war.'

'All right. Let's get into bed and give Zeus a run for his money. Would you like first go with the bathroom?'

'Yes, please, I shan't be long.'

'Take as long as you like. I'm not going anywhere.' He waited while she used the bathroom, wondering, as Eileen had, what his destination might be. Such evidence as there was pointed to the Far East, which would mean a long time for them to be apart. On the other hand, though, and looking at it from a purely selfish point of view, he had a score to settle with the Japanese, and that was a prospect he could relish. He was still thinking about it when Eileen came into the room.

'Right,' she said, 'it's all yours, but you don't need to linger. I'm not quite as shy as I was.'

'Noted.' He brushed his teeth and emerged to find her loosening her stockings.

'These things are so precious,' she said, 'they have to be handled very carefully.' Looking up at him, she asked, 'Is something wrong?'

'Not in the least. Far from it. I was just thinking about Betty Grable, and wondering what makes her all that special.'

'Don't. You'll make me shy again.'

'Well, we can't have that.' He removed his uniform and hung it up. As he did so, he heard her pull back the bedclothes and climb in. He switched on the bedside lamp and turned off the main light. Then, shedding the rest of his clothes, he joined her in bed and asked, 'Did you remember to...?'

'Everything's in place,' she assured him.

One day, he thought, someone would invent something much more discreet that would enable true spontaneity. Until then, he would ask clumsy questions and feel all the clumsier for it. He put the thought behind him and took her in his arms.

'I hate the idea of being without you again,' she said.

'I know, but if you marry me, you'll find, even in peacetime, that you'll spend much of your life as a grass widow.'

'Oh, please don't use that word.'

'Try not to think about it.' He kissed her, partly as a distraction, but mainly because it was hard not to.

After a short time, she said, 'You're very fond of them, aren't you?' She was referring to her breasts, which were currently receiving his earnest attention.

He broke off to say, 'I love them. I love every part of you.'

In an abrupt change of subject, she asked, 'Have you a different address now?'

He stopped what he was doing and said, 'Your heart's not really in it, tonight, I can tell.'

'I'm sorry. It'll be all right. I just have a feeling that I shan't see you for a long time, and I find it unsettling.'

'Neither of us can be sure of that, darling.'

'It's just a feeling. That's why I asked about your address.'

'I'm sorry. Of course, you won't have seen my letters since I left America. It's *HMS Invincible*, BFPO Ships.'

Seemingly content to talk, at least for the time being, she asked, 'Isn't it a coincidence that they called the ship in *Ships With Wings* "*Invincible*"?'

'I suppose it is.'

'Is she similar to your old ship?'

'They're both carriers, but *Invincible* is bigger and faster, and she carries more aircraft. She's brand new and she's a beautiful ship, but that's all I'm allowed to tell you.'

'Will you write to me regularly?' As the words left her mouth, she closed her eyes, regretting her foolishness. 'Of course you will. That was stupid of me.'

'With every spare moment – well, nearly every spare moment, because there are times when I have to stop for a drink – I'll write to you, dearest beloved. You can depend on it. I can't guarantee a regular collection or delivery, but letters will leave the Underwood cabin at frequent and regular intervals.' He kissed her, more in reassurance than in hope of renewed interest, but she responded readily, so he continued, kissing and exploring until, eventually, parting and separation were temporarily forgotten.

As they lay together in darkness, he asked, 'When you said you'd spend the night in a hotel, do you think they suspected anything?'

'Ted didn't say anything, but as I was leaving, Lorna asked me if I was taking proper precautions.'

'Women are just too intuitive for words.' It had been a source of personal regret for some time.

'She was very nice about it, and she only mentioned it when we were alone. She was just concerned for me.'

'She's not the only one. You will look after yourself, won't you, darling? I love you.'

'I love you too, so you'd better take care of yourself as well.'

20

Letters and a Posting

Based now in Message Handling, Eileen learned of Reg's whereabouts before his first bundle of letters arrived, simply by monitoring signal traffic whenever possible. *HMS Invincible*'s first call was Gibraltar, which meant one of two ultimate destinations. She was either on route for the Italian coast to provide support for the land forces there, or she was heading for the Suez Canal, and that could only point to the Far East. If it turned out to be the latter, they might be separated for a very long time indeed. In the meantime, however, she had his letters, which she read repeatedly. Her favourite, because of its final paragraph, coincided with his arrival at Gibraltar. She knew that from its date and *Invincible*'s last signal.

Dearest Eileen,
I hope everything is well with you, Ted and Lorna.
For obvious reasons, I can't tell you where we are, but some of us had a glorious swim this afternoon, after which, Guy and I enjoyed a bottle of chilled wine. The war seemed far away, I can tell you, but I've no doubt it'll catch up with us soon enough.

A fairly distant explosion reminded Eileen of the fact that the war was still very much a fact of life in London. There seemed no end to the 'doodlebug' offensive; she had counted four such explosions that morning.

When we went ashore, I discovered that a poet had been practising his art in the officers' heads. I don't usually read mural offerings, let alone relay them, but this one is a cut above the usual:
This bloody roundhouse is no good at all;
The seat is too high and the hole is too small.
Beneath that, in different handwriting, were the following lines:
To which I must add the obvious retort,
Your arse is too large and your legs are too short.
If only I were gifted in poetry, prose, or anything, really.

To change the subject, as I feel I must, I've thought a great deal about our last night together. We were both sad about parting, however temporarily, and I think we should look on the bright side and think about our future. Here's something to consider. I should get a reasonably long leave after this deployment, so why don't we get a special licence and get married? I look forward to reading your thoughts on the subject. Meanwhile, I await our next meeting eagerly.
Yours, with absolutely all my love,
Reg XXX

The letters had taken almost two weeks to come from Gibraltar, but that wasn't surprising. She replied immediately, not knowing how long hers might take to reach him.

Dearest Reg,
You really must find something more challenging to read. What was the name of that comic you told me about? The one with the man whose table manners are so appalling he'd never pass the 'knife and fork' course? That might do for a start, just until you get the hang of reading in places other than the heads. But seriously, I love you despite your uncouth taste in literature, and I look forward to taking charge of your education.

Meanwhile, doodlebugs continue to fall in and around London, but we can take it! With Ted and his mates up their ladders, hosepipes in hand, how could we do otherwise?

Last evening, a friend and I saw The Way Ahead, *starring David Niven. It follows the fortunes of a platoon – I think that's the word – of soldiers from basic training to their first spell of enemy action. It ends with David Niven leading them through a cloud of smoke into goodness-knows-what, and it had the same effect on me as the end of* Ships With Wings. *I went through three hankies. I always have plenty, as my parents give me them for Christmas and birthdays; at least, when they remember my birthday.*

I know you're waiting for this, so I saved it until last. Yes, yes, yes, let's get married! I'll keep an eye out for parachute silk so that I can have a dress made. That was what people did in the Blitz, wasn't it? I remember Ted telling me about it. Here's to it!

Keep safe.

All my love, too,

Eileen XXX

The short stay in Gibraltar had enabled Reg to read Eileen's earlier letters, but the rest would have to follow, because *Invincible* had sailed again, stopping briefly at Malta, and was now heading for Port Said and the Suez Canal.

The ship's company, including the Air Group, spent the voyage exercising, and the time was particularly useful for Reg's squadron, because of the new pilots flown in from training in Rhode Island to replace the two casualties. That leg of the voyage occupied only nine days, but Reg was able, in that time, to build a cohesive team with a sense of identity. Another development was the way in which the squadron had come to view the Corsair. The Americans had introduced it as the 'Bent-Wing Bastard from Connecticut' and a 'goddamned death-trap', but their allies across the water saw it in a different light. Blessed for the first time with a fighter that could hold its own against all-comers, the Fleet Air Arm had been determined to make it a success, and that resolve had paid off. No one would deny that the Corsair was tricky to land on a flight deck or that it had less than favourable stalling characteristics, but that was where the criticism ended. They were devoted to it, and they flew it with unquenchable enthusiasm.

It was universally accepted that postings and drafts occurred without any perceptible reason and followed no recognised pattern, so Eileen was only a little surprised when Second Officer Curwen told her of her new appointment.

'You're going to *HMS Flowerdown*, near Portsmouth,' she said.

'But it was only five months ago that I came here, ma'am. Why am I suddenly surplus to requirements?'

Miss Curwen gave her a stern look and said, 'No one is surplus to requirements, Third Officer. The fact is that, since the invasion took place, naval activity in the Channel and its approaches has become increasingly intense, and the "Y" stations, the listening stations, are shouldering an extremely heavy workload. That is the reason for your posting.'

'I see, ma'am. Naturally, I'll go wherever I'm posted. It just seemed odd, that's all.'

Miss Curwen smiled unexpectedly. 'Welcome to the ways of Postings and Drafts, a department that could spring further surprises on you before this war is over.' Folding her hands in her lap, she said, 'I believe you've been living at home on Ration Allowance.'

'At my brother's home, ma'am. He's with the NFS in Whitechapel, and he has a flat in Hoxton.'

'How very convenient, but you'll be vittled and accommodated on board, so things won't be so bad; in fact, you'll find that *Flowerdown* has some remarkable facilities for recreation.'

'That's something to look forward to, ma'am.' She was determined not to come across as feeble, unwelcome though the posting was.

***

Invincible's Fighter Group Commander was a vastly experienced lieutenant commander called Lionel Sanderson. Reg had known him briefly in *Ark Royal* before Sanderson was given the job of creating a new squadron, and the two were soon back on friendly terms. He would operate also as commander of Baker Squadron.

It was Lionel Sanderson's job to make the two squadrons work together as one unit, a demanding task in so short a time, but he achieved wonders, staging mock battles between the squadrons, and dreaming up a diverse range of situations for them to address.

Time spent in Port Said was all too brief before *Invincible* had to enter the Suez Canal. In his spare moments, Reg would stand on the observation platform as the ship passed through the Canal, flanked incredibly by desert on either side. On such occasions, his admiration and sympathy went out to the officer of the watch and the coxswain, who had to maintain a careful and narrow course with 23,000 tons of aircraft carrier to manage.

Another concern was the unremitting heat, which became gradually more intense as they approached the Gulf.

'Honestly,' complained Guy one morning, 'I put this shirt and these shorts on five minutes ago, and they're soaked. It's a waste of time dressing.'

'Don't walk about naked, whatever you do,' said Reg. 'There's enough unpleasantness waiting for us out there, without you providing yet more horrors.'

'You're only jealous of my manly torso and bulging biceps.'

'Of course,' agreed Reg, 'but you can keep the rest. Let's go to breakfast and find out what's still solid.'

Eileen waited at the Main Gate of *HMS Flowerdown* until, in response to the sentry's telephone call, a determined-looking second officer arrived.

'Third Officer Dewhirst? I'm Second Officer Tremaine. I'll show you around myself, as you're going to be in my unit.'

'How d'you do, ma'am.'

'How d' you do. Follow me, and I'll take you to your quarters so that you can leave your things.' She led Eileen through a labyrinth of passages and rooms until they came to the sign that read: *WRNS Officers*. 'You'll be sharing with another three-oh.' She checked the name on the door and said, 'Jane Dixon. You're in different watches, so you won't see much of each other. Anyway,' she said, opening the door, 'Put your things in there. You can unpack later.' She waited for Eileen to leave her bag on the unused bunk, and then led her back along the passageway. She asked, 'How much do you know about this station?'

'Very little, ma'am. I suppose that's not surprising, considering its sensitive nature.'

'Quite. We're a listening station – I'm sure you know that much – and our purpose is to intercept German and Japanese transmissions.'

'Japanese? I'm afraid I've had no experience of that, ma'am.'

'In that case, you'll be relieved to know that you're to be based in the German Department, with me.'

'That is a relief, ma'am.'

For the first time, Miss Tremaine's features relaxed, and she smiled at Eileen's reaction. 'Japanese Morse is complex, and it's transmitted at the equivalent of thirty words a minute, which is too fast for any operator to handwrite, so it has to be recorded on a wire recording machine and played back slowly enough to be read, or "copied" as our American allies call the process.'

'It sounds impossible, ma'am.'

'Thankfully, we have telegraphists trained to cope with it, although the Americans are now dripping about our traditional telegraphists, because they're not trained to touch-type, as theirs are. They like to operate at twenty-fives and above, which makes hand-writing impossible. Of course, it doesn't help, as well, that they use the automatic Morse key, which only lends encouragement to the speed merchants.' She stopped outside a door marked *German W/T* and opened it. 'I wonder, sometimes, if we're on the same side. Remove your hat, Three-Oh.'

'Of course, ma'am.' Eileen doffed her hat as she entered the room, looking around her at the ratings, who were hard at work. 'There are some very young-looking POs and Chiefs, ma'am,' she commented.

'Linguists are given accelerated promotion to PO or PO Wren. I don't know why, but they're doing an important job, so I've no argument with the practice. Come into my office and I'll explain the watch system to you. You'll find it's not quite what you're used to.'

Eileen followed her into the glass-panelled office at the end of the room.

'Come in and take a seat.' She waited until Eileen was settled, and said, 'The watches are basically what you know from Whitehall, but with one important difference, which is that we split them into work and rest periods. That's why we possibly appear to have more personnel than we need.'

'How does that work, ma'am?'

'Because monitoring requires intense concentration, no telegraphist is allowed to work longer than four hours. They do four on and four off, purely as a means of preserving their mental health. Even then, we keep a close eye on all ratings in case they begin to show signs of fatigue. War can be cruel enough without adding the nervous breakdown to the list of injuries.'

'That makes perfect sense, ma'am.'

'Good.' Conversationally, she asked, 'What was your accommodation in London?'

'I was on Ration Allowance, ma'am. I lived with my brother and his wife.' Quick to avoid embarrassing questions about a man resident in London in wartime, she said, 'My brother's a fireman in the East End.'

'Is he really? Was he there during the Blitz?'

'Yes, ma'am, both he and his wife served there throughout the Blitz.'

'In that case, I'm full of admiration for them.'

'He wanted to join the Navy, but he was turned down by all three services because he's allergic to soya.'

'Poor man. I hope you're not.'

'No, ma'am, I'm not.'

'It's just as well. We get the wretched stuff all the time at this place.' Quite unexpectedly, she said, 'I see you're wearing an engagement ring. It's nothing to do with the job. I'm just being nosey.'

'Yes, I'm engaged, ma'am. My fiancé is a fighter pilot, and he's away somewhere, serving in *HMS Invincible*.'

'I sympathise, Three-Oh. My husband's in *Indomitable*. Take my advice and keep yourself busy.'

21

Heat and Stress

For security reasons, incoming mail was collected at HMS Nelson, the naval barracks in Portsmouth, and then delivered by naval transport to *Flowerdown*. Portsmouth, however was only the second stage for Eileen's mail, as any letters from Reg were addressed to Ted's and Lorna's flat in London. In any case, after such a recent appointment, she wasn't expecting anything, so she was surprised and delighted when she received several letters from Reg, forwarded apparently from Malta.

'Every picture tells a story,' Second Officer Tremaine told her confidently in a spare moment. 'You're next lot will probably come from Alexandria.'

'Why do you say that, ma'am?'

'Mine did. You see, the Army in Italy is now covered by the RAF, based on Malta, so there's no longer the need there for carriers. Instead, they're sending them through the Suez Canal to Trincomalee.'

'Oh.' She'd rather closed her mind to the possibility that Reg would be sent to the Far East. It just seemed so distant.

'Chin up, Three-Oh. You and I are in the same boat, so to speak, and it's always good to know that we're not alone. Anyway, how did you and he meet?'

'We were on Orkney, ma'am.' It seemed only a short time ago. 'Because we were short-handed, I was ordered to install a transmitter in a Fulmar night fighter. I was a Wren telegraphist at the time, and I was completely flustered because I'd never done anything like that, but Reg

154

was terribly patient. He helped me through the installation and told me what to do if we had to bale out, and then he took me on a bird's-eye-view tour of the Fleet Anchorage at Scapa Flow. It's the only time I've ever flown, and it was wonderful, and then, a few days later, he asked me to join him for a drink. It was rather naughty, and we were found out, but my divisional officer just told me to keep my mind on the job and not be distracted.'

Miss Tremaine smiled at the disclosure. 'It happens all the time, here,' she said. 'With a naval air station next door, it's unavoidable, so no one really cares.' Confiding again, she said, 'That's how I met my husband, except that it happened at Lee-on-Solent. He's a fighter direction officer.' In the sympathetic way she had, she said, 'Just hold on, Three-Oh. The war can't last for ever.'

It was a great comfort, just as Miss Tremaine had said, to know she wasn't alone, and Eileen still had Reg's letters to read. Her first opportunity occurred at the end of her watch, when she opened the most recent one.

Dearest Eileen,

It seems all wrong that you should be working so hard, while I'm on this pleasure cruise. Still, 'Into each life some rain must fall', or something of that kind, and before you jump to conclusions, I didn't read that in the heads. I've moved on from that kind of thing.

Speaking of moving, where are we going to live after the war? I really haven't given it much thought until now. Shall we be terribly conventional and 'live over the shop', as 't were, whilst keeping a pied-a-terre *wherever your seat of learning happens to be, or shall we be independent and live wherever our hearts are drawn?*

Another burning question that occurs to me is that of perpetuating the Underwood name. I mean to say, I'm sorry to be stuffy about this, but I am the last of the line, so if we can manage an occasional addition to the family among everything else, that would be splendid. Seriously, though, where do you stand on children? I'm not suggesting that you actually stand on them; in fact, the thought appals me, but what I'm saying is that I wouldn't dream of forcing one upon you if you were otherwise inclined. When all's said and done, life's too short to spend it thumping the table.

How are Ted and Lorna? I do feel that someone should write a book of some kind about the work of the Fire Service in this war. I saw them at work in London during the Blitz, and they have my fullest admiration. Is 'fullest' a proper word? If it isn't, please substitute an acceptable alternative. At all events, I'm sure you know what I mean.

Now for the serious bit. I miss you like the blazes, but we shall be together, whatever that old spoilsport Zeus thinks.

Take care of yourself.

Yours with all the love I can scrape together,

Reg XXX

She folded the letter and placed it in its envelope. It was Reg through and through. She thought about their earlier exchange about what they could and could not write about, and it seemed to her that he'd got the hang of writing doting nonsense, because although it was nonsense, there was no doubting the love that came with it. She needed to check on one thing, so when she next saw Second Officer Tremaine, she asked, 'Does the expression "living over the shop" mean anything to you, ma'am?'

'Yes, it does. In service parlance, anyone who has a house near Portsmouth, Plymouth, Chatham or any of those places is "living over the shop". Is it something you've read in a letter?'

'Yes, it's just a bit of nonsense, ma'am, but I wondered.'

'Nonsense is all you're allowed to write, I'm afraid.'

'It's better than nothing, ma'am.'

The ship refuelled at Aden and set off across the Indian Ocean. At times, the temperature seemed unbearable, and Reg had to remind himself at such times of the air mechanics and artificers working below in the hangar, which resembled a huge, steel oven. Then, when he was appointed Squadron Maintenance Officer, he had no need to remind himself, because he was obliged to spend most of his time with them.

After one watch, he discussed the matter with Guy, who was suitably sympathetic.

'Hard for them, old man, but harder for you because you're not used to it.'

'I don't know, Guy. They have a great deal to endure. I mean, you know how the average matelot likes to drip?'

'Don't I just.'

'He drips about his quarters, his duties, the food and the pay. It's normal behaviour on the lower deck, but it doesn't mean a thing. When things go wrong, the air mechanics are on the job whatever the conditions, and they stay there until it's done. We can always rely on them.'

'That's very true, Reg.' He lifted his hand to summon the steward. 'Two pink gins, Groves, if you please. I'll sign for them as Lieutenant Commander Underwood has suffered more than I have today.'

'Thank you, Guy. I appreciate that.'

'It's true, what you said about the braves. We inside the tepee should appreciate their efforts more than we do.'

'I think it was at Dartmouth,' said Reg, peeling himself from the back of his chair, 'where I read something that Lord Nelson once said, to the effect that the true hero of any naval engagement was the ordinary British seaman.'

'And they had it much harder in those days,' said Guy, taking the drinks from the steward's tray and signing the mess chit, 'but, what are you saying, old chap? Are you thinking of resigning your commission and joining the lower deck? If so, I think the heat must have affected your brain.'

'Of course not. I'm just saying that we have a hell of a lot to be thankful for.'

Guy considered that statement and said, 'It's difficult to appreciate that fully in these conditions, but yes, I suppose you're right.' He tried his pink gin and declared it satisfactory. 'It'll be better when we're flying again.'

'There'll be no flying until we reach Trincomalee.'

'None at all?'

'No, but it'll only be five days, Guy, and then we'll have the enemy to contend with as well as the heat.' It wasn't the only thing on his mind at that moment. He'd been studying his friend covertly, and he suspected all was not well. 'Guy, tell me to mind my own business if you will, but you've not been quite your jovial self since the mail arrived.'

'That's all right, old man. I received a letter from my mother's solicitor, telling me that she is no longer. She'd been frail for some time.'

'Oh hell, Guy, I'm sorry.'

'Thanks, old man, but we were never particularly close. Not at all close, really. I just feel that another door on my past has closed.'

'Had she no other close relatives?'

'None whatsoever. She's left me all her worldly wampum, as well as the family wigwam, a modest but pleasing abode in Hampshire.'

There was no more Reg could say, so he patted Guy's shoulder and went to his cabin to read Eileen's last letter. He'd read it several times, but its appeal had never faded.

I know you're waiting for this, so I saved it until last. Yes, yes, yes, let's get married! I'll keep an eye out for parachute silk so that I can have a dress made. That was what people did in the Blitz, wasn't it? I remember Ted telling me about it. Here's to it!

Keep safe.

All my love, too,

Eileen XXX

He could see himself reading that same letter for months to come, and if that were the case, whose business was it but his?

———————

One aspect of serving in a 'Y' station that Eileen found frustrating was that she was no longer able to keep an eye on allied signal traffic, which meant she could only guess at Reg's whereabouts. All she could do was act on Second Officer Tremaine's advice and concentrate on her work, which offered a useful distraction, sometimes in the most unexpected way.

She was checking one of the signal logs when a Wren came to the office in some agitation.

'It's Wren Stewart, ma'am. She's unwell.'

Eileen left the office and crouched beside the unfortunate girl. 'What's the problem, Wren Stewart?'

'Stomach... pain, ma'am.' She was clutching herself, and her features were contorted with distress.

'It's not the usual, is it?' It would have surprised her. When a number of women lived in close proximity, nature had a curious and remarkable way of synchronising their natural rhythms.

'No, ma'am. It's something... else.'

Turning to the girl who had alerted her, she said, 'Wren Barnes, take Wren Stewart to the Sick Bay.'

'But, ma'am, the German broadcast....'

'It's all right. I'll read it.' She took the girl's place at the bay, donned her headphones and picked up a pencil. The German Navy headquarters at Kiel were busily transmitting coded groups, and Eileen began reading them. She continued to do so until the end of the broadcast, when she completed the log. She'd been so occupied with the task that she hadn't noticed that Wren Barnes had returned from the Sick Bay, and was now standing behind her, waiting patiently for her officer to vacate the bay.

'I'm sorry, Wren Barnes. I didn't see you come in. What's the story with Wren Stewart?'

'I don't know, ma'am. A sick berth attendant took her in to see the surgeon lieutenant. He sent me away.'

'Of course.' It made perfect sense. 'Thank you for your help, Wren Barnes. I've logged the broadcast.'

The girl was looking at her with a kind of wonder. 'Thank you, ma'am.'

When Eileen returned to the office, Second Officer Tremaine asked, 'What was all that about, you on the WT bay?'

'I had to send Wren Stewart to the Sick Bay, ma'am. Wren Barnes took her, so I read the broadcast.'

'What's the matter with Wren Stewart?'

'Stomach pain, ma'am. It looked quite dramatic, and she's normally a quiet sort of girl.'

Miss Tremaine nodded. 'It's possibly a stomach ulcer. They're not unusual. As I told you earlier, these girls are working under a lot of pressure.' Reflecting briefly, she said, 'Under normal circumstances, you might have done better to take the girl to the Sick Bay yourself and leave the Wren on the WT bay, but you're new to this establishment, and it probably did no harm for the girls to see you confidently reading the broadcast. It would serve as a reminder to them that officers are not all strutting amateurs.'

'Do they really think that, ma'am?'

'Some of them do. Be honest, Three-Oh. I bet you did when you were a rating.'

'Not all of them, ma'am, but I see what you mean about letting them know we can still do their job.'

The phone rang, and Miss Tremaine picked it up. 'Kriegsmarine WT. Second Officer Tremaine speaking.' She listened to the caller, occasionally acknowledging something. Finally, she said, 'Thank you for telling me. Goodbye.' Putting the receiver down, she said, 'That was the Surgeon-Lieutenant Phillips. They're taking Wren Stewart to Haslar Hospital for tests. They suspect a peptic ulcer. I was probably right, poor girl, and on top of that, I'll now have to find a spare Wren telegraphist.'

22

Punishment, Pity and Silliness

All aircraft were flown off, to be based at Trincomalee Airfield while
Invincible lay at anchor. Pilots and other aircrew were billeted
almost at the edge of the jungle in huts roofed with woven coconut
leaves. There, they learned about the local wildlife, sometimes the hard
way, finding their clothing destroyed by rodents similar to squirrels,
that entered the quarters without invitation and plundered the drawers
and cupboards. Snakes, including cobras, were common, and night
time brought mosquitos to torment the inhabitants. It was a relief to get
into the sky, and during that time, Lionel Sanderson wasted no time in
preparing his fighter group for action.

As dawn broke over the island, Reg sat in his cockpit, going
through the drill. There were no fewer than 110 gauges on the Corsair's
instrument panel, but the checks took no more than a few minutes.

He looked to the Control Tower, where a steady red light told him to
remain where he was for the time being. The cooling gills on the engine
compartment were open, allowing air to be drawn in to keep the engine
from overheating, a precaution made even more necessary than usual
by the fierce, tropical heat of Ceylon. A green light replaced the red, and
Reg closed the gills and moved forward on to the runway, increasing his
speed as he did so. The tail of the aircraft lifted off the runway, and he
opened the throttle further. At about 130 knots, he became airborne. He
closed the Perspex hood and raised the undercarriage. As he climbed,
he described a wide spiral, keeping an eye on his squadron, until the
last aircraft was in the air. He led them through the clouds to 10,000

feet, enjoying the sweet taste of oxygen. When they were assembled, he spoke to them.

'Able Squadron, this is Able Leader. Execute to follow, Victor formation. Over.'

When the last pilot had receipted his signal, he ordered, 'Stand by, stand by, execute!' The Corsairs under his command formed up on him, and he led them down the coast of Ceylon, towards Batticaloa, ready to do 'battle' with Baker Squadron whilst revelling in the excitement of flying at more than 320 knots. The Corsair was capable of a great deal more when speed was required, but fuel had to be conserved.

So the preparation continued. It was announced that the two squadrons would fly as a wing, carrying out strafing attacks on Japanese airfields. Such attacks were not without danger, firstly, from enemy action, and secondly, because diving and low flying were inherently dangerous practices, anyway. For several weeks, Sanderson had them fly low over the fields and forests of Ceylon, terrifying the local animal life and probably quite a lot of local inhabitants as well, but emerging infinitely better equipped to fulfil their temporary role.

As far as enemy action was concerned, it stood to reason that the best way to approach an enemy airstrip was lengthways, and that was where they placed themselves in danger of being shot down, because the Corsairs would be visible during their approach, and the Japanese anti-aircraft gunners were known to be particularly adept at defending their bases. Only the prodigious speed of the Corsair could safeguard the attacker from ground-based gunfire.

The time came for the fighter group to be flown on to *Invincible* again, to be taken up the coast, in company with her sister ship *HMS Insatiable*, to carry out attacks on enemy aircraft.

At first, they simply hung around the coast, rather as a bullfighter entices his quarry. Unfortunately, and unlike most fighting bulls, the Japanese weren't in a hurry to give battle, so a strafing attack had to be carried out.

The position of the nearest airstrip was known to the nearest mile, and its orientation had been established by reconnaissance aircraft, so with Seafire fighters from *Insatiable* guarding the carrier group, the Corsairs headed for the reported position.

They found it within ten minutes of crossing the coastline. The aircraft, some dozen of them, which Lionel Sanderson identified as 'Val' dive-bombers, were parked in a herringbone pattern at the end of the runway. 'Val' was the convenient name given to the Aichi D3A by the Americans, who struggled to pronounce Japanese names, but the important fact remained that, whatever its label and however it was pronounced, it spelt trouble, and its destruction was vital.

Sanderson went in first, his six Browning machine guns wrecking the rearmost aircraft and destroying another. His squadron followed, causing so much damage that it seemed at first that Able Squadron would be surplus to requirements, but then Reg saw the water tower and the bomb and petrol dumps.

'Able Two, take the water tower,' he said. 'Able Four, take the petrol dump. The rest of you concentrate on the accommodation while I attend to the bomb dump.' As he spoke, a lone, brave soul crawled out of the wreckage and was training a 'woodpecker' machine gun on the attackers. As lost causes went, his was hopeless from the start.

Accordingly, Guy attacked the water tower, puncturing it so that the deluge from above brought several figures running from the bamboo control tower to avoid immersion or worse. Meanwhile, the petrol dump was exploding as Sandy McGregor's bullets tore into each drum. Then, in response to Reg's attentions, there was a massive multiple boom from the bomb dump, and he felt the Corsair being hurled violently upwards by the explosion. For a moment, he was afraid he would be thrown into a spin, which would have been fatal, but he managed to correct his trim, turning through 180 degrees, and it was then that he saw the machine gunner still steadfastly firing. He was very brave, or at least, committed, but it was no time for chivalry. Reg's thumb closed on the firing button and he saw the man and his gun blown apart.

Leaving the carnage behind, he made height and ordered the squadron to form up on him. Carrying out a roll-call, he was subsequently relieved to learn that Able Squadron had suffered no casualties.

Whether or not the Hereafter provided the means to monitor earthly goings-on, no one could possibly say, but if it did, he hoped his father had been watching.

⎯⬥⎯

Mindful of the stress of working in a 'Y' station, the Admiralty had the foresight to retain and maintain the recreational facilities at *HMS Flowerdown*. Consequently, officers and ratings were able to take part in various sports and even hold dances in the extensive ballroom. *Flowerdown* was also host to ratings being rested from the transatlantic convoys, so the facilities were always in demand.

Eileen's preferred place of exercise and relaxation from her work, however, was the swimming pool, and having noted the days on which the pool was allotted to members of the WRNS and female civil servants, she made regular use of it.

She was returning from a session in the pool when she came across a rating. He was sitting on the grass outside the tennis courts, and he was completely alone. His head was bowed, possibly in thought, although Eileen thought she should check in case he was unwell.

'Hello,' she said, 'are you all right?'

The rating, who was very young, looked up suddenly.

'I'm sorry,' said Eileen, 'I didn't mean to startle you.'

'Yes, I'm okay, thanks, Miss.'

She crouched beside him to ask, 'Have you been here long?'

He shook his head. 'Only about ten minutes, Miss.'

'I meant here, at Flowerdown.'

'Oh, right. Sorry, Miss. No, we only arrived last week.' His speech was nervous, coming in bursts. He lapsed into silence again, and Eileen was about to walk away and leave him in peace, when he asked, 'You're from up north, aren't you, Miss?'

'Yes, my home's in Cullington, near Bradford.' For the purpose of conversation, she used the word 'home' loosely.

'I thought so. I'm from Denholm.'

'I know it well.'

After a brief silence he said softly, 'We've been in the North Atlantic, on Russian convoys.'

164

'I see.' It seemed he wanted to talk, so she lowered herself on to the grass beside him.

'I've seen some horrible things.'

'Do you want to tell me about them?'

He eyed her discreetly and said, 'Maybe I shouldn't talk like this, you bein' an officer an' that.'

'If you want to talk, just go ahead.' She was about to tell him to forget she was an officer, but that was possibly a risky thing to say. Instead, she asked him, 'What's your name?'

'Ackroyd, Miss, Thomas Ackroyd.'

'Not "Tom"?'

'No, Miss, Thomas.' Absently, he plucked a blade of grass and rolled it between his hands. 'Do you know what's the worst thing?'

'No, Thomas, tell me.'

'It's seein' blokes in the water. I'm not scared of water. I'm fairly good at swimming, but the idea of bein' in the oggin....' He shook his head, unable to finish the sentence.

'Go on,' she prompted him gently.

'They say, if you abandon ship up there....' He stopped again. 'They call it "down north". I don't know why.'

'Do you mean the North Atlantic?'

'That's right, Miss. They say it's so cold, you don't last more 'n a few seconds. I know how cold it is up top, so I can believe it.'

'Presumably you serve in a carrier?' The badge on his right shoulder identified him as an aircraft handler.

'Escort carrier, actually, Miss.'

Now she could offer him some kind of comfort. 'You stand a better chance than the merchant ships,' she reminded him.

'That's true.' Incredibly, it was as if he'd never considered that possibility.

To lighten the conversation, she said, 'My fiancé served in an escort carrier, *HMS Yorker*, until earlier this year. He's in a bigger one now.' She thought it advisable not to name his current ship.

He nodded, recognising the name. 'Yorker's one of the new ones.'

Recalling an earlier conversation, she said, 'Maybe you can tell me which aircraft is the one the Japanese call "Whistling Death"?'

He smiled at the name. 'I've heard of that,' he said. 'They're talkin' about the Corsair, a Yankee fighter. Is your fiancé a pilot?'

'Yes.'

'I don't suppose you know where he is, but chances are he'll be in the Far East. That's where most of 'em are going.' He smiled again. 'At least, that's the buzz, and it'll be warmer there.'

It was her turn to smile. She asked, 'Do you feel better, now, Thomas?'

'Yes, thanks, Miss. I feel better now I've talked to somebody. You're ever so nice. I reckon your fiancé's a lucky... officer.'

'That's very kind of you,' she said, getting to her feet, 'but I must be off.'

''Bye, Miss. Thanks again.'

'Goodbye, Thomas, and good luck.'

Invincible's next target was to be Sabang, a harbour on a tiny island to the north of Sumatra, which served the ships supplying the Japanese army in Burma. There was also an airfield further inland that required the attention of the task force, which included a battlecruiser, two battleships and several cruisers as well as the aircraft carriers.

The Japanese were caught largely by surprise, and a number of hastily-manned anti-aircraft guns were put out of action by the Corsairs' machine guns, the attackers going on to sweep the airfield, destroying all the aircraft on it. As Guy pointed out later, the Japanese would just have to develop a sense of humour. There was nothing else for it.

Back in his cabin, Reg wrote to his mother, to Vera, and finally to Eileen.

Dearest Eileen,

First of all, I hope everything is perfect in your various places of work, rest and amusement.

Ray Hobbs

Things would be pretty boring, here, if it weren't for the misfits, eccentrics and lunatics of this parish. Let me try to describe some of them, so that you know what I'm up against. Where shall I begin? Yes, with Guy, my wingman, who speaks fluent Red Indian, at least, when he's sober. When he's drunk, he simply talks nonsense.

Moseying further into the Wardroom, I spot Sandy McGregor, a Canadian and a giant among men. He's only just able to fit into a cockpit, but when we're ashore, we send him to get the drinks, as he towers above the populace, thereby gaining the barmaids' immediate attention. His attitude towards naval etiquette is entertaining, to say the least. When we were inspected, the senior officer complained that Sandy's wings were crooked. He said, 'They look okay from this angle, and that's how they were when I sewed them on.' They still reside at the same crooked angle.

Next is Daniel Fisher, our resident Romeo. If we had wooden bedposts, his would have collapsed by now, weakened by the countless notches carved in them to record his carnal triumphs. I don't approve of that kind of thing, as you know, but I've long since given up trying to control his lascivious ways. Live and let lech, I suppose.

Another maverick imposed upon me by the Wavy Navy is Timothy 'Cloth-Ears' Clayton, so nicknamed because of his selective hearing. When he's supposed to be listening, he's usually found quoting long passages of Shakespeare and other assorted poets. Mind you, I'm not convinced that everything that proceeds from his lips is authentic Bard, Keats or Newbolt. I mean, no one's going to persuade me that Shakespeare wrote, or said, even in an unguarded moment, 'Whitebait my Aunt Fanny! These poor little blighters should have been thrown back!'

The abovementioned brings me to the end of the second side, and so, Light of My Life, Flower of My Dreams, I must say au revoir.

Oceans of love, honestly,

Reg XXX

23

January 1945

New Directions and a Dead End

After the briefest of Christmas leaves spent, naturally, with Ted and Lorna, Eileen returned to *Flowerdown*, where the New Year passed almost without notice, and life continued as before. That was until Second Officer Tremaine called her into the office on the morning of the fifth.

'Close the door, Eileen, and take a seat.'

Eileen did as she was told, although she couldn't help wondering a little. In the past, Second Officer Tremaine had only addressed her by her Christian name when they were both off-watch.

Miss Tremaine made herself comfortable and said, 'You've acquitted yourself well in the short time you've been here, and you and I have got on well.'

'Thank you, ma'am.'

'Unfortunately, however, we have to part. I'm destined for Trincomalee, which may possibly be a good thing, although I'll have to wait and see about that.'

'Congratulations, ma'am. Trincomalee sounds like a good posting, and I hope you see your husband soon.' It would be a shame to see her go, but it was no time for selfishness.

'I'm not the only one who's leaving, Eileen, although it's a case of *déjà vu* for you. Your new appointment, believe it or not, is Whitehall Wireless Station. You must have left quite an impression there.'

Eileen was more surprised than ever. 'Whitehall again,' she said, 'and so soon.' Counting her service prior to being drafted to Orkney, it would be her third spell of duty there.

'To coin a well-worn phrase, Eileen, there's a war on, and more astute minds than ours have tried to fathom the ways of Postings and Drafts, but without success.' She picked up the document that was on her desk and handed it to her. 'You're to report on Monday. I'll see you before then, of course, because we must have a drink together before we go our separate ways, but I do wish you the best of luck.'

'Thank you, ma'am. I wish you the same.'

Intensive preparation and exercises involving the carriers of the East Indies Fleet off Ceylon had been in progress for some time, so a major operation was now expected. On the fifth of January, the Captain of *HMS Invincible* made a broadcast to the ship's company.

'You must have wondered about the exercises that have been taking place recently, and I can tell you now that we shall be participating in a series of large-scale strikes on oil refineries in Sumatra. These provide more than half the oil required by the Japanese Navy, and about three-quarters of the aviation spirit needed to keep their Air Force in operation. It is as important as that. You'll be given more detailed information in due course, but for the time being, just let me offer my thanks and appreciation for the excellent work you've put into preparing for the operation. That is all.'

'On the warpath again,' said Guy. 'How long will it take the Japs to learn that if they don't like the consequences, they shouldn't have started it in the first place?'

'They don't think as we do,' said Reg. 'If they did, they'd behave very differently. For one thing, they'd eat sensibly with a knife and fork instead of trapping their food between two sticks and hoisting it up to their mouths.' He shrugged at the absurdity of such a practice and said, 'Naturally enough, they cheat by holding the plate almost up to their chin, but it's still a bloody silly and long-winded way of keeping body and soul together.'

'Seriously? Is that what they do?'

'I saw it in a film.'

That set Guy thinking. 'I wonder how they tackle soup,' he said.

'Search me. Maybe they haven't invented it yet.' The thought took root, and he said, 'That could be a significant turning point, you know. Just as primitive man invented the wheel, and it led to everything else, the knife, fork and spoon could symbolise a new age in Japanese civilisation.'

'Speaking of civilisation,' said Guy, 'what about those V-Two rockets? I mean, the Doodlebugs are bad enough, but at least they can be heard. The V-Twos hit the ground with no warning.'

Not for the first time, Reg was struggling to follow his friend's logic. 'What has civilisation to do,' he asked, 'with rockets?'

'Just that the Nazis are sending them over, and that, in my book, is bloody uncivilised behaviour.'

'Agreed.' The topic appeared to be exhausted, so Reg's thoughts returned to more immediate matters. 'Pink gin?'

'Very civilised of you, old man.'

Bewildered though she was by the ways of Postings and Drafts, Eileen was delighted to be at home again with Ted and Lorna, and they made her as welcome as ever.

Whitehall Wireless Station was like an old friend, too, although, if Eileen's experience were any indication, she was unlikely to meet any old friends serving there.

She stopped at the desk and gave her name.

The Wren on the desk looked at her identity card and then at a document on her desk, before picking up the telephone and reporting Eileen's arrival. Replacing the receiver, she said, 'Second Officer Underwood is sending someone to meet you, ma'am.'

For a moment, Eileen thought she'd misheard her. 'Did you say Second Officer *Underwood*?'

'Yes, ma'am.' She waited, as if poised to carry out some unexpected order.

'That's all right,' Eileen assured her. 'I recognised the name, that's all.' She would know soon enough, because a Wren emerged from the familiar, sloping passage to approach and salute her.

'Are you Third Officer Dewhirst, ma'am?'

'That's right.'

'I'm to take you to Second Officer Underwood, ma'am.'

'Thank you. Lead the way.'

She followed the girl to the WT Room, where she thanked her and made her own way to the glass-panelled office. The officer inside was standing with her back to the door, but her fair hair looked familiar. She turned when she heard Eileen's knock, and greeted her with a beaming smile.

'Come in, Eileen. I'd have come down to the desk myself, but I had to deal with a hitch in Coding. Sit down and I'll organise some coffee for us.' She opened the door and hailed a convenient Wren to charge her with that errand. 'They must have decided they were fed up with me at Faslane,' she said, closing the door again, 'but you made a good impression at *Flowerdown*.'

'I was lucky, Vera…. I'm sorry. I should call you "ma'am" now, shouldn't I?'

'Only when we can be overheard.' She made a dismissive gesture. 'Don't worry about it.'

'Thanks. I was going to say that I had a particularly good two-oh there, and it seems my luck is holding.'

'I hope so. I wouldn't want my future sister-in-law to think ill of me. Tell me, when did you last hear from Reg?'

'I had a letter from him last week. My two-oh at Flowerdown thinks he must be in the Far East, but it's difficult to tell.'

'He is.' Vera was confident. 'He's based on Trincomalee. I keep going into Message Handling and having a nosey through the log. I learn a great deal that way.'

'It's one of the perks of being in authority, I suppose.'

'As you'll discover, because Message Handling is to be your destination for the time being.'

'The main refineries are Pang Kalan Brandan and Palembang in Sumatra,' Commander (F) told them, 'and the targets that have been chosen are at Palembang. The two main installations are at Pladjoe, which is the largest in the Far East, and therefore the most important, and Songei Gerong. The task for *Invincible*'s Corsairs will be to carry out a sweep on the airfields at Palembang, Talangbetoetoe and Lembah.' He indicated each on the map behind him. 'You'll be assisted in that task by Corsairs from *Insatiable*.'

The operation was well-conceived and planned minutely; in fact, the only snag came about because of something no one could help: namely, the weather, which was quite atrocious, rendering the first two attempts impossible. However, conditions improved towards the end of the month and, finding a convenient window between storms, the Commander-in-Chief ordered the strikes to go ahead.

Lionel Sanderson led *Invincible*'s Corsairs across the coast to the airfield at Lembah, where they achieved total surprise, destroying or damaging every aircraft on the ground. By the time they reached Palembang, however, warning had been given, and they were intercepted by Zero fighters coming at them from below. Reg's first intimation of them came from Sandy McGregor.

'Rats, Boss, three o' clock down!'

'I see 'em. Able Squadron, rats at three o' clock down. Immediate execute, choose your targets and... break!'

One by one, the Corsairs of 1846 Squadron peeled off to attack the enemy fighters, which were simply outclassed by the Corsair. One by one, the Zeros either went down in flames or exploded in the sky. The squadron was then in a position to attack Palembang airfield, Baker Squadron having already made for Talangbetoetoe.

Anti-aircraft fire was fierce and accurate, and Reg felt the juddering impact as his machine was hit by bullets from the machine-guns below. So far, though, he'd not seen any of his squadron go down, and they managed to silence the woodpeckers.

'This is Able Leader,' said Reg. 'Form up in line ahead at ten thousand feet. Over.'

There was no response. As far as he was aware, he had a full squadron, but none of them was answering. Switching to 'Transmit' and then back again to 'Receive', he heard nothing. He tried again, but without success. Knowing they would all have the sense to head back to *Invincible*, he started to climb, and it was then that he realised something was horribly wrong. His engine simply wasn't responding as it should. The two thousand horsepower that should have made short work of climbing to ten thousand feet was seriously depleted. Moreover, the engine was faltering.

'Able Squadron, this is Able Leader. Over.'

Again, there was no response. He switched to 'Transmit' again and said, 'In case anyone can hear me, I've got engine trouble, and I may have to ditch.' The receiver was silent, with not even the usual atmospherics. Clearly, his radio had been hit and rendered unserviceable.

With no other aircraft in sight, he pressed on, making little more than 85 knots, barely sufficient for the Corsair to remain airborne, and then the engine faltered again. He looked around, and his eye fell on dry land, which was surprising, as he hadn't noticed it on the way in. It seemed, however, to be an island or atoll, and the squadron had made its approach at ten thousand feet, so it wasn't so strange that it had escaped his notice. He nursed the stricken aircraft closer, pulled back the canopy and released himself from the safety harness. He was close enough to the island to see the coconut palms, and he reckoned he still had enough altitude to jump, so he rolled the Corsair over and launched himself into the air.

With the air rushing past his ears, he pulled on the ripcord and was relieved when the parachute opened and filled with air. He knew he was going to fall short of the island, but there was nothing he could do about it except get as close as he could. Using the control lines, he edged his way towards it as he rapidly lost height. Then, sooner than he expected, he hit the water with such impact that the shock left him momentarily too winded to inflate his lifejacket. Instead, he hit the self-inflation device on his dinghy, and it quickly filled with air beneath him. Still attached to the parachute, he thrust his hand into the canvas paddle, hoping desperately that the stretch of ocean in which he found himself wasn't hugely popular with sharks, and made for the island, which must have been something close to a quarter of a mile distant. The parachute hindered his progress through the water, and he considered releasing it, but then elected to persevere. He might easily need it for shelter from the sun or rain.

By the time he reached the island, he was almost exhausted, but he managed to drag the dinghy and the parachute up the beach, where he rested for a few minutes in the shade of a coconut palm. At least, that was his intention, but the respite from his labours was so welcome that he made no attempt to move. His clothes were soaked and needed to be dried out, but he could muster neither the energy nor the will to do anything about it. When he'd rested, he would go in search of an enemy patrol or establishment and give himself up, even though the option had little to recommend it. Pitifully few had ever succeeded in escaping from the Japanese, but the fortunate exceptions told of unspeakably barbaric conditions as well as the harshest treatment imaginable. On the other hand, though, he had to eat and drink, and no other obvious way presented itself.

Vera read the decoded signal and passed it to Eileen. 'They're off the coast of Sumatra,' she said. 'We shan't hear from him for a while.'

'As long as he's safe,' said Eileen, 'I can wait.' She completed a double-take and asked, 'Where's Sumatra?' She'd never been keen on geography and had dropped the subject as soon as she could.

'Indonesia. Near Malaya,' she prompted, placing the signal in the tray, from which it would be taken shortly and delivered to the appropriate addressee. 'Whatever its exact position is, it's a long way from here.' After a moment's thought, she said, 'You and I are in need of a distraction. They're showing *A Canterbury Tale* at the Odeon. It comes highly recommended. Do you fancy seeing it?'

'Haven't you got a chap you'd rather go with?'

'Good heavens, no. I haven't been here long enough to see anyone worth a second glance. Honestly, it'll do us both good.'

'Okay, what's it about? Not one of Chaucer's, surely?'

'No, as far as I can make out, it's about a modern-day pilgrimage. Eric Portman's in it, and he's always worth seeing. At all events, a spot of make-believe will do us no harm at all.'

A brief reconnaissance on foot revealed that, not only were there no Japanese on the island, but that Reg was its only human inhabitant. His recce had been brief because it was a very tiny island, no more than about half a mile square. It was little wonder he'd missed it on the way to Lembah. As he sat beneath one of the numerous palm trees, attempting to break open a coconut with the hilt of his clasp-knife, he finally realised what a hopeless position he was in. He was alone on an uninhabited island, his squadron could have no idea where he was, and would probably have drawn the conclusion that he'd been shot down. He would never see Eileen, his mother or Vera again. In his utter despair, he reflected that the Japanese must really have it in for the Underwood family.

24

Castaway

It wasn't long before Reg discovered that the butt of his service revolver was more effective than his service clasp-knife in breaking a coconut shell, although it was advisable that he gained access first to the milk inside it. This he did with the aid of the corkscrew device on his knife, having first penetrated the outer, hard layer with the point of the blade. The milk tasted sweet and not entirely pleasant, but it seemed a reasonable assumption that it contained water, of which there seemed no alternative source, at least until that evening.

At a time when Invincible might have mounted a search for him and, for all he knew, other missing aircrew, it was particularly cruel that the wind and rain that had delayed the strike on the oil refineries should make an unwelcome return, lashing the island and causing the palms to bend, their leaves flying like the hairs of a demented paintbrush.

For what seemed like most of the night, he crouched, wrapped in his parachute, against a palm tree, neither of which afforded any real shelter from the driving, tropical rain. There was a cruel irony in the fact that the parachute was one of the old, silk ones, the kind Eileen had mentioned in one of her letters. That, and the knowledge that the storm must surely have led *Invincible* to give him up as lost, made it the most miserable night of his life. As the rain hammered down with unremitting, tropical violence, he thought of his family and fiancée on the other side of the world, now lost to him.

The rain eased a few hours before dawn, and exhaustion led

mercifully to sleep, so that when he eventually emerged, his first sensation was the warmth of the sun, and then the blue sky between the shifting palm leaves. He stretched his aching limbs before finding his way out of the folded parachute. His watch, which had survived its brief immersion in the ocean, told him it was almost half-past nine, although that knowledge was of no use to him. Checking the time was no more than a habit. Something that was useful, however, was the rainwater that had accumulated in his dinghy, and he lost no time in dipping the empty coconut in it from the previous evening, and drinking fresh water. It was a blessing in itself.

The storm had brought down countless palm leaves, and he wondered for a while if he might be able to use them to rig some kind of shelter, possibly including the parachute, although he had no idea how to begin, so he looked further afield, and was surprised to find the beach littered with debris. There were the inevitable branches and foliage, and even some timbers, presumably from an unfortunate native craft that had foundered. He pitied anyone who was at sea when the storm came, although death must have come with merciful swiftness. For want of anything more pressing to do, he set about carrying the detritus up the beach, where it could continue to dry in the sun without being washed away at high tide. The previous night had been very cold, and a fire would be useful, albeit in the short term.

The mood had been bleak among the fighter group when it assembled aboard *HMS Invincible*. Reg was a popular squadron commander and colleague, and Guy Davidson was naturally affected by his loss.

'I saw him fall back,' he told Lionel Sanderson, 'and I called him on the intercom, but I couldn't raise a reply.'

'I know, Guy. You told me that when we returned.'

'I went back to look for him, but I found nothing, and then I had to return because my fuel was low.'

'You did all you could,' said Lionel, 'but if he baled out over the sea, he wouldn't stand a chance in that storm, and if he was over enemy territory….' He left the rest unspoken. Naval aviators were particularly unpopular with the Japanese, and reports had been received of summary executions, although most aircrew avoided the subject.

Eileen and Vera had both enjoyed *A Canterbury Tale* and, with a free day ahead, Vera suggested meeting at her home the next day. So it was that Eileen rang the front doorbell, expecting a warm welcome. Instead, when Elsie opened the door, it was immediately apparent from the redness around her eyes that all was not well.

'Elsie, what's the matter?'

'I'll take your coat, Miss Dewhirst. Mrs Underwood will want to see you.'

Eileen handed her gloves and hat to Elsie and let her take her coat. Not surprisingly, as a servant, Elsie was disinclined to comment. Instead, she said, 'I'll tell Mrs Underwood and Miss Vera you're here, Miss.' She went to the morning room and made the announcement, only to make way for Vera, who came into the hallway looking equally distraught.

'It's too awful for words, Eileen,' she said. 'The telegram came this morning. Reg has been posted "Missing in Action".'

25

A Precious Virtue

The three women sat together, too shocked and dismayed to eat very much, but each feeling that she should introduce a note of optimism, if only to bolster one another's hopes.

'Surely,' said Vera, 'they'll mount a search of the area. It seems obvious, doesn't it?'

'Reg can't be the only one who was shot down,' said Mrs Underwood. 'They're bound to go out and look for them. I mean to say, "missing" is only the first level of casualty.'

'I suppose he could have been taken prisoner,' suggested Eileen.

'Don't,' said Vera. 'That would be too awful.'

'Why?'

'I'll tell you later.'

Mrs Underwood was oblivious to her daughter's cautionary words, insistent as she was that a search must be under way.

In truth, all three knew they were trying to fool no one but themselves.

***

The fleet had been attacked by Japanese dive bombers, happily, with no success. The Seafires defending the fleet had shot down all but one of them, that one falling to the warships' anti-aircraft guns.

'A bloody good thing, too,' said Guy, still understandably vengeful on Reg's behalf. 'Let's get after the bastards.'

'There's going to be another strike tomorrow, and you'll get your turn soon enough,' Lionel promised him. 'You're Acting Squadron Commander in Reg's place, now.'

'Am I?'

'You're the most senior, Guy, and you're the only remaining RN officer in the squadron, so you can stop looking round the room.'

'Okay, sir, but I'd be happier if we could find Reg.'

'Wouldn't we all?' Lionel spoke with obvious sincerity, 'But we have to be realistic, Guy, and the likeliest of possibilities is that Reg was drowned in the storm.

———

As the sun began its descent, Reg gathered a pile of wood from the beach and took out the magnifying glass that Eileen had given him with the pencil at Christmas, never suspecting how useful it was to become.

A blue wisp of smoke curled lazily upward from the kindling at the base of the pile, the centre glowed red and then gave way to a flicker of flame. As it grew stronger, Reg lay down and blew, so that the flames burned brighter, and before long, the pile of wood was ablaze. He sat back to eat the last coconut of the day. In less tragic circumstances, he would have expressed his boredom with coconut as his staple diet, that and the inconvenient way in which it was already affecting his digestive system. He'd gone to the trouble of weaving an elaborate lavatory seat, using palm leaves, to make his frequent visits less uncomfortable. Palm leaves being as sharp as they were, he nevertheless found it safe as long as he remained perfectly still whilst *in situ*. Otherwise, boredom and irritation were meaningless. He could only feel cheated and desolate.

———

Eileen made her way home, offering only a bald and factual explanation for her obvious distress, before going to bed, where she buried her face in her pillow so that Ted and Lorna wouldn't hear her desperate sobbing.

After some time, there was a tap on the door and Lorna came in with a cup of tea, which she placed on the bedside table. Sitting on the edge of the bed, she put her arms around Eileen and held her while she wept.

'Don't write him off,' she said gently. 'He's only "missing". When Reg – I mean my late husband Reg – was killed, the telegram said, "killed in action". The next one below that is "missing, believed killed", and there's a lot of difference between that and just "missing in action".'

For a while, Eileen was unable to speak; her breath was coming with a series of shudders, but eventually, she said, 'He told... me a story... about Ancient Greece.' She went on to tell the story of the complete people Zeus had separated and banished to distant lands, and how mankind still searched for the ideal love-match. 'We used to... drink a toast. "Confusion to... Zeus!" If he exists, the... old tyrant must be... laughing up his... sleeve by now.'

'He never existed,' Lorna told her, holding her tightly, 'and you mustn't assume that you've lost your one and only. Keep an open mind.'

'I'll... try.'

'I've brought you a cup of tea. Drink it while it's hot.' She took the cup and saucer from the bedside table and waited for Eileen to raise herself into an upright position. 'There. You've probably dehydrated yourself, anyway.'

Reg thought he must be dehydrating himself with his repeated diversions to the palm-leaf throne, and he was glad of the rainwater in the dinghy, because coconut milk was likely to intensify the effect of solid coconut on his internal goings-on. Having established that, it just might possibly keep him alive until some passing ship or aircraft witnessed his plight, because that was all he could hope for. With that thought, he built a beacon in readiness for such an event, starting with dried grass and shavings, and progressing to kindling, branches and palm leaves. The latter were poor fuel, being slow to dry, but they were likely to smoke well, and that was what he wanted.

Guy was frustrated. He wanted desperately to fly over the route where Reg had been lost, but *Invincible*'s Corsairs were required to neutralise the airfield at Talangbetoetoe before a second strike could be made on the refinery at Pladjoe. Still, orders were orders, and he still hoped someone might find Reg floating in his dinghy. He was a man of great spirit but little imagination. Carefully and methodically, he prepared to lead the squadron for the first time.

With the Seafires circling overhead, ready to repel enemy aircraft, the Corsair pilots waited on the flight deck. Guy taxied on to the steam catapult, where the handlers attached the sling to his aircraft. With the engine running, he waited, and was rewarded when the Corsair was hurled into the air. It flew over the bows and dipped slightly before climbing again. He spiralled up to 10,000 feet and waited for the rest of the squadron to join him.

With the squadron intact, he led them towards the coast of Sumatra, but to the west of their previous route, as they were to attack Talangbetoetoe. It was too frustrating for words.

This time, they took Talang by surprise and destroyed what aircraft they could see, as well as setting fire to the petrol and bomb dumps.

'Able Squadron, this is Able Acting Leader,' he called. 'Form Victor formation on Able Two, fly on 284 magnetic and return to Mother. I have a little matter to attend to, but I'll see you all soon. Over.'

Each pilot receipted, and Guy altered course.

The sky was perfectly clear, a deep, tropical blue, and it seemed to Reg, as it increasingly did, that the ocean belonged to him. The only sounds were the lapping of the waves on the beach and the call of the seabirds. In different circumstances, it would have been an idyllic setting. Unfortunately, the waves on the beach and the seabirds' cry were of no use to him. He decided to ignore them.

He was busily ignoring them when another sound came to his notice, one that led him to fear, at first, that he was suffering some kind of coconut-induced delirium, because the sound was unmistakably that of the Pratt and Whitney Double Wasp aero engine.

Frantically, he took out the gold magnifying glass and focused the sun's rays on the dried grass and shavings at the foot of his beacon. In an agony of agitation, he watched the smoke curl upward and give way to a tongue of fire. The aircraft was now clearly visible. He lay down, as before, and blew encouragement into the fire, exulting as it blazed ever higher. The aircraft seemed to be approaching. It was time to attract their attention in any way he could, so he seized the parachute and wrapped it round the two palm trees closest to him.

Guy swept the horizon anxiously. Fuel consumption dictated that he had no more than half-an-hour before returning to *Invincible*. The coast seemed featureless at first, but then he sighted what could only be an island and, as he approached it, he was rewarded with a column of smoke. Such a thing seldom happened without human agency, so he had cause to be excited. He lost height quickly and investigated. As he drew level, he saw a figure beside the fire. He was waving frantically, and something that looked like a parachute was draped across the trees behind him. Flying as low as he dared, he opened his canopy and waved back. It was as much as he could do before re-joining the squadron and leading it back to *Invincible*.

Happier than he could remember, he made his way to the Observation Tower, where he found Commander (F).

'I've located Lieutenant Commander Underwood, sir,' he reported. 'At least, I found a pilot with a British parachute. He's on a very small island about thirty miles south-west of Lembah.'

Commander (F) eyed him coldly. 'And just how,' he asked, 'did you happen to see that on your way back from Talangbetoetoe?'

'I made a small detour, sir.'

'You defied orders and deliberately jeopardised your life and a valuable aircraft. You also abdicated responsibility for your squadron.'

Guy was determined to defend his position. 'I calculated that I had sufficient fuel for the dogleg, sir.'

'And how could you be sure of that, Davidson?'

'Experience, sir.'

'Nonsense. You could easily have come a cropper this afternoon by acting on a schoolboy whim.'

'I'm sorry I put up a black, sir, but if you have me court-martialled for it, it will still have been worth it for the sake of locating my squadron commander and closest friend.'

The commander suddenly abated. 'You're a bloody fool, Davidson, and I'll have to report your behaviour to the Captain. Before I do that, though, I'm going to report the location of the flier you saw, because, whoever he is, he's bound to be more sensible and reliable than you are. Carry on, Davidson.'

'Aye, aye, sir.'

Reg could scarcely have believed his eyes when he recognised Guy's Corsair, and now, a little less than two hours later, he was heading back to *Invincible* in the good old Walrus amphibian, escorted by three Corsairs. It was like that special moment after waking from a nightmare, when everything falls into place and the horror has drained away. He accepted a mug of tea from the telegraphist air-gunner and sighed deeply.

'Are you feeling all right, sir?'

'More than all right, thank you. I'm just pinching myself to make sure I'm not dreaming.' He sat in the after part of the fuselage, nursing his precious parachute.

'Right enough, sir. You weren't easy to find on that island.'

'No, I don't suppose I was. All I know is how Robinson Crusoe must have felt when he woke up that morning, the poor bugger.'

The TAG peered through the canopy and said, 'It looks as if they're going to let us land first, sir.' He strapped himself into his seat. 'Brace yourself, sir.'

Reg wriggled into position with his back to the TAG's seat and waited for the hook to catch the wire. When it happened, it felt tame after landing a high-powered fighter, but he kept that to himself.

Guy was waiting for him in the hangar. 'Are you all right, Reg?'

'Thanks to you, Guy, I'm fine. I've never been so pleased to see you as I was when you flew over the island.' He shook his hand vigorously. 'Thanks, old man.'

'Think nothing of it, Reg. Any bloody fool would have done the same.'

'Is that what you've been called?'

Guy nodded. 'I sent the squadron home and made a diversion to find you. I'm waiting to be sent for, so if you've ever fancied the role of Prisoner's Friend, you may soon get the opportunity.'

'With any luck, it may not come to that. I'll speak to Commander (F), but first of all...'

'You need to let the doctor examine you.'

Reg winced. 'Before that, I need to visit the heads. Believe me, I'll be happy if I never see another coconut.'

When Reg spoke to Commander (F), he learned that the matter was now out of his hands, which made an appointment with the Captain both necessary and urgent. Fortunately, the Captain was generous enough to agree to see him the next day, and Reg presented himself at the cabin at the agreed time.

'Ah, Lieutenant Commander Underwood. Welcome back. I trust you're not experiencing any lasting ill-effects?'

'Not now, thank you, sir.' A couple of doses of kaolin and morphine had finally laid the demon to rest.

'Unfortunately, Casualty Section would receive a signal on the second day after your ditching, posting you as "Missing in Action", but I do know that a signal was released today, rectifying that state of affairs.'

'Thank you, sir. My family and fiancée will be very relieved.'

'Of course.' Coming to the immediate point, he said, 'I imagine you're here to plead Lieutenant Davidson's case.' He shook his head sorrowfully. 'He behaved like a midshipman, and a particularly stupid one at that.'

'Speaking as an operational pilot, sir, I can't disagree with that, but I've known Lieutenant Davidson for almost four years, now. He's my wingman, and I've depended on him more times than I care to recall, always in the knowledge that I was in safe hands. He's become my closest friend, as well, sir.'

'I know, but you come from an old naval family, don't you, Underwood? I knew your father, and I'm sure he would have had plenty to say about Davidson's cavalier behaviour.'

'I've no doubt he would, sir, but there's something else he told me a long time ago, that I've never forgotten, and that is that one of the most precious virtues known to man is loyalty. In acting as he did, Lieutenant Davidson displayed that virtue in abundance, sir. He also enabled the rescue of an experienced pilot and squadron commander.' For a moment, he wondered if he might have gone too far, but then the Captain smiled.

'You're no stranger to loyalty, yourself, Underwood. You've no doubt been told at some time that the apple hasn't fallen far from the tree.'

'Once or twice, sir.' For the first time, he felt he was making progress.

'I'm glad you came to see me. You've given me something to think about.' He stood up, signalling that the interview was about to end. 'I shall see Lieutenant Davidson shortly. I'm not going to tell you what my decision will be, because that would be wrong of me, but I can tell you to stop worrying on his behalf.' He extended his hand to Reg and said, 'Welcome back, Underwood.'

Looking remarkably cheerful, Guy duly reported back. 'Reprimanded and logged,' he said.

Reg was also relieved. Logging wasn't a punishment, but simply the recording of the incident in the Captain's Log. It was unlikely to harm his career. 'Let me get you a drink. I owe you that at least.'

'I shan't argue with that, Reg. Then I'll buy you one for saving my career.'

26

Fresh Orders and Good News

That afternoon, Reg was digesting lunch and enjoying his deliverance from the wilderness and return to civilisation, when the Tannoy crackled.

'D' you hear there, d' you hear there? Action stations, action stations! Enemy aircraft approaching!'

Amid the shouts and running footsteps, there was nothing he could do. The Corsairs were all in the hangar with their wings folded. Air defence was the task of the Seafire squadrons, which were already airborne. When the rushing and shouting had died down, he made his way to the Observation Platform and joined Commander (F), who greeted him with a smile.

'The "Owner" says you should leave the service and take up the law,' he said.

'I was only doing what I could for an old friend, sir.'

'Well, it did the trick.' Peering through night glasses, he said, 'Here the bastards come. "Kates", by the look of them.' He handed his night glasses to Reg, who identified them, also, as Nakajima dive bombers. 'They're Kates, all right, sir.'

One of the enemy bombers dived into the sea, prompting the Commander to say, 'Just watch those Seafires, Underwood. Once they're airborne, they're a match for anything the Japs can send us. They're only a problem when they come in to land, with that spindly undercarriage of theirs. The RAF make a big joke of it, but they've pranged plenty Spitfires on their grass runways.' Seemingly dispassionate about the drama being enacted above him, he asked, 'Are you okay after your experience?'

'Fine, thank you, sir. I'm just grateful to be back.'

'I'm glad to hear— Oh, splendid!' Another Kate plummeted into the ocean. 'They're knocking them down like ninepins.' He handed the glasses again to Reg, who took them readily.

'The Seafires are breaking off now, sir,' he reported.

'Yes, they have orders to do that as soon as the enemy come within range of our close-range guns.'

As he spoke, the fleet's Bofors and Pom-Poms opened up, creating what looked like an impenetrable wall of fire, and two more bombers were hit, one of them hopelessly out of control and, it seemed, heading for *Invincible*. As it plunged ever nearer, Reg lowered the night glasses and instinctively raised his arm to cover his eyes. Next, there was a huge explosion as the aircraft struck the ship somewhere below the platform where Reg and the Commander were standing. Reg was about to leave the compartment, but the Commander stopped him.

'No, Underwood,' he said. 'Leave it to Damage Control. You'll only get in their way.' A pipe sounded, calling fire and first aid parties to the base of the island superstructure and the WT Office. It seemed to bear out Commander (F)'s advice, but Reg felt helpless and useless at the same time.

Meanwhile, the last of the enemy attackers was shot down. That, at least, was no longer a problem, but the piped orders from the bridge confirmed, as if confirmation were needed, that a major on-going incident was still taking place below. As far as Reg could ascertain, the fire party had smothered everything in foam, and Damage Control were struggling to clear the wreckage.

Much later, Reg heard the full story. The dive bomber had struck the superstructure with its bomb intact, and the resulting explosion had destroyed part of the WT Office, killing five ratings and injuring three more, two with horrendous burns.

The next day saw the fatalities buried at sea. Nothing remained of the two Japanese crew members. Otherwise, the burned-out section of the WT Office was temporarily sealed off to relieve the remaining telegraphists of the lingering stench of burned flesh. The lost equipment would be replaced at some time, victims of the intense fire, as were the decoded signals waiting to be distributed, and those awaiting transmission.

Salt was rubbed into an already agonising wound when mail from Reg, written at least a month earlier, arrived at the flat.

'I left it in your room,' said Ted, 'for you to decide what to do with it.'

'Thanks. I shan't look at it yet, if I ever do, but thanks for doing that.'

Later, Lorna said, 'They're showing *Arsenic and Old Lace* at the Empire. It's Cary Grant, and he's usually good for a laugh. We're going. Would you like to come with us?'

'No, thanks. I wouldn't be very good company for you.'

'Okay, I understand.'

Eileen knew she understood. She'd been through the same agony, herself, but going to the pictures was out of the question. Oddly, the only emollient she knew was Vera's company, because they were both suffering the same loss simultaneously. Neither had any need to wonder what the other was feeling, or to explain anything at all. They were like twin sisters, sharing their sensations almost by telepathy, and they shared the same counter-irritant: namely, work. It was there to be done because duty demanded it, and there was never any shortage of it at Whitehall. Also, they were spared interaction with other officers, having the excuse that they were simply busy. Then, at the end of each watch, they could go home and steel themselves until their next watch.

Following its successful assault on the Sumatran oil refineries, the fleet did not return to Ceylon, but sailed almost 1900 miles to Fremantle in Western Australia, to take on stores and oil before preparing for further operations in the Pacific. The journey took rather more than a week, but for the crews, who had been operating under pressure for some time, it came as a period of relief, and it helped everyone to recover, as far as possible, from the shock of the bomber incident.

Fremantle was like the Promised Land. After months of powdered milk and canned vegetables, the ship took on fresh milk, eggs, vegetables, fruit and meat, all of which resulted in a massive surge in morale.

After all that, the journey round the coast to Sydney was sheer pleasure.

One day, Guy remarked, 'This is why I joined the Navy.'

'To sail round the south coast of Australia?' Not for the first time, Reg struggled to follow Guy's logic.

'No, to see foreign parts, exotic creatures and compelling sights.'

'You could have done that in the Merchant Navy.'

'I know, but they go in for hard work, and there are never enough hands on board.'

'What made you decide to join the Fleet Air Arm?' It was always interesting to hear the stories the others told.

'Alan Cobham's Flying Circus. It was my first taste of flying, and I was hungry for more.'

'Me, too.'

Guy looked at him in surprise. 'Really?'

'Yes, and as soon as the Branch was restored to its rightful owners, I volunteered for it.'

Guy was impressed. 'You're a pioneer, Reg, a trailblazer in a blue suit.' One thought evidently led to another, and he asked, 'Have you ever wondered what it must have been like for the pioneers of the old west?'

'No, but I'll bet a pound to a pinch of you-know-what that you have.'

'What days they must have been, Reg, and for these chaps, too.' He waved a hand airily in the direction of the Australian coast, which was currently out of sight.

Such were the easy conversations that took place between Fremantle and Sydney that spring, when the war seemed temporarily far away.

As the ship approached Sydney harbour, the air group flew off, its destination being Nowra in New South Wales. Here they found a Mobile Naval Air Base, short title: MONAB, actually the first of its kind, designed to be packed up and transported to wherever it was required. There seemed to be no limit to man's ingenuity. All it took to fuel the mind and put it in top gear was a world war. It was a terrifying thought.

After a few weeks' flying, they could resist the fleshpots of Sydney no longer, and they yielded unto temptation and had a truly memorable time, in spite of their total confusion regarding Australian licensing laws. Then, it was back to Nowra, which was the perfect place for Guy, resembling as it did a street in the old wild west, complete with wooden shacks, shops and pubs, each with a wooden rail for tethering horses.

'Leave me here,' pleaded Guy, knowing that what he asked was impossible.

'Places like this have to grow up, eventually, into modern towns,' Reg told him. 'It happened in America, and it will happen here. Come back in twenty years' time and then tell me I was right. Meanwhile, let's get on with the war.' Someone had to be grown up.

After a spell of drinking, merrymaking, swimming and generally taking advantage of Sydney and all it had to offer, the fleet sailed under the immediate command of Admiral Sir Bruce Fraser, but under the operational command of Admiral Nimitz, Commander-in-Chief of the US Pacific Fleet.

Eileen had a sheaf of unopened letters from Reg. She simply hadn't the heart to look at them or even to discard them, so when a fresh packet arrived from the Postal Service, she put it in her bedside drawer, wishing the stream of correspondence would come to an end and stop tormenting her.

'I can't believe,' said Ted, standing in her bedroom doorway, 'that mail can take more than a month to arrive.'

Eileen shrugged dismissively. 'As far as I'm concerned, it can take as long as it likes,' she said. There was clearly something on his mind. So much was obvious to her, even in her preoccupied state,

'I wouldn't normally ask this, Eileen,' he said, 'but do you mind if I open one, just to check the date? I shan't read it.'

'Please yourself.' She really hated herself when she was horrible to the people who meant most to her, but it had become almost a reflex action.

Ted took the packet from the drawer, slit it open and inspected its contents. Something, probably the dates stamped on the envelopes, prompted him to take the nearest and open it. When he saw the handwritten date, he gave a start.

'What is it, Ted?'

'Reg was posted "Missing in Action" on the twenty-fifth of January, wasn't he?'

'Yes.' She had no need to be reminded of it.

'But he wrote this letter on the twenty-eighth.' He looked at it again and handed the single sheet to her. 'I think you should read it,' he said. Then, seeing that she was reluctant, he said, 'Honestly, you should.'

Puzzled, she took it and began to read.

Dearest Eileen,

You must have had a hell of a shock when you heard I was posted 'Missing' – I imagine my mother would tell you – and I'm sorry you were troubled. By now, you must have been told I'd been picked up. Obviously, I can't go into details, but

She stopped reading when tears clouded her eyes, making it impossible to continue. 'I can't believe it,' she sobbed. 'He's alive.' She heard footsteps and then Lorna's voice.

'What is it?'

'Reg is alive, after all,' Ted told her.

'There, I knew it. Hutch up, Eileen.'

They sat on the bed, one on each side of her as she continued to sob with relief and joy.

'What I don't understand,' said Ted, 'is why there was no notification that he'd been found, or whatever the circumstances were. The mail can go astray in wartime – we expect that – but his ship must have signalled the Admiralty.'

'I don't... care,' said Eileen, still sobbing. 'All I care... about is that he's... safe.'

'Well,' said Lorna, ever the fount of common sense, 'read the rest of the letter, and then you can tidy yourself up and speak to Vera on the telephone.' They left her to read the letter.

Obviously, I can't go into details, but my old chum Guy came looking for me, and everything was right again. Let me know if you're all right. This has to be a quick one, because there's so much going on, but I'll write again soon.

Confusion to Zeus, and oceans of love, as ever,

Reg XXX

She washed her tear-stained face and did what she could with the make-up that Reg had brought her from New York, and then went to the telephone kiosk at the end of the road.

Her hand trembled with excitement as she put two pennies in the slot and dialled Vera's number, and her finger even slipped off button 'A' when Vera answered.

'Vera, it's Eileen. You'll never guess. Reg is alive and back on board ship.'

'What?'

'I got a letter from him today, about how his friend Guy went back to look for him, and he was rescued.'

Vera's response was unintelligible as she, too, sobbed for joy and relief.

It was a house of happy women, that afternoon and evening. Mrs Underwood even invited Elsie, the maid, who was as overjoyed as anyone, to join with them in drinking to Reg's rescuer, and then to Reg himself.

'I met Guy once,' said Vera. 'Reg's leave and mine coincided for once, and all three of us ate at a restaurant in Portsmouth. He's an unusual chap, but very nice, and he wins my vote for rescuing Reg.' After a moment's thought, she said, 'I wonder what they're doing now.'

27

The Final Assault

US forces were all set to invade Okinawa, the most southerly of the main Japanese islands. The operation was given the name *Iceberg*, and the task given to the British fleet was to neutralise, as far as possible, the airfields in the Sakishima islands and to prevent enemy aircraft reaching the US invasion fleet. To do any lasting good, it was necessary to attack the airfields continuously over a period of time, and to make that possible, a fleet 'train' of supply vessels had been set up to provide the fleet with whatever it needed.

1846 Squadron was involved from the beginning, on the 26th March, flying patrols over the airfields to prevent any enemy fighters from taking off, while others attacked the aircraft on the ground, leaving the bombers and rocket-carrying aircraft to attack the various installations and crater the runways with high explosive bombs. The islands were heavily defended with anti-aircraft fire, and losses were inevitable. Reg's squadron lost two Corsairs and their pilots in the first week.

Before long, aircrew were weary and in need of being rested. Unfortunately, however, there was no rest to be had, except for a few hours each night, before they were shaken, shortly before dawn, in readiness for the first morning strike, and then the next, and so on.

With so little sleep, some pilots in other squadrons skipped breakfast and even neglected to wash, shave and dress, flying only in their pyjamas. On the other hand, Reg made it a necessity to maintain standards, insisting that his squadron arrived at breakfast by 0330, washed, shaved and dressed. Any slackening in personal standards, he maintained, would be reflected in their work, and there was no room for carelessness. Also, whenever he could, he called on the fitters and riggers in the hangar to remind them that they weren't forgotten in their toil and their oven-like enclosure. He knew his gesture was appreciated, because they told him so.

Because of the threat of Kamikaze suicide attacks, from dawn until nightfall, all watertight doors were kept closed and ventilation was shut down, making life on board ship scarcely bearable. Then, after dusk, precautions were relaxed, and it was possible to have a shower and a bottle of beer before turning in.

The strikes went on for a month, after which *HMS Illustrious* was sent back to Sydney to be refitted. In her place came *HMS Formidable*, another of the *Illustrious* class, after which strikes were resumed.

It was during this second month that Kamikaze attacks began in earnest on the British fleet, and Reg, who remembered the incident off Sumatra vividly, was relieved to find that the attacks were largely unsuccessful. One reason for this was that the British carriers, unlike those of the US, had armoured flight decks that were able to withstand such assaults.

Eventually, *Invincible* was detached to steam south to the supply train for replenishment. For almost forty hours, her ship's company enjoyed the respite from operations, and the stores that awaited them were an added pleasure. Mail was waiting for them, too, but not, unfortunately, for Reg. Eileen's last letter was dated in late January, shortly before his Robinson Crusoe episode, as were his mother's and Vera's. He couldn't understand why they'd suddenly dried up, although accounts of the V1 and V2 rocket attacks on London came to mind until he forced himself to dismiss them.

All too soon, it was time to return to *Operation Iceberg*, and the assault on the islands of Ishigaki, Iriomote and Miyako continued, sadly, with the loss of a number of aircraft.

Kamikaze attacks intensified, as well, and some damage was done to the British fleet, although it was quickly, if temporarily, repaired.

The greatest sadness for Reg was the loss of several friends, some of longstanding. It was inevitable in an operation such as *Iceberg*, but it was no less painful for that.

Soon, it was time to return to Sydney, this time for permanent repairs and a much-needed rest. In the relentless pressure to keep the enemy air force from reaching the US fleet, Victory in Europe had passed almost without notice, and by the time they reached Sydney, celebrations would probably have ended. Some wondered if there would be any beer left in the city, but Reg could only hope there would be mail waiting for him.

At home, VE Day celebrations gave way, for some, to plans for the future, and Ted and Lorna were already discussing the next stage in their lives. For Eileen, however, the war was far from over. No one could say when the Japanese were likely to surrender, although the news, such as it was, from the Far East was encouraging. The Americans had taken Okinawa and were now using it as a base to bomb the Japanese homeland. The trouble at home was that any news about the war in the Far East formed a tiny part of the general bulletin. It really was the 'Forgotten War'.

Vera had taken up with a captain in the Royal Marines she'd met quite by accident in Trafalgar Square and, although she was careful not to cut Eileen entirely out of her life, he was nevertheless a new and exciting distraction for her.

On one occasion, Eileen went with Ted and Lorna to see *The Halfway House*, starring Mervyn and Glynis Johns. It was an enchanting ghost story of the best kind and, surprisingly for a ghost story, it made a great deal of sense.

Eileen was conspicuously quiet on the way home, to the extent that Lorna remarked on it, saying, 'You seem subdued, Eileen.'

'Not subdued, Lorna, just thoughtful.'

Sensitive as ever to his sister's moods, Ted said nothing, but waited until Lorna had brewed tea and brought it into the sitting room.

'Now,' said Lorna, 'a penny for them, unless, of course, your thoughts are too private to be aired, in which case, forget I asked.'

'They're not terribly private. It was the film that set me thinking.'

'It was a good film,' said Ted, who'd been rather taken with certain female members of the cast.

Keen to keep the conversation from straying, Lorna asked, 'What did it make you think about, Eileen?'

'Only that all those people were drawn to the inn so that they could reflect on how they were dealing with their problems and how they saw their lives. As the landlord said, they'd each been given a pause in which to examine their situation. I think there must be an awful lot of people in that position, but they have no ghostly landlord and daughter to set them right.'

Lorna handed her a cup of tea. 'It obviously rang a bell with you,' she said.

'Yes, it did. At twenty-two, I'd been thinking about all the things I wanted to do with my life once the war was over – I mean apart from marrying Reg – and suddenly, my world was torn apart. Instead of being drawn to a ghostly inn that only exists when it's needed, I thought I'd lost the man I loved.' She closed her eyes, remembering the shock. 'But it was really the news that Reg was safe that concentrated my mind, and I realised what was important, what was *most* important to me. It was my future life with him. No matter what happens during that time, that is what matters.'

'It seems to me,' said Ted, in an effort to lighten the conversation, 'that when Eileen takes a seat in the one-and-threepennies, she gets a lot more than her money's worth. It was the same when we were children. Felix the Cat always had a hidden agenda, and Tom Mix, the cowboy, was usually making a statement about the meaning of life.'

'Beast.' Eileen took the cushion from behind her to throw it at him, but thought again, as he was holding a cup and saucer. 'Anyway, you two know what you're going to do, now the war's over, don't you?'

'It's always been there, in the background,' said Ted. 'The City Council have been obliged to hold my job for me and, apart from putting out fires and rescuing damsels in distress, that's the only job I know. Lorna wants to study, and Leeds University will be only a short train journey away. It all seems very straightforward, really.'

'It won't be long, now,' said Lorna. 'The children who were evacuated will be coming home, and the fire station will assume its original role as a council school.'

'The lucky little blighters,' said Ted. 'They'll be able to use the showers I installed in nineteen-forty.' He reflected briefly and said, 'On second thoughts, knowing how young lads usually feel about soap and water, they're not likely to feel all that lucky.'

'That shower room's paid its way over the years,' observed Lorna. 'All those exhausted firemen coming off-watch must have appreciated it. I know I did when the water here was cut off, and the Sub-Officer let me use it.'

'You and all those firemen, Lorna?'

'No, Eileen, it was all done very decently. The Sub-Officer left Ted to stand guard over the door, so that no one came near, and to turn off the water when I'd finished. I was in doolally-land at the time – I'd just received the telegram – and I was hardly aware of what was going on. Ted came back when I was dressed, to make sure I was all right, and he found me in a daze, so he dried my hair for me.' Her eyes became wet at the memory.

'It was my *forte*, wasn't it, Eileen?' He reached for Lorna's hand and held it.

'I've always maintained,' said Eileen, 'that no one could dry hair quite the way you do it.' Turning to Lorna, she said, 'Just be careful he doesn't spoil you, Lorna. He was always accused of spoiling me when he dried mine.'

'Well,' said Ted, 'we all know the truth about that, don't we?'

Lorna asked, 'Will you invite your parents to your wedding?'

'We'll invite them,' said Eileen, 'on the basis that we went to see them after we got engaged. If they don't want to come, it's their affair, but if we didn't invite them, it would be on our consciences. I think they'll come, because our mother's an awful snob, and she'll want to see her daughter married to a man whose family keep servants.'

'She's probably practising her curtsey in readiness,' said Ted.

It was a light-hearted note, and a suitable one for bedtime, now that serious matters were dealt with.

28

Home Again

It was towards the end of the fleet's stay in Sydney that Reg received three welcome surprises. The first was that he had been awarded the Distinguished Service Order for his part in the Sakishima raids, and he knew, as a professional officer, that a healthy war record could only be beneficial to his career. The second was that Guy had been awarded the DSC, and the final surprise was a sheaf of letters from Eileen, the first of which explained the hiatus since he was shot down.

Dearest Reg,

I've just received your 28th Jan, and I'm still walking on air. Why, oh why didn't the authorities tell your mother you'd been found? For more than a month, we'd no idea what had happened to you, but now you're safe!

'I thought a signal had gone to Casualties Section, telling them I'd been found,' he said.

Guy gave the anomaly some thought and said, 'It was about the time I was in the hot seat, waiting to hear my fate. Could that signal have been in the WT Office the day the Kate paid us a visit?'

Reg thought hard. 'You know,' he said, 'it might have been. "Routines" have until the next day to be dealt with, so it's more than likely.'

'And all that time, your family and Eileen were in limbo, wondering what had happened to you. That's too cruel for words, Reg.'

Reg looked at the envelopes Guy had picked up, which were mainly of the business kind, and said, 'You don't get a lot of mail, do you?'

'Don't rub it in, old man. There was only my mother until she did a bunk.'

'No girl?' He stopped himself guiltily. 'Of course not. I remember now.'

'No such luck. Cupid has passed me by.'

It was too bad. 'If we're ever allowed to go home, I could always introduce you to my sister. That's if she's still the three Fs.'

Guy asked warily, 'What are the three Fs, old man?'

'I'm sorry. That must have sounded outrageously coarse. I meant footloose and fancy-free.'

'I should have realised. If you remember, I met your sister one leave. It was in Portsmouth.'

'Of course.'

'A very charming girl, if I may say so.'

'You may, and yes, she has certain qualities. Just don't let her near the family porcelain and glassware.'

'Mm. Let's have a drink, shall we?'

Within days, the fleet left Sydney, once again to take up station in Japanese waters. On this occasion, they were to join US forces in bombing and strafing coastal installations in an attempt to persuade the Japanese to surrender. They were hindered for some time by adverse weather, which included typhoons and, incredibly, in view of Japan's proximity to the equator, dense fog.

'This climate doesn't recommend itself to me,' remarked Guy one day. 'I'm inclined to look elsewhere for a place to come home to.'

'I'm just sick of the Far East,' said Reg. 'I wish the Japs would throw in the towel. They just don't know when they're beaten.'

Strikes went ahead when the weather allowed, with the advantage by that time that the enemy was devoid of aircraft and ships.

'Food can't be all that plentiful in Japan,' said Reg.

'Maybe the plan is that if we starve them long enough they'll eat each other and solve the problem that way. Having heard about the goings-on in their prison camps, I must say I've no sympathy for the bastards.'

Reg chuckled. 'Did you hear about the signal the skipper of *Formidable* sent to Admiral Vian after she was hit by a Kamikaze?'

'Go on, spill the beans.'

'He signalled the flagship, "Little yellow bastard", and the Admiral sent back, "Who, me?" '

Guy considered the story briefly and said, 'It's a sign you're growing older, when admirals begin to seem human.'

'No, I think you're confusing them with policemen looking younger.'

'Quite likely. I've seen more admirals than policemen during the past year.'

Early in August, all ships were ordered to leave Japanese waters, but no explanation was offered. Subsequently, it was announced that nuclear devices had been dropped on Hiroshima and Nagasaki, resulting in a request from the Emperor Hirohito, for peace.

Guy asked, 'What's a nuclear device, Reg?'

'Other than a means of getting the Japs to see sense, I've no idea. I imagine we'll find out at some stage. Meanwhile, we've run out of enemies. Surely, they'll send us home now.'

Recently demobbed, Ted and Lorna had moved to a house on the outskirts of Cullington, where he had resumed his duties as English Master at the Boys' Grammar School. Eileen had been obliged to move in with Vera and Mrs Underwood, which was a pleasant enough arrangement, although she waited anxiously to hear about Reg's return.

She'd noticed that Vera was around more than of late, so she waited until Mrs Underwood had gone to bed, before asking Vera, 'Is Victor no longer the man of the moment?' Victor was the Royal Marines officer Vera had met in Trafalgar Square.

'Certainly not. He's gone back to his wife.'

'Good grief. I didn't know he was married.'

'Neither did I until a few days ago. The bugger took me for quite a ride.'

'What a rotten trick.'

Vera toyed with her drink before draining her glass. 'I'm done with men,' she said. 'I've never had much luck with them, anyway.'

'I wonder why.' Vera was attractive, personable and good fun to be with. It seemed all wrong.

'Now that they've bombed the Japanese into submission,' said Vera, changing the subject for a pleasanter one, 'Reg must be home soon.'

'That's what I keep telling myself.'

Reg was also wondering when they would be allowed to return home. Orders had been received for *Invincible* to use her aircraft to patrol the Japanese coastline, looking for evidence of prison camps. Such camps as had been liberated had displayed evidence of horrific treatment of prisoners, and their rehabilitation was more than urgent.

Accordingly, Reg's squadron searched the area allotted to them, but without success, and finally, after weeks of waiting, *HMS Invincible* was ordered back to Sydney. The Captain ordered, 'Splice the mainbrace,' and Reg and Guy had their very first taste of rum. Everyone knew how popular it was with the lower deck, but it wasn't long before the two reverted to pink gin.

As they approached Sydney, the entire air group flew off to Bankstown, where they left their aircraft and returned to Sydney to join in the strangely muted celebrations. After all that had happened, the end of the war was an anti-climax.

Eileen spotted a signal to Invincible, ordering her to leave Sydney, and she lost no time in telling Vera. 'He's on his way home,' she said. 'They'll refuel at Aden, wherever that is, and continue to Port Said.'

'At last.' So that Eileen wouldn't remain in total ignorance, she explained, 'Aden is in the Persian Gulf, and Port Said is in Egypt. He really is on his way home.'

At the end of the watch, they relayed the news to Mrs Underwood, who was just as delighted. 'I've been giving some thought to a place for you and Reg to live,' she told Eileen. 'If you're going to be married soon, you'll need a place of your own.'

'It's very kind of you to take the trouble, Mrs Underwood.'

'Not at all. It was something to do while I was twiddling my thumbs and wondering when I would see my son again. I'll speak to you both about it when he arrives. That's only fair, isn't it?'

After refuelling at Aden, *Invincible* continued to the Suez Canal and, eventually, Port Said, where the local taxi-owners and boatmen demonstrated that they had lost none of their *penchant* for extortion. After a drink at the Officers' Club, Reg and Guy were being borne back to the ship, when the boatman stopped and said, 'More money to go to ship.'

'They never learn,' said Guy, taking out his revolver and pointing it at the offending boatman. 'Start rowing again, and make it *muy pronto, hombre. ¿Entiende?*'

'I don't think he speaks Mexican Spanish, Guy,' said Reg.

'He understood me well enough.'

As if to bear out Guy's assertion, the boatman pulled urgently towards the ship.

With stops for provisions at Malta and Gibraltar, *Invincible* turned for home, taking the Bay of Biscay in her stride, and by the time she reached the English Channel, September had dawned.

Guy surveyed the anchorage at Portsmouth dispassionately. 'It seems like another anti-climax,' he said, 'returning to an empty house.'

'Don't return to your empty house,' Reg urged him. 'Come to my not-so-empty house instead. There'll only be Vera, Eileen and my mother, so there's ample room.'

'Are you sure, old man? I mean, won't your mother mind?'

'No, she's a generous old stick, and the circumstances are rather special.'

After all the goodbyes and the leaving routine, they headed for the dockyard telephone, and Reg dialled his home number.

'Hello?' It was Vera's voice.

'Vera, it's Reg.'

'Reg! How wonderful! Where are you?'

'Pompey Dockyard, and I'm bringing Guy with me. Do you remember Guy?'

'The officer who saved your life? Of course I do. Yes, bring him.'

He wondered what Guy would make of his new reputation. 'We'll get the first train we can to Waterloo.'

'Wonderful. We'll see you soon. There go the pips. 'Bye'

''Bye.' As he replaced the receiver, he said, 'You're assured of a warm welcome, Guy. In fact, you'll probably get star billing.'

The train journey to Waterloo Station was remarkably quick and, in what seemed only a short time, the two men left the taxi and walked into the house to be greeted ecstatically by Vera and with a little more restraint by Mrs Underwood, although Reg was aware of her true feelings.

'Allow me to introduce Lieutenant Guy Davidson. You and he have already met, Vera.'

'I remember. Hello, Guy, the officer who saved my brother's life.'

'Hardly that. I found him,' he said, shaking hands with Mrs Underwood, 'but others carried out the rescue.'

'He broke the rules to find me,' Reg told them, 'and narrowly avoided a court-martial.'

'It was Reg's appeal to the Captain that earned me that reprieve,' insisted Guy.

'Anyway,' said Reg, 'where's Eileen?'

'She's in her room,' Vera told him, 'preparing herself for the grand reunion.'

'I'm here.' The voice from the staircase was Eileen's. Even after a year, Reg recognised it in an instant and, as he held out his arms to her, he heard Mrs Underwood say tactfully, 'Come into the morning room, Lieutenant Davidson, and we can have a chat.'

For what seemed a blessed age, Reg and Eileen clung to each other, treasuring the moment, each reluctant to break the spell. Eventually, they relaxed, and Reg saw that Eileen's face was wet with tears. 'Here,' he said, taking a handkerchief from his breast pocket and putting it in her hand.

'I'm just so relieved and happy and....'

'I know.'

'I spent ages doing my face....'

'And now you look like a panda, but a very fetching one.'

They kissed until she broke away and said, 'I must tidy myself up, and then we can join the others.'

'All right. I'll go in there and do the civilised thing, and you can make your grand entrance when you're ready.' He kissed her briefly before going into the morning room, where, in a rare show of exuberance, his mother hugged him again. He felt awkward, being the focus of attention, and he kept up polite conversation, relieved when Eileen came in with her make-up intact.

'I left a bottle of champagne to chill, last night,' said Mrs Underwood, ringing for Elsie. 'I think the time has come.'

'We haven't tasted champagne since war broke out, have we, Guy?'

'I certainly haven't. I didn't know you then, Reg.'

Elsie opened the door and gaped when she saw Reg. 'Mr Reg!'

'Well spotted, Elsie,' he said, drawing her into an illicit hug.

'Oh, sir, you'll get me the sack.'

'I'll let it go this time,' Mrs Underwood told her, 'as it was Mr Reg's fault, anyway, but now your feet are back on the floor, Elsie, will you bring the champagne that's on ice, and six glasses, please?'

'*Six* glasses, ma'am?'

'You're going to join us in celebrating Mr Reg's and Lieutenant Davidson's safe return, aren't you?'

'Of course, ma'am. Thank you, ma'am.' Still embarrassed, she left the room to carry out her mistress's instruction.

Smiling at a state of affairs that could never have taken place at one time, Mrs Underwood asked, 'How long have you two known each other?'

'It was *Operation Pedestal*, the Malta convoy in 'forty-two,' said Guy, 'so that makes it more than four years.'

'Four years,' echoed Reg. 'I think I can safely say that our flying days are over. It'll be general service for us, now that we've been allowed to "live this day and see old age".'

'You had me thinking you were a literary dud,' said Eileen.

'*Henry the Fifth* is the only one I know,' he told her modestly. 'There wasn't much time for literature at Dartmouth.'

The door opened, and Elsie came in carrying a tray. On it was a bottle of Veuve Clicquot surrounded by six glasses.

'Thank you, Elsie,' said Mrs Underwood. 'Reg, will you open the bottle?'

Reg peeled off the foil and loosened the cage. 'This is another job that used to be my father's,' he said.

'Get used to it, Reg.'

The cork came away with a discreet *phut*, and he poured the champagne carefully into each of the glasses, handing the first to his mother.

'Here's to the wanderers' return,' she said, 'and that's plural.'

'I should think so,' said Vera. 'If it hadn't been for Guy, Reg would never have returned.'

They all drank the toast, including Elsie, who then retreated self-consciously into the kitchen, and Guy was relieved when Mrs Underwood changed the subject, saying, 'Now, this evening, I thought we could all eat together. Then, tomorrow, you can all go off and do the things you youngsters like to do.' With that dealt with, she said, 'Now, Lieutenant Davidson, come and tell me about yourself.'

Eileen took Reg over to the bay window and said quietly, 'Vera's chap gave her the heave-ho last week, and she's currently without.'

'Poor girl. What was he thinking?'

'No, she's all right. He was a total you-know-what, but I'm just thinking about tomorrow evening.'

'I'll speak to Guy. He's hardly been able to take his eyes off her since we arrived.' He grinned at the thought.

'Don't be awful. She's lovely, and it's quite natural that he finds her attractive.'

Later that day, when Guy and Vera were alone, Guy seized his opportunity. 'Vera,' he said, 'for some reason best known to them, Reg and Eileen are expecting company tomorrow evening. I've no doubt they'll want to be alone later on – I mean it's only natural – but I wondered if you and I might join them for cocktails and dinner. Then, we could go on somewhere else and give them a sporting chance.'

'What a lovely idea, Guy. Thank you, I'd like that very much.'

29

The Final Score

To comply with hackney carriage regulations, it was necessary to take two cabs, although, as Eileen pointed out, four passengers would have been an awful squeeze.

In the event, both cabs arrived at the Savoy within a few minutes, and the four went straight to the American Bar.

Vera looked at the menu in bewilderment. She asked, 'What did you two have last time you were here?'

' "Eight Bells",' Reg told her, 'but if you don't fancy rocket fuel, you could always have something traditional, such as gin and tonic or pink gin.'

'I think I'd like a pink gin, please.'

'And Eileen?'

Eileen gave an excited squeak and said, 'They do an orange blossom cocktail.'

'Does that excite you?'

'Yes, but only because I thought you invented it when we were at Hatston.'

'You credit me with being more inventive than I am. Is that what you'd like?'

'Yes, please.'

'Guy?'

'I fancy an "Eight Bells", but why don't I get Vera's and mine, and you get Eileen's and yours? That way, we won't get confused.'

'A sound idea.' They put down the menus, and a waitress came to the table.

'Are you ready to order, gentlemen?'

'Yes, we'd like an orange blossom cocktail and an "Eight Bells", please.'

'A pink gin and an "Eight Bells, please,' said Guy.

'Very good, gentlemen. I see the Senior Service is well represented.'

'More than you'd think,' said Vera.

'Oh?' The thought evidently appealed to the waitress. 'Are you ladies in the Wrens?'

'Only just,' said Eileen. 'They'll have to manage without us soon.'

'Well, you won't go unappreciated.' She smiled and turned away to get the drinks.

Vera looked around the bar appreciatively, noticing the line drawings of famous people who'd spent time there, and said, 'This is all new for me. I must say I'm terribly impressed.'

'I was when Reg brought me here,' said Eileen, 'in fact, I still am.'

'We're just thankful to be home,' Guy told them.

Mention of home led Vera to ask, 'Where's your address, Guy?'

'I have a place in Rushmoor, near Aldershot, where I'd have been lonely and all forlorn, had Reg not invited me to your home. Instead, I find myself in the company of my close friend and squadron commander, and two truly lovely and charming ladies.'

'Well said, Guy.'

The waitress arrived with the drinks and placed them as requested. 'Thank you,' said Reg.

'Thank you, sir.'

'It seems an age since we were here,' said Reg.

'It *has* been an age,' said Eileen.

Vera asked, 'Where are we going next?'

'Edouard's in Greek Street,' Guy told her. 'As I remember it, it was a friendly, cosy place, but Reg and Eileen have been there since I last knew it.'

'It probably is,' said Reg. 'It used to be frequented by Americans, French, Poles, Czechs, and every nationality under the sun, and welcome though they were at the party, the place must be quieter now that most of them have gone home.'

Vera nodded sadly. 'The first party was over well before you came home. It's a shame you couldn't have the kind of reception the forces got on VE Day.'

'Not at all,' said Guy. 'We're the Silent Service, discreet at all times.'

'What I don't understand,' said Vera, 'is how you spotted Reg on an island, and from goodness knows how many feet, miles, or whatever.'

'I'm glad you mentioned that, Vera,' said Reg, 'unpleasant though the whole thing was.' Taking the magnifying glass from his pocket, he removed the pencil and re-inserted it. 'Without this wonderful present that Eileen gave me two Christmases ago,' he said, reaching for Eileen's hand, 'I wouldn't have been able to light the beacon that attracted Guy's attention.'

'I never realised that,' said Eileen. 'It means so much more, now, much more than just a pencil and a magnifying glass.'

'Another thing is that I managed to hang on to my parachute, which is one of the old-fashioned silk ones that we had before the Americans brought those nylon arrangements over. If you can get a dressmaker on the job fairly smartly, Eileen, you can have a new wedding dress.'

'Wonderful! Thank goodness for your parachute!'

'You can say that again.' Reg looked at his watch and said, 'Edouard's awaits us. Shall we go?'

They finished their drinks and made their way to the foyer, where the doorman hailed two taxis, which arrived promptly.

Before joining Eileen and Vera, Guy asked Reg quietly, 'Are you sure about this, old man? I mean, wouldn't you rather be alone, just the two of you?'

'We shall be, Reg assured him. After dinner, we'll go on to the Blue Lagoon. Where you two go, then, is up to you.'

'Understood and appreciated, old man.' They boarded their respective taxis.

'Edouard's in Greek Street, please.' Reg told the driver. They drove on through the unaccustomed, brightly-lit streets of London. It seemed unreal after the last time.

Eventually, they arrived at the restaurant, and Raoul showed them to their table, where Vera and Guy were waiting.

Reg asked the perennial question, 'What's not on the menu?' As usual, the answer was in the form of game, in this case, partridge, which they all chose, and the meal continued in the same spirit of amiable agreement.

The night was mild and, having taken their leave of Vera and Guy, Reg and Eileen walked to the Blue Lagoon.

'It was lovely to have them with us,' said Eileen, 'but I'm glad we're alone again.'

'For the first time,' agreed Reg.

They left their coats and hats with the door staff, and a girl in a revealing outfit took them through. 'I'm afraid we're no longer serving food,' she told them.

'That's all right, thank you. We've eaten.' Looking around, he said, 'An alcove would be good.'

'Of course, sir.' She led them to a table and lit the candle. 'Would you like to see the wine list, sir?'

'Yes, please.' It would be interesting to see if things had improved in the five months that had elapsed since the end of the war in Europe.

Eileen took her seat and said, 'I can hardly believe it. I've been waiting for this moment.'

He reached across the table and took her hand. 'So have I, many times.'

With the air of someone full of news, she asked, 'Did your mother tell you about the house she's been looking at?'

'She tried to, but I confess I've been distracted. What do you know about it?'

She waited until the waitress had left the opened wine list on their table. Reg gave it a cursory glance and said, 'A bottle of the Dom Perignon '37, please.'

'Very good, sir.'

'Your mother's been in communication with an old friend and shipmate of your father, a man called Arthur Connolly.'

'Captain Connolly?'

'Vice-Admiral Connolly, now, I believe. He has a *pied à terre* in

Fareham, but he's retiring from the Navy, so he no longer needs it, and he's giving us first refusal. Naturally, I don't know the first thing about the financial arrangements, but your mother seems very determined on our behalf.'

He nodded. 'She's like that, and it would be convenient for Pompey and London. Did she say when we can look at it?'

'The day after tomorrow. The admiral's sending a key in the post.'

'Where's the old boy now?'

'Sheerness. He's Flag Officer Nore Command, just until he retires.'

'Sheer-nasty-ness, eh? Poor bugger.' Correcting himself immediately, he said, 'I'm sorry. It's a reflex action in the service. Just the mention of Sheerness triggers an outburst of profanity.'

'You're forgiven, but only if you ask me to dance.' The band were playing 'I'll be Seeing You,' and it seemed too appropriate to be ignored.

'May I?'

'By all means.' She allowed him to lead her to the dance floor, where they luxuriated in each other's proximity and the music, but most of all, the joy of being together again.

When they returned to their table, they found a bottle of champagne in an ice bucket. Reg inspected it and gave his approval. 'Stand by,' he said, removing the foil and the cage, 'because this is a special moment.' The cork left the bottle with a gentle *pop*, and he poured two glasses. ' "Confusion to Zeus" is a little out of date, isn't it?'

'Yes, how about, "The rest of our life together"?'

They drank to that.

'Actually,' she said, 'we must have done more than confuse him.'

'I imaging he's grinding his teeth, and I've no sympathy for him.'

Eileen cocked an ear. 'They're playing "Till Then",' she said.

'And why not?' He stood and offered her his hand.

The floor was almost empty, so they enjoyed it to the full, sharing it with just two couples. The song was a year old, but it was still popular.

As they returned to their table, Eileen asked him, 'Did you really mean it when you said your flying days were over?'

'It's not up to me, but they probably are. I'm twenty-five, now, and that's old for a pilot. Also, there's talk that the service may get jet aircraft – at least, once the RAF have had their pick – and that's another world altogether.' He gave a reassuring smile and said, 'Sufficient unto the day. Anyway, what are you going to do, apart from marrying me?'

'I'd been thinking of university, but then, when I heard you were missing, and then when you were found, it made me adjust my priorities, and I decided that the main thing was that I had you.'

He was following her argument with difficulty. 'It's not an "either or", he said. 'You can still have me and plough your own furrow as well. Don't forget, I'll be at sea for quite long periods, and flower-arranging and the Women's Institute don't sound like your kind of thing at all.'

'You're probably right.' She took her place again at the table. 'Just let me get used to having you back safe and sound, and then I'll start making decisions.'

'Good. Have some more champagne,' he said, topping up her glass.

She took a sip and said, 'At the risk of sounding like a matchmaker, I'd say Vera and Guy were getting along rather well when we left them.'

'It was always on the cards,' he said. 'Naturally, I've warned him to keep her away from the porcelain and glassware, so there shouldn't be any unpleasant surprises.'

'You're horrible about your sister. She's lovely, and I couldn't have had a better superior officer at Whitehall.'

'Oh, I can believe that. All I'm saying is that when she went into the retail trade and then the Wrens, the world was denied the services of a born demolition contractor.'

The bandleader had announced, 'I Remember You', and Eileen was never going to win the argument, so she asked, 'Shall we dance?'

'I'm game, but the floor's looking full.'

'Let's do our old thing and dance here.'

'Why not?' He stood up and offered his hand, which she took. As he looked around, he saw other couples doing the same thing. The song was four years old, but it was still popular. As they danced, he kissed her beneath her ear.

'Mm,' she said, 'that's lovely.'

'I know.'

'How do you know?'

'It was one of the things we learned at Dartmouth. It's listed in BR Ninety-Nine, the service handbook of places where women like to be kissed. If we had time, I'd take you through the whole book from cover to cover, kiss by lecherous kiss.'

'I'll hold you to that, some day.' She moved closer to him, still only half-convinced that he was home and safe. 'Did you ever find out,' she asked, 'why Casualties Section let your mother and Vera and I go on believing you were missing?'

'Not officially. We can only imagine that the signal from *Invincible* was destroyed by fire.'

'By fire?' Suddenly, she was alarmed. 'When did that happen?'

'Shortly after I was rescued, a force of dive-bombers attacked us. One got through, but it was hit by anti-aircraft fire, and it hit the ship between the flight deck and the superstructure. Part of the WT Office was burned out, and a lot of signals probably went with it.'

'Horrible.'

'It wasn't nice,' he agreed, trying not to let himself be reminded of the stench and the chaos.

'I shan't mention it again.'

'That's my girl.'

The number reached its end, but they made no move to take their seats. Instead, Reg blew out the candle, as before, making the alcove a place of seclusion.

Unhurriedly, they kissed, as they had at Christmas, almost two years earlier, when they made their covenant.

Eileen said, 'We put one over on Zeus in the end, didn't we?'

'We certainly did. We beat the blighter fair and square, one – nil.'

'Reading the signs when we left Vera and Guy, I shouldn't be surprised if it were to happen again.'

'Oh, yes?'

'Oh, yes,' said Eileen confidently, we could conceivably be celebrating a two – nil result.'

They kissed again on the strength of it, and because they finally could.

The End

If you enjoyed this story, here are two more by Ray Hobbs that may appeal to you. Both are published by Wingspan Press.

A Chance Sighting

It is January 1944. Pilot Cliff Stephens and linguist Laura Pembury meet for the first time on a rain-swept night in Hampshire and are immediately attracted to each other. They meet again three times and their relationship blossoms. The future looks inviting until Cliff is posted missing over the English Channel.

Unknown to those searching for them, Cliff and his crew are picked up by a German patrol vessel. Meanwhile, a storm in the Channel leads to the search being called off, and Laura believes Cliff has been killed.

Now a prisoner-of-war in Germany, Cliff has no address for Laura, and the need for stringent security means that he cannot write to her at the wireless station where she is based. It seems that their relationship is over.

Destiny, however, follows its own agenda.

A Worthy Scoundrel

Four years have elapsed since Fred Fuller returned from New Zealand to join the Royal Naval Air Service. It is January 1918, and he is at Dover Seaplane Base in Kent, searching the English Channel for U-boats in a vital struggle to keep the approaches open.

He meets Agnes Morley, the young widow who runs the Navy and Army Canteen, and surprises her with his liberal attitude towards society and his cavalier disregard for authority. Their relationship grows ever stronger. One significant hurdle stands in their way, however, and that is her reluctance to leave her familiar surroundings after the war and take up a new life with him in New Zealand.

As the war continues with no sign of resolution, they wonder if they, too, will ever reach agreement.

Ingram Content Group UK Ltd.
Milton Keynes UK
UKHW011020300323
419408UK00001B/55